CW00419552

The Tunnel

and everything after

Leaving

The seat was cold, rigid, uncomfortable. She adjusted herself, shuffling sideways, trying to find a position that didn't result in some lump or bolt poking her in the back. It was no use. The seat had not been designed for comfort. It had barely been designed at all, just thrown together at the last minute when someone realised a seated traveller might feel more secure. At least while seated you could strap yourself in, lean your head back, hold on tight. Standing could lead to limbs being in unexpected positions. It could lead to a traveller arriving with their arms and legs not exactly where they had left them.

Still, they could have chosen something a little more accommodating than this cobbled-together monstrosity. Someone should really say something. Thankfully, the journey was fairly short. If it could really be described as a journey at all. It was called a trip and they were called travellers, but in reality they weren't going anywhere at all. It was the rest of the universe that was revolving around them. When done correctly, travellers would barely feel a thing. When done incorrectly, they would feel many terrible things all at once and then nothing at all ever again. But she had faith in her team. They would not let her down.

The countdown began, the machine vibrated, and she closed her eyes. She was nervous - who wouldn't be? - but excited. She had seen many others do this. Most of them had come back. And when they returned, she had witnessed that look on their faces, that wide-eyed wonder as they spoke of the places they had been and all the miracles they had seen. She wanted so desperately to share in all that. That was why she was here.

A voice boomed in her ears - three, two, one.

She held her breath, slipped into the light, and then she was gone.

The Tunnel

Scuffed up running shoes, caked in dirt, on top of pristine metal grating. Susan looked down and tutted. This was embarrassing. What had she been thinking? She never came into town wearing her running gear. And these weren't even her good running shoes. These were the spares, the pair she'd pull out of the cupboard on particularly grotty mornings when she didn't want to get her number-one running shoes dirty. How had she ended up in town wearing *these*?

She glanced up from her flaky footwear to the man standing directly before her - a shiny bald head atop thick muscular neck, both forcing their way out of a high viz jacket. Like Susan, he was standing with feet firmly planted on the travelator, his back straight, right arm outstretched and hand gripping the handrail for support. His stance made it impossible for anyone to get past. Susan was about to scowl at him for breaking the number-one rule of the Underground before she suddenly realised she was doing exactly the same thing. She quickly let go of the handrail and flung her arm to her side, hoping to God no one had been angrily eyeballing her the way she had been the bald man. Cautiously, she looked over her shoulder to check.

Fortunately, no one behind her was trying to get past. In fact, the nearest person was some feet away, almost exactly the same distance behind Susan as she was the bald man. A middle-aged woman with a tired face, also with arm outstretched, gripping hold of the handrail. She caught Susan's eye. Susan raised half a smile, and was just about to turn back to face forwards, when she realised the woman was wearing a dressing gown. A garish, pink dressing gown, with grubby, black, tattered edges. Down below, her pale legs poked out, her feet encased in aged, matted slippers, which also had their fair share of dark black stains. Jesus, Susan thought, and I thought knackered old running shoes was bad - what kind of person would be seen dead in town wearing *that*? And was that a cigarette in her hand? It was! The woman was trying to shield it from Susan's line of sight behind the hem of the grotty old dressing gown, but it was definitely there. A half-smoked cigarette. How disgusting.

Susan turned away from the woman, only allowing her judgement to show through fully when she was sure no one could see. Some people… Below her the travelator continuously chugged away, edging her forwards ever so slowly. She sighed, thinking she could probably walk faster than this. Up above the dull metal plating of the tunnel roof glided by at a snail's pace, the monotonous grey ceiling stretching on into the distance. Someone should really try and liven up the design down here, she thought. Would it be too much to ask to add in a little colour? Provide a bit of inspiration for the morning commute? Having the same dull surroundings stretching on forever is surely just going to depress the hell out of people. Speaking of which, she thought, this whole journey is getting a little boring. How long does this travelator go on for, anyway? She peered around the bald man to get a better look.

Before him stood a queue of people, all equally spaced out a few feet apart, stretching on and on along the travelator as far as she could see. They all stood in exactly the same position - right arm out, hand gripping the rail, all facing forwards. No one seemed to be talking to each other. All in their own little worlds, staring ahead, just waiting for the journey to end. Susan glanced over her shoulder, past the middle-aged woman who should be ashamed of herself, and saw exactly the same scenario behind her - just a queue of people staring forward, holding onto the handrail, waiting in silence. In fact, now she thought about it, the only sound at all was the gentle hum of the travelator, the machinery working away below her feet. Not one voice, not one tinny tune bursting out from a headphone turned up too loud, not one ping of a high score achieved on a mobile phone. No sounds at all. Nothing.

OK, this is a little weird, Susan thought. People can be a little standoffish on the Tube, sure, but this was taking it a step too far. Not one person talking to another was definitely unusual, even for the Underground. And now she was looking for it, she realised she couldn't even *see* a headphone or a mobile phone. Just an endless queue of people stood in silence on this travelator, staring ahead, waiting patiently to go wherever this thing was going. And where *was* it going? Susan glanced around again - this dull metal tunnel, basically featureless, just grey walls arched over her and stretching on in both directions. It looked kind of familiar, sure, but then so much of the Tube looked the same these days, especially the new builds. What line was this again? She tried to think back to the station she had gotten on at.

She couldn't remember. Susan shook her head, closed her eyes and gave them a rub. She must be tired. To not remember something that happened all of five minutes ago? That was bad, even for her. She brushed it off. Just a blank spot in her memory. Nothing to worry about. She hadn't been paying attention, had been on auto-pilot and had missed it completely. It happens all the time. And especially on the dull morning commute, the same journey day after day, just going through the motions. You don't always take it in. And why would you? It would be pointless, clogging up your memory with boring nonsense like that. It was more than possible to forget which station you boarded at. She relaxed slightly, opened her eyes, content to have reassured herself that not remembering how she got on the travelator was nothing to worry about at all. Only...

"I was on my run," she said to herself. The bald man in front of her stirred slightly, no doubt curious as to why the young woman behind him had suddenly started talking to herself. But Susan didn't care about that right now. She was lost in a trail of thought, sifting through her memories to try and piece together events of the day so far. The alarm had gone off - 6AM. She'd got up, checked the weather, put on her running gear (opting for the old trainers, as the damp conditions would ruin her new ones), downed her protein shake, left the flat, started her run and then... She let out a frustrated sigh. That was as far as it went. The run and then here, in the tunnel, with these silent people, on this travelator, which seemed to stretch on forever. Her stomach sank a little. It just didn't add up.

"Excuse me," she said, leaning towards the bald man ahead of her, taken aback slightly by the echo her voice made bouncing off the walls of the cold, dull tunnel. No one else seemed to notice, though. Not even the one person she was trying to get the attention of. Susan cleared her throat and tried again.

"Sorry, excuse me."

Still nothing. The man continued to face forward, down the tunnel, seemingly oblivious to her or anyone else around him. She glanced around at the woman in the dressing gown to see if she could get a response out of her. Their eyes met and the woman shook her head frantically, nodding forcefully for Susan to turn back and face the front. Susan paused for a second, a little unsure as to what she was seeing. Was that fear on the woman's face? She certainly seemed quite insistent that Susan turn back around. What was she afraid of?

No matter. This was getting ridiculous now and Susan had had enough. She needed answers. And aside from barging her way through the queue (which, of course, she would never do - Susan was many things but a queue jumper was not one of them), her only option appeared to be getting the attention of the bald man just ahead of her. Time to up my game, Susan thought. After taking a deep breath to build up a little courage, she reached out and gave the man a little prod on the back.

"*Excuse me,*" she said again, and this time he finally seemed to get the message. His head moved to the left, then to the right, darting around in an attempt to discern the source of the noise. Something seemed to connect in his brain, telling him the contact had come from behind. He peered over his shoulder, looked Susan up and down, and frowned.

"Are you talking to me?"

"Er, yes, sorry, I was just..."

"No need to apologise, love," he smiled warmly to her, "Was in a world of my own there."

As he took his hand off the handrail, the woman in the dressing gown gave a little squeak. Out of excitement or panic, Susan wasn't quite sure. She would come back to that. Right now she needed some answers from the bald man. He turned to her and leant against the side of the travelator, hands in his pockets. Susan could see now he had a deep purple bruise on his forehead, which to her looked like it would be very painful. But the man didn't seem to mind. He just continued smiling merrily to her.

"Something troubling you?" the bald man asked.

Susan gave a nervous laugh, shrugged, and wondered what she could say to him that wouldn't sound like she had completely lost the plot. I don't know where I am and I don't know how I got here. It didn't sound good, did it? Maybe start small and build up to that, she thought.

"Do you know where this goes?"

She pointed down the travelator, into the far distance, to the very end of the queue. People as far as the eye could see, standing motionless and staring down a grey metal tunnel that seemingly went on forever. The bald man followed her finger, stared down the tunnel for a second, and then looked back to her. He smiled. The smile, Susan considered, of someone who has just realised they are talking to an imbecile. He nodded down the tunnel.

"Well, it goes that way, doesn't it, love?"

Susan nodded, smiled back, opting to keep things as polite as possible for now. Keep your frustrations to yourself.

"Yes, I can see that, just I wasn't sure which way *that* was. Where are we?"

The man shook his head, gave a little chuckle.

"We're in the tunnel, love. Where do you think we are?"

Susan decided to take a moment, think things through. It felt very much like she was missing something blindingly obvious about her current situation. At least, that was the impression she got from the way the bald man was looking at her. OK, retrace your steps again, she thought. Logic will solve this. I woke up, got up, had my protein shake, left the house, started running, jogged across the road towards the park and… then here. That was it. She was sure of it. There was nothing in between. Nothing she could recall, anyway. Her mind was just jumping from her morning run to being on this everlasting travelator, in this infinite tunnel, talking to this strange bald man. Whatever was going on here was not normal, she was sure of it. If somebody was missing something here, it certainly wasn't her. Time to get some answers.

"The thing is," she began, thinking for a second that she had heard an uneasy murmur coming from the woman behind her, but quickly opting to ignore it, "I don't remember how I got here, and I don't know where *here* is, and I don't know where this thing is going, and I really don't know what is going on."

The bald man nodded, this time offering up a more sympathetic expression, one that gave Susan some hope that he wasn't just going to come out with another completely unhelpful non-answer. She had got through to him. He finally understood.

The bald man smiled to her.

"I wouldn't worry about it, love. None of us do."

Susan felt a headache coming on.

*

The alarm goes off at 6AM. Susan reaches over to the side of the bed, flicks it off. She was pretty much awake anyway. The alarm is just her signal to stop lying in bed while worrying. On goes the light. Her bedroom remains admirably pristine, the surfaces clear, not one item out of place. All clothing is tucked away in the appropriate drawer or cupboard. Since Sam left, ensuring everything is in its right place has become part of Susan's nightly routine. If I can't be happy, she thinks, at least I can be organised.

She downs the glass of water left by her beside and then moves to the bathroom. Toilet flushed, teeth brushed and face washed, she returns. She heads for the running gear laid neatly out from the night before. A quick glance out of the window. The weather isn't looking so good this morning. Best not to risk those new trainers. It's still pretty much dark and no one will be able to see them anyway. Go with the old pair, the back-up pair, and that way she doesn't have to worry about dodging muddy puddles when she heads through the park. She dresses, ties her hair back, looks at herself in the mirror. A nod of approval. This will do for now. Unless she runs into Sam. But the chances of him being up at this time are slim to none, and he certainly won't be out running in the park. No, she should be safe.

To the kitchen, to the fridge, to grab the protein shake ready mixed from the night before. Organisation is key. It tastes disgusting, but the guys at work swear by it, and it certainly seems to be working for them. She downs every last drop, stifles a burp. She rinses out the plastic container and leaves it to dry on the side. She moves towards the front door, does her stretches, hops on the spot, preparing herself for the blast of cold air when she pulls it open. She checks her time - 6:20 AM. Perfect. That's exactly how long it *should* take. She would never be able to fit all of that into 20 minutes if Sam was still around. She'd never be up this early going for a run. But look at her now. Look at her go.

She pulls open the door and jogs out into the cold.

*

Susan took a step back to recalibrate. The bald man just continued to smile at her, as if what he'd said had been completely clear and should have put her totally at ease. But she was not at ease. She was trapped in a tunnel that didn't appear to end, using a travelator that didn't appear to go anywhere, and talking to a strange bald man who apparently didn't have a problem with any of it. She was about as far from being at ease as she thought she could get.

"No one knows how they got here?" Susan asked.

"Well, I don't know about *no one*," the bald man replied, "*I* don't know, that's for sure. Truth be told, I haven't actually talked to anyone else. So I guess *they* might know…"

He tailed off, seemed to contemplate what he had just said for a couple of seconds, and then shrugged it off. He resumed grinning at her. Susan sighed, trying and for the most part succeeding in using her frustration to bury her fears. There's no

7

point getting too worked up, she thought, not until we've gathered all the information we have available to us. So she turned away from the bald man, to the middle aged woman in the tatty dressing gown, hoping conversation with her would prove more enlightening. Susan made eye contact and smiled, as warmly as she could, before opening her mouth to speak.

"Shh!" the woman hissed.

Susan paused, slightly taken aback. She tried again.

"I…"

"No!" the woman interrupted, this time turning her head away. Susan persevered.

"Can I just…?"

"Don't talk to me!"

"But…"

"Don't talk to *anyone!*"

"I just…"

The woman thrust up a finger, putting it to Susan's lips. Susan froze. This had never happened to her before - a complete stranger touching her on the face, on the mouth, in such a forthright manner. She really didn't know how to react. Susan just stood stock-still, staring wide-eyed down at the woman, trying desperately not to think about how clean that finger was. The woman started to lean in towards her. Oh, God, Susan thought, what is happening? Is she going to kiss me? Bite me? Vomit on me? *What is this?*

The woman then spoke in a low whisper, so only Susan could hear.

"Don't speak to any of us, OK? Not to me, not to him," she nodded over Susan's shoulder, to the still grinning bald man, and then focused back on Susan, "Not to a soul, OK? Just stand in line, face forward and *be quiet.*"

The woman nodded to Susan, her stare deathly serious. Susan frowned back, feeling her stomach sink, as the fears slowly began to overtake the frustrations. The woman's eyes were wide, tired, red, and most concerning of all, scared. She removed the finger from Susan's mouth and stepped back, mouthing two words up at Susan as she did. Trust me. The woman in the dressing gown then moved back into position, right arm out onto the handrail, back straight, facing directly ahead. Susan looked beyond her, to the man behind, standing in exactly the same pose - his right arm holding the handrail, his left down by his side, gripping hold of an extremely scuffed-up motorcycle helmet. The bike leathers he wore, covered in scratches and showing some extreme signs of wear and tear, didn't make a squeak. Not one tiny sound. He was standing so still as to not move a single muscle. And his eyes - oh, God, Susan thought, finally catching sight at his eyes - were exactly the same as the woman in the dressing gown. Red around the edges, wide, full of terror, not wanting to look anywhere but to the end of the tunnel into which they were all heading.

Susan looked beyond him, to the queue of people, and noticed for the first time that their eyes all seemed to be saying exactly the same thing. Their body position was calm and rigid, uniform and straight, but behind the eyes... behind the eyes was uncertainty and worry. Behind the eyes was fear. She saw now that all these people wore exactly the same expression. They were all absolutely terrified.

*

Susan puts one foot in front of the other and starts to pick up speed. Her first thoughts are about running itself. The way it clears the mind. She has always liked running for that reason - the way it empties out her brain. Sometimes Susan feels like her head is too full up. Too many thoughts, too many ideas, all competing and overlapping with each other, so it is impossible to select just one and focus on it in isolation. And so they all add up. Too many unresolved concepts, a collection of unfinished ideas. She becomes overwhelmed. But running is her escape from all that. It is a way of clearing out the clutter - albeit temporarily. Put one foot in front of the other, her brain says to her. Just breathe, her body replies. Just run, just keep on going. Nothing else matters.

As always, the first section is the worst section. The pavements, the roads, dodging around pedestrians, waiting at the traffic lights. It is impossible for Susan to get into her rhythm and so her mind wanders. It brings up Sam. It brings up heartbreak. It brings up loneliness and regret. It endlessly repeats worries she could really do without.

Susan is relieved when some revellers left over from the night before cut across her path. Susan skirts to one side to avoid them. They barely even notice she is there. She pretends to herself she is annoyed with them, but deep down she is glad for their intrusion. It is a welcome distraction. Next come the early risers, those unfortunate enough to have jobs that drag them away from a nice warm bed on a chilly winter's morning. Dodging them requires Susan to concentrate and the bad thoughts are temporarily ejected. She trots around these half-asleep zombies, thinking to herself that they are less a sign of a city that never sleeps, more of one that is never fully awake. Like herself, they have been deprived of a full night of relaxation. Although she suspects the reasons for their sleep being cut short are very different from her own.

Susan shakes off that train of thought, focusing on the upcoming park. It's the park where Susan's mind can truly be free. Away from all these people. She picks up speed. But something isn't right. Something isn't working. A nagging feeling. A tiny trickle of anxiety slowly drip, drip, dripping its way into her brain. She can sense it all beginning to pool. Soon it will be a puddle. Soon she won't be able to avoid it...

What if I *do* see Sam? What if he has *her* with him? What will I *say*?

She knows these worries are pointless. They don't make any sense. What would they even be doing out here at this time of the morning? And what did it even matter if she *did* see him? See them? It wouldn't bother her.

Susan is fine. She feels good. She *looks* good (apart from the grubby trainers). She can cope with bumping into him. Into them. She isn't worried about it in the slightest. She can cope with the nagging feeling that the only reason her relationship with Sam crumbled was because he had become bored with her. It doesn't bother her at all. She is OK with it. She can cope with the fact that she was totally unprepared for him leaving, and that when he sat her down and told her, it all came out of nowhere and hit her like a train. She doesn't worry about it. It is all behind her now. She can cope with the punch to the gut that was him moving on so quickly. So quickly, in fact, that she can't help but suspect that he had probably moved on before he had even left. That's OK. It is what it is. Life moves on. She can cope now he has left her behind, with her tattered heart, and her loneliness, and her nagging worries that somehow she is now broken, unable to recover, never to be herself ever again. She can cope with all of that. It doesn't get to her in the slightest. She is absolutely fine.

The park is coming up on the other side of the road. Susan moves to cross. I shall not think about Sam, she says to herself. I shall not think about any of it any more. I am done. Put one foot in front of the other, her brain tells her. Just breathe, her body replies. Just keep going. She heads out into the road. This is working brilliantly, Susan thinks. My mind is totally clear. I'm not thinking about what happened. I'm not thinking about being alone. I'm not thinking about Sam at all. I'm not thinking about him *so much,* in fact, that I haven't even noticed that bus.

*

Susan slowly turned away from the woman in the tatty old dressing gown and faced forwards. She peered around the bald man - still smiling at her - and looked to the row of people facing away from her into the distance. How many were there? Susan believed she could see maybe a couple of hundred ahead of her, probably the same number behind. How long was this tunnel? Well, she'd been on this travelator a good while now, and hadn't seen any signs of it ending. Nor could she remember it beginning. She simply had no memory of getting on the thing. So as impossible as it might seem...

Susan shook her head, not wanting to admit it, but struggling to come up with any better suggestions. She grimly accepted - that is the answer, no matter how insane it sounds. As impossible as it may seem, this thing may not *have* an ending. Just hundreds, thousands, maybe even millions of people stuck on this travelator that apparently goes on forever. It began to dawn on Susan why everyone was looking so scared. Everyone except...

Susan looked to the bald man, who nodded warmly to her.

"Why aren't *you* scared?" she asked him.

He gave a shrug.

"Que sera sera."

Susan groaned, suddenly feeling extremely alone. She was surrounded by all these people but not one of them seemed able to explain to her what was going on. In fact, only one of them seemed willing to communicate with her at all, and the information he had provided had been less than helpful. She slipped to the side, propping herself up against the rail. Deep down a feeling of helplessness began to grow. A feeling of despair. Of fear. She shut her eyes, trying to fight it. Breathe, just keep going. Breathe, just keep...

"The way I see it, love," the voice of the bald man sliced through her attempts to calm herself, simply increasing the panic, "If you can't fight 'em, might as well join 'em."

11

What did that even *mean*? Susan groaned again. The bald man, not taking his cue that he really wasn't helping, continued on.

"I mean, this place is a little odd, no doubt. Confusing, even. I'll give you that. But compared to where I was before…"

Susan's eyes flashed open. She held her breath. Where he was before. Before the travelator. Before the tunnel. If he could remember before all this, maybe that could help. Maybe somewhere in his recollections she would discover an answer.

"..this place is a considerable step up," he continued.

"Where were you before?" Susan asked eagerly, pulling herself upright.

"Oh," the bald man said with a grin, "Just down on the site."

"What site?" Susan persisted, doing her best to not let his frustratingly vague answers tip her all the way over into a full blown rage. He smiled curiously to her, offering up another little shrug. His expression seemed to suggest that he thought the answer would be obvious. He nodded down to the high viz jacket and the tool belt around his waist.

"The building site," he replied.

Now we're getting somewhere, Susan thought. Maybe he could remember what she had forgotten. Maybe he could piece together the series of events that had led to them all being here. Let the investigation commence.

"Right, OK," Susan began, preparing to release her inner Miss Marple, "You were at the building site and then what happened?"

"Well, just the usual, really. Standard morning. Nothing out of the ordinary. Break time rolled around. Nipped out for a cuppa and a smoke. I came back to the scaffold after, I dunno, about ten minutes? I shouted at Lucas to turn his bloody radio off - the stuff that boy listens to, well, it's not what I'd call music. So Lucas, he looks over the platform, he's looking down at me, and I'm looking up at him, he shouts something and then…"

For the first time the bald man's smile dropped.

"And then?" Susan prompted.

"And then…"

Distant now, his eyes flicking around for the answer, his face blank.

"*And then?*" Susan tried again.

He shook his head, folded his arms.

"I don't want to talk about it," he said, suddenly looking away.

Susan sighed, preparing to step things up from good cop to bad cop, but then cut herself short when she saw the look on his face. The bald man now looked genuinely distressed. What he had been trying to remember was troubling him. Something had been clawed back from the edge of his mind that he would rather have left there, preferred to have forgotten completely. Should I stop? Susan considered. How would she feel if a complete stranger had started quizzing her? Would she want to tell them about what had led her here? If they had asked about her life, her past, about Sam? Would she want to open up about all that?

She didn't think so. She'd maybe say that she'd gone for a run, but she certainly wouldn't mention that the reason she'd gone for a run was because she was sad. That was the truth of it, after all, wasn't it? She'd been running to get away from how she felt. Running to hide from her clouded mind, to escape that thick fog of terrible thoughts. And she'd kept running because it just wouldn't go away. It had chased her. She'd just run and run, trying to free herself, one foot in front of the other. She'd shot out across that road - just keep running, just keep breathing - without even looking, without even thinking of anything else. She'd just blindly stepped out - keep running, keeping breathing - straight into the path of that bus…

Susan froze. Her eyes widened.

That was it. The last thing she could remember before being here. Stepping off that curb, jogging into the middle of the road. And only then seeing the bus. She hadn't even had time to scream. She'd not managed to do anything at all, because she already knew it was far too late.

The colour drained from Susan's face. Her hands began to shake. Her mouth went dry. She glanced up to the bald man, as everything slowly slotted into place. She looked to him and knew the answer before she had even asked the question.

"There was an accident?"

He nodded, glancing away, no longer wanting to look at her. And that bruise on his head. She saw it clearly now. It wasn't just the colour of the skin, it was the shape. The bruise was actually caved *into* his head. His skull was cracked. How had she not noticed that before?

Susan turned to the woman behind her, the woman in the tatty old dressing gown, with grubby black stains around the edges. Stains or burn marks? She looked down to the half-smoked cigarette in the woman's hand. She looked down to the slippers. The black patches upon them. It wasn't dirt - they were charred.

Susan glanced beyond her, to the man behind in the motorcycle leathers, with the helmet in his hand. The scuff marks across it, across his jacket, over his trousers. Those leathers weren't old and tatty - they had been bounced across tarmac.

The travelator glided along, further and further down the tunnel, which edged by in silence, on and on and on. The same blank metal walls stretching on in either direction as far as the eye could see. The bald man with a hole in his head turned away from Susan, put his hand out to the handrail, held it gently, and stared blankly ahead. Beyond him the queue of people stretched on forever, all standing silent and terrified, facing the same way and awaiting their fate. Old people in hospital gowns. Young people in military gear. People with ripped clothes, bruised bodies, blooded faces. People with bald heads and tubes up their noses. People with empty eyes and empty bellies. People with bodies all crumpled and torn. The queue of the dead, stretching on forever, as far as Susan could see.

She looked down to her own body and saw the bruises, saw the cracked skin, saw the scrapes and the scratches. She saw the indentation in her own chest that had crushed her lungs and ended her life.

Susan slipped to the floor and screamed. The travelator just kept on rolling.

*

The bus hits and Susan feels herself being thrown into the air. Everything happens too fast, too quickly to register. A thump and then flying. A more brutal force than she has ever encountered, could ever really imagine. And then the ground is gone. Her breath leaves her as she rises. For a brief second she imagines herself waking up. That's all this is, the jolt you have when you start to drift off, when your body spasms and you kick out. A brief moment of panic that then blends into relaxation, as you realise you are safe at home, simply experiencing the comfort of a nice, warm bed.

But then she hears the crack.

A shuddering slap that jolts right through her. She *feels* it. Her body against the road, her bones unable to take the strain and snapping. This is not the comfort of a nice, warm bed. This is agony.

Susan stares up at the streetlamps, still brightly lit against the dull morning sky. She can just about make out the top of the bus, pulled to a stop. Something nearby screeches and skids. Tyres against the road, maybe. She can't lift her head. She can't bend her neck to look. She can't move at all. A car door slams. Footsteps clack against pavement. And then the faces arrive, peering down at her. Their mouths open and shut but she can't hear anything. They look worried and upset. She realises they are scared for her. Something pulls her along. She knows she isn't moving but she can feel it anyway. Something moving her forwards. Moving her on.

Maybe it's not that bad, Susan thinks, taking in a deep breath. But no air enters her lungs. Only pain. She tastes blood. She feels it clogging up her throat. She feels it seeping from her mouth. The faces above her shout and scream at each other, but Susan doesn't hear a word. Behind them grey walls covered in dull metal panels. Behind them a tunnel which stretches on forever.

Susan wants to get up but she can't. She wants to scream out but there's no air left in her body. She wants to shout at herself, berate herself for crossing the road without looking. How could she be so stupid, so distracted? She had let her thoughts about Sam overwhelm everything else in her life and now they were going to kill her. She regrets that this moment of clarity only comes to her now, when she is lying in the middle of the road and dying.

But it's too late. The bus has smashed her open and her life is seeping out. It won't be long before it's all gone. She doesn't want that. She doesn't want to leave. She wants to stay. This isn't fair. She wants a second chance. She wants to fight.

But she can feel herself being dragged forward. She can see the grey walls passing her by. She can see her scuffed-up running shoes on pristine metal grating. She can't see the streetlamps any more, the top of the bus, the concerned faces looking down to her. She can't see any of it.

All she can see is the tunnel.

*

Susan reached up a hand and grabbed the handrail, pulling herself to her feet. Her screaming had stopped. There didn't seem to be any point to it any more. No one was listening. No one cared. They just stood there, locking in position, waiting for God knows what. Waiting for something that might never come. Susan took one deep breath in, let it flow out slowly and looked around herself. This was it, then. The answer to the great mystery. And yet it answered nothing. An everlasting travelator that went nowhere? A vision of the afterlife inspired by a particularly dull section of the London Underground? Whose idea was that?

She began to compose herself, thinking things through, taking stock. What had her life been like? Ups and downs. Like everyone's, she presumed. It had ended on a down. Quite a significant down, really, being hit by a bus. But even before that, she hadn't been happy. It wouldn't have been too far from the truth to describe the last few months as a bit of a downward spiral. She could admit that now. There was not much point lying to herself any more. But that wasn't to say she couldn't have turned things around. That wasn't to say there wasn't some hope in there somewhere. She wasn't a complete write-off.

Although now I am, I suppose, Susan considered with grim acceptance. The end has arrived and the end is… She looked around the grey, monotonous tunnel, and to all the silent, sad people. She shook her head. The end is really quite boring, isn't it? What even is this place? Hell? Purgatory? People had talked about paradise and pearly gates, or flames and torture, but an everlasting nightmare of rush hour commuting? What had she done to deserve *this*?

She didn't think she was a bad person, but she wasn't sure if that was what all bad people thought. She knew she hadn't been perfect but… had anyone? Regardless, this didn't seem right, being trapped here forever. Of all the possible options, to be given this one. She was fairly sure she hadn't done anything so bad as to deserve that.

An idea began to form, a niggling concept that gnawed away at her until she could no longer ignore it. *This wasn't fair.* Her life with Sam, her life *after* Sam. The bus. And then being here, ending up like this. It just wasn't acceptable. The world might be an upside down place where bad things happen to good people, good things happen to bad, but wasn't the afterlife supposed to correct all that? Wasn't there supposed to be some sort of divine justice? Not this everlasting, bleak monotony. For her to end up here… No, that didn't seem right at all. The fear and despair upon first realising her fate had now been replaced by something else, something much more powerful and harder to ignore. Anger. Susan realised she was extremely pissed off.

"Hey!" Susan shouted, shocking herself as much as everyone else around her. The bald man looked over his shoulder with a frown. The woman in the dressing gown shushed her. But Susan didn't care. She had started now and she had no reason to stop. She was already dead. What did she really have to lose?

"Hey! Who's in charge here?"

"Shh!" the woman behind her hissed. Susan looked to her, shrugged, turned back to no one in particular and shouted again.

"I demand to speak to someone in charge!"

The travelator continued to roll on in silence, not a sound except for the light hum of the machinery below. A few people in the queue glanced around to see what the commotion was. The bald man turned slightly to get a better look at Susan, curious as to what she was going to do next. Susan herself was curious as to what she was going to do next. This was definitely uncharted territory. But whoever or whatever was out there was ignoring her and she wasn't going to put up with it any longer.

"I'm serious!" she called out. "I want to know what the hell is going on and if someone doesn't explain things soon I'm going to…"

She looked around, searching for inspiration. What *was* she going to do?

"I'm going to…"

There was nothing *to* do. Nowhere to go. Just the travelator and the tunnel and the dull grey walls and all these people and…

"I'm going to…"

"Better let it go, love," the bald man said to her, his tone sympathetic. But that did nothing for Susan. She was fed up with letting it go. She was fed up with putting on a brave face and just coping with things. She wanted to scream and shout and let the world know that she was here and she deserved better. And suddenly she knew what she was going to do. The only thing she could do.

She was going to get off this fucking travelator.

Susan sidled over to the handrail and pulled herself upwards. The woman in the dressing gown gasped, putting her hands to her mouth. Susan lifted up her right leg, her scuffed-up running shoe coming down onto the top of the handrail, and jumped up. The bald man wheeled around and stared at her, his mouth forming an almost comedic O of shock. Susan hauled herself up over the handrail and stretched out her left leg, looking down to the metal flooring below. Here goes, she thought, and with a smooth swivel, Susan pulled her body over the edge and let go.

Both feet landed firmly on the metal grating. She put an arm out either side for balance. When her body had adjusted to no longer moving forwards, she looked up. The woman in the dressing gown was leaning over the side of the travelator, still with a hand over her mouth, still with a look of sheer panic in her eyes. The bald man jumped forward, also leaning over the side, looking back at her. The travelator just kept on chugging away. Off it went, down the tunnel, away from Susan, taking the bald man and the middle-aged woman with it. Into infinity, into oblivion, into whatever, Susan didn't much care. It was heading one way and her only act of defiance was to head the other, so that was exactly what she was going to do.

Susan turned away from the direction of the travelator and began to walk. For as far as she could see the dull grey walls stretched ahead of her, the queue of the dead sliding out of the narrow horizon one after the other. She didn't know if heading backwards would be any better than heading forwards, but at least it was her choice to do so. The faces glanced at her as she walked - wrinkled and old, young and pale, discoloured, bloody, some even disfigured - and every one of them changed their expression slightly as she passed. Their fear was momentarily replaced with curiosity. Who was this woman and where was she going? Susan smiled to each and every one as she passed. Maybe they'd follow her, maybe they wouldn't, it was up to them. But she had made her decision and she would see it through.

Susan quickened her pace, stepped it up to a jog, and then a full-blown sprint. One foot in front of the other, just keep breathing. Her footsteps echoed all around her as each scuffed-up running shoe pounded down onto the metal flooring. The sound gave her an easy rhythm to keep up with. One foot in front of the other. Just keep breathing. I know what I'm doing now, she thought, with some satisfaction. I'm in control. *I'm in charge.* Just keep running, just keep breathing, one foot in front of the other, and let's see where this thing goes.

*

Susan's eyes flick open. Her head hurts. Her arms hurt. Her legs hurt. She coughs and realises that even her throat hurts. *Everything* hurts. But this is a good sign. Pain means she is home. Pain means she has made it back. She coughs again and it brings on a chuckle. A cough is a good sign. A great sign. It means she has air in her lungs. It means she is able to breathe. It means she is alive.

"She's awake!" someone calls.

The faces are back, the bus is back, the streetlamps are back. She thinks for a second - back from where? As she lies injured in the middle of the road, surrounded by all these concerned pedestrians, she pushes a thought to the back of her mind - an idea being shelved, a memory filed away. Something about a tunnel…

"The ambulance is here!" someone else calls.

Susan sucks air into her lungs and her body responds well. She has been winded terribly by the bus, and from the feel of things must have a fair few broken bones, but she is alive. The faces above her are concerned but relieved. She can hear the siren. She tries to look out for it. Someone tells her not to move. It'll be OK, just stay still. Don't worry, you're going to be fine.

She worries she is forgetting something important. Some essential information about somewhere she has just been. For a reason she can't fathom, she thinks of the London Underground. But it's nonsense. She hasn't been anywhere. She's been lying in the middle of the road. She almost died, maybe she passed out, but she hasn't moved from this spot. Of that she is certain. She considers these bizarre images of metal walls and moving floors just her mind's way of trying to understand what has just happened. It is simply trying to make sense of these traumatic events. It doesn't take long for her brain to move on to other things.

God, this is embarrassing, Susan thinks. What was I thinking, running out into the road without looking? What an idiot. I was obsessing again. Obsessing about Sam. And it nearly killed me. He is a fog that has clogged up my brain. I can barely see anything else because of it. I couldn't even see that bus. Enough is enough. This has to stop.

The paramedics arrive and lift Susan onto the trolley, before wheeling her into the back of the ambulance. They reassure her, tell her everything is going to be fine. She will be out of action for a few months ("You certainly won't be running any time soon!"), but there won't be any lasting damage. They pump her full of drugs for the pain. She finds herself spouting all sorts of nonsense to them as a result, most of which they take in good humour. She tells them about Sam. How she loved him, still does love him. But it's over now and she is sad. But that's OK. Being sad is to be accepted. It is normal. She'll recover in time, she is sure of it. If she can escape the tunnel, she can escape him, that's for damn sure. And then she thinks to herself - what tunnel? Susan laughs. She's talking nonsense. The drugs must really be kicking in now.

As she drifts off into a peaceful sleep, Susan continues to babble away to the paramedics. She boasts about her escape, how she ran home, ran back to her body, and to the new life she is now going to live. The paramedics don't really listen. They are used to this sort of thing. They don't think anything of it. They have heard all sorts of crazy stories in the back of their ambulance. They forget. Susan does as well. The memory fades. Those strange recollections of cold metals walls, and of a travelator that stretches on forever, they completely disappear. The paramedics forget, and Susan forgets. Everyone always forgets. Because until they get there and see it for themself, no one can know about the tunnel.

Dictator Dating

Adam's story begins in a small room, a room he's been told is his bedroom. More accurately, it is simply the room in which he's being kept. It's dark, it's cold, and he's sitting on a mattress with a young woman. The woman is smiling at him, playing with him, keeping him occupied. He's been told that this woman is his mother. Adam is happy. He doesn't often get this much attention.

The woman is wearing a vest. Adam can see the whole of her arms, right from her knobbly shoulders all the way down to her bony little fingers. Her skin is pale. That sticks in his mind as clearly as anything. He repeats it to me, like it's important. So very pale. Colourless skin, reflecting the lamplight. She waves her hands before him, her palms dancing in front of his eyes, playing a little game of hide and seek. As they do, he catches glimpses of her drawings, two dark shapes just above each wrist. Later he would learn that they were tattoos. To him they just look like two strange black worms having a fight, or maybe a cross running backwards. And they aren't just on her wrists. They are everywhere. All over his room, all over the house too. The woman he's been told is his mother tells him that they are a symbol, one that he must learn to know and love. He doesn't really know what she means.

Also in his room, all over the walls, are pictures of a man Adam doesn't like the look of. Black and white pictures, one after the other, of this man and his friends. They are all covered in the very same symbol - that cross running backwards. He's a very serious man, the man on Adam's wall, with very angry eyes. Adam doesn't understand why these pictures have to be there. Why is this nasty man up on Adam's wall, glaring down at him, being so scary? The woman pretending to be Adam's mother just smiles at him, takes hold of his hands, tells him he doesn't need to be scared. There's no need to worry. This man up there, he's a very great man, very important. We all love him, she says. Never forget that. She then reaches up her bony fingers and rests them gently on either side of Adam's head, turning him away from the scary pictures, turning his head so he is looking right at her. And then she tells him, with beaming smile, with eyes full of so much love, she tells him that the man on the wall is the man Adam will grow up to be. He doesn't understand. But then she kisses him, holds him tight, and in the warmth of her skinny, pale body, he forgets that the man is even there.

But then the noises start.

Men shouting, screaming, barking orders at each other, just outside his room. Adam hears thumping footsteps, sounds of panic, the clunking and clattering of people scrambling in all directions. He can hear doors slamming, things being pushed over, furniture crashing to the ground. So much commotion. Adam starts to get scared, and he asks the woman who claims to be his mother what is happening. But she doesn't say anything. He asks her and he asks, begging her to tell him, but she just keeps staring up at the door. Her hold on him is way too tight now. She's squeezing him too much, squeezing the air right out of him. He tries to tell her that too, that she's hurting him, but she doesn't seem to hear. She just keeps on staring at that door.

And then loud bangs outside. Pop, pop, pop. And the men are shouting again. They are screaming and stomping and making so much noise. And all the while, those awful bangs just go on and on. Pop, pop, pop. He has no idea what it could possibly be, but it is just so *horribly loud*.

The woman is screaming now, squeezing him too tight and hollering in his ears. And Adam is crying. He has absolutely no idea what is happening. He just wants to go back to playing games, to hide and seek. Stop all these terrible noises, all these pop, pop, pops. Make it go away. But suddenly there is a thud at the door. Someone is outside. They are shouting, screaming, kicking and thumping. And more loud bangs. Pop, pop, pop. The woman screams, and Adam screams, and then with an almighty crack, the door bursts open. The shouting stops.

Adam can't see. There's too much light. Someone is shining a torch in his eyes. He can still feel the woman he's been told is his mother next to him. She is still holding onto him, far too tight. And she starts to talk to him, whispering something into his ear. She is trying to calm him down, comfort him, tell him everything is going to be alright. Don't listen to them, she says. Remember that you are special. You're going to lead us. You're going to change the world.

Then she kisses him gently on the forehead, and with a terribly sad sob, she finally pushes him away. Adam falls back onto the bed, still crying, still wailing at the top of his lungs, as the woman slowly rises to her feet. He remembers this image clearly - her standing there, right above him, her body a silhouette in the glaring light from the torches. She is holding her right arm high into the air, totally straight above her, palm completely flat. And then she shouts something, two defiant words Adam doesn't recognise, bellowing them out into the light. There is one final ear-shattering pop, one last bright flash. And then the woman who wasn't his mother drops to the floor with a hole in her head.

*

I do remember thinking, that night we first met, that there was something familiar about his face. As if I'd seen it before. I hadn't really noticed, looking at his profile pictures. But you select those, don't you? You pick out the best version of yourself, all sparkling smiles and perfect angles. But face to face, when there's nowhere to hide, that's when you have to revert to just being you. And that's when I noticed, for the first time, that there was something about Adam I recognised.

He definitely wasn't my usual type, looks-wise. But his messages had made me laugh. They'd been engaging. And he'd actually asked about me. Who I was, what I did, what I liked. Not everybody did. There's a whole army of people out there who think just talking about themselves is enough. Like that should seal the deal on its own. I find me fascinating, so why shouldn't she? There was none of that from Adam. He genuinely seemed interested in what I had to say. To be honest, by the time his message popped up, my bar had already been set pretty low. He hadn't referred to me as babe, he hadn't asked what I was wearing, and he hadn't sent me a beautifully filtered picture of his cock. At the time, that was enough to earn a reply.

"Hi, Adam? It's Kate."

He put out his hand. I remember that. I liked it. He didn't immediately go in for a hug, or a kiss on the cheek. There was none of that awkward finding out where the boundaries are, or just ploughing through them without a second thought. He just said hello back, and then we shook hands. It must have looked horribly formal to anyone watching. Maybe it was. But to me, I don't know, it just felt comfortable. Like there's no pressure here, let's just see what happens.

It helped that I could tell he was more nervous than I was. He kept on fiddling, rubbing his nose, scratching his neck. All these awkward gestures. When he held the pub door open for me, he slammed it right into the wall way too hard. When we got to our table, he bumped his leg up against the chair, struggling to pull it out properly.

23

He probably thought it was a disaster, but it actually warmed me to him straight away. He was as clumsy as I was, a kindred spirit in the art of making a twat of yourself.

We sit down, opposite sides of the table, and I get a good look at his face straight on. And again, there's something there that's ringing a bell with me. I just can't put my finger on it. It's weird. Something shouts out to me that he should have a moustache. Like, if he had a moustache, I'd be able to tell who it was he reminded me of. But I don't want to stare too much, so I try my best to throw the thought away. Forget it, it doesn't matter. It'll come to me later.

"This is a nice place," I say, when he finally makes it back from the bar, "Do you bring all your dates here?"

It's a shit line, I know, but I throw a cheeky little smile in with it. I say it mainly just to see how he reacts. Maybe that's cruel, I don't know, but I see it as my little test. You do this enough times, with the sort of luck I've had, you just want to have a little bit of fun before it inevitably goes tits up. Adam just nods, blank face, and then raises his eyebrows in the direction of the exit.

"Uh-huh. There's a clear run to the door, so it's easier for them to sneak out when I go to the toilet."

Not a bad reply. Not the best I've heard, certainly not the worst. I've had some absolutely terrible responses in the past. Some guys get flustered, they lie, say they don't bring everyone here. Like this place is somehow special, they've saved it up just for me. Others boast, say of course they bring girls here all the time, like I should somehow be impressed they've dated so many. Here's a tip - you tell someone you've been on that many dates, it kinda just suggests that you're not very good at it.

But Adam, he clocked my silly little line for what it was - a dumb joke. And he threw another right back at me. That was a promising sign. It showed he wasn't going to take himself too seriously. And it showed that he could take part, join in, that this wasn't going to be too hard work.

"That's very considerate of you," I say, playing along.

He smiles at me, raising his glass to his lips. It's a nice smile, somewhat playful, with a little twinkle in the eye thrown in for good measure. It pushes his cheeks out a bit, shows off his dimples. I wouldn't say I was blown away by his pictures and, to be honest, even in person, the first thing I thought when I saw him was that he was a bit mousey. His ears stuck out way too much. He was a bit

24

squidgy. His face was lacking in edges. But I have to admit, as the night went on, and the conversation started to flow, I started to find him more and more attractive. The wine helped, obviously. The wine always helps. But Adam was funny, told a good story, and actually listened to my stories. He asked all the right questions, and then seemed genuinely interested in the answers. And the flirting was easy, just silly and fun. Nothing forced. I liked him a lot.

We slept together for the first time that night. I know some people have these rules, don't they? Don't go giving anything away, not on the first date. They won't respect you, they'll never call you back. Maybe that works for some people, but it's not for me. I wanted to sleep with him, and I didn't want to wait. So I did. And if he didn't call me, or if I didn't call him, well, we'd had a fun night, what did it matter?

I won't go into any details. You don't need to hear the details. Although I will say this - afterwards, when the light was off, and Adam had fallen asleep, I do remember catching a little glimpse of him which threw me for a second. Again, I couldn't put my finger on it exactly, but when I saw him there, eyes closed, mouth slightly open, head back on the pillow, it started to bug me. The moonlight caught him on the side, casting these little shadows across his face, one tiny dark patch over his top lip. It made me sit up in bed, stare down at him. I had that little pang of recognition. Something out of a memory, perhaps, or a dream. Maybe out of a film. I couldn't place it. But I just stared down at him for ages, trying to work it out, just thinking to myself over and over again...

I know that face.

*

We're three dates in when Adam tells me he's adopted. We were out for dinner somewhere, some fancy restaurant he'd picked out. And when I say fancy, I mean the sort of place where they serve abalone soup and caviar omelettes. Proper swanky. Or pretentious, depending on your point of view. To be honest, I tend to fall into the latter category. I'd much rather just a curry or a burger. But at that stage, Adam was still trying to impress me, treat me how he thought I'd like to be treated. And I was more than happy to go along with it. It was sweet that he thought I was worth it.

It was over the main course that he mentions it. Or maybe I asked him. I can't quite remember (blame the wine). I'm tucking into my sea bass, chilli and sizzled ginger (*that* I do remember, because it was absolutely delicious), and somehow it just comes up. I think I mentioned my family first. Well, moaned about my family. I don't know what I said exactly, but chances are it involved complaining about my brother being an idiot, my mum being annoying, or my dad just generally being a pain in the arse. And then I'd just blurted it out, as you do, just making conversation with someone I still didn't know all that well.

"You can't choose your family, can you?"

"No, but they can choose you."

And that reply threw me. I didn't really get it. So I just asked him straight up. And Adam explains it all to me, tells me how he was adopted when he was four years old, taken out of foster care. That he didn't know his real parents - his biological parents. They were part of some sort of commune that got shut down by the authorities. Now, I am not shy in asking questions, especially when I'm feeling a little more relaxed (again, the wine…), and so I just start firing them at him, one after the other. How? Why? When? *And a commune*? Don't get me wrong, not in a mean way. There was no judgement. I didn't grill him. This was no interrogation. I was just curious, genuinely intrigued. It was not a story I was familiar with and I just wanted to know how the whole thing worked. And Adam being Adam, he's just chilled, relaxed, and happily comes out and tells me.

He doesn't remember much about this commune, he says. A bunch of very strange people with some pretty out-there views, that's all he knows. Or all he's willing to tell me, anyway. Social services came calling, took him in, and he was placed in foster care until he was four. He tells me he doesn't really remember much of that either, only that it was a considerable step up from being in this commune. But then along comes this couple. They already had a kid of their own, the normal way. Sorry, not normal, I shouldn't say it like that. The *biological* way. Anyway, they have this kid, and they want them to have a little brother or sister, as you do. But they think to themselves, you know, there's too many kids out there without a home to go to, without a family. They want to do their part, help out. So they go through the system, they find Adam, and they totally fall in love with him. They take him in. They become his parents and that's that. Adam suddenly has a family.

You can tell by the way he says it, the look he's giving me while he's telling his story, that he absolutely loves them to bits. It's written all over his face, clear as day. There's that little twinkle in his eyes again, those cute little dimples. It's adorable.

26

When he's finished, I kind of just wanted to fling myself at him right there and then, jump right across the table. But I expect it would be frowned upon in that kind of establishment. Plus I didn't want to get chilli and sea bass all over my brand-new dress. But I did find it attractive, I have to say. It was sexy as hell, that he had all that love in his heart. And it was then that I realised, for the first time, that I was properly starting to fall for him. Obviously I didn't tell him that.

"They sound amazing," I say of his parents, "They kinda make me wish they'd adopt me too."

He nods, flashing that cheeky smile of his.

"I could ask them," he replies, "But that might make *our* relationship a little awkward."

I laugh at that. And then I notice that he just used the word 'relationship'. I wondered if he meant to. I hoped that he did.

*

We're four weeks in when we have our first proper argument. And it's so stupid. I couldn't even tell you what it was about. Well, I could, but it still wouldn't make any sense. It was over the History channel. Or, more specifically, me watching the History channel and Adam freaking out about it. And so there it was. Our first row, over the fucking History channel. How dumb is that?

Now, I like history. Historical films, historical fiction, documentaries, podcasts - I can't get enough. I even like watching those Time Team repeats on All 4. You know, when they're messing around with that geofizz machine, someone says there's a wall under there, or a small structure, and all of a sudden it starts to take shape in dodgy '90s computer graphics, the past coming to life right before your eyes. It's fascinating to me. Where we've come from, what we've been through. All these things that have shaped us, made us who we are. I love it. But I do understand it's not for everybody. If it's not your thing, I won't force it on you. If your idea of a good day out isn't a trip down to your local quadrangular castle followed by a visit to the nearby pottery museum, I won't make a point of dragging you along just for the hell of it. In short, I am not a dick about it. Which is why it was so ridiculous when Adam got all uppity about me watching the stupid History channel.

"Turn that off!"

He pretty much shouts it from the kitchen, completely out of the blue. It made me jump. He must have shocked himself too, because he spills the bag of ice he was holding, all these chunks of it flying out and scattering over my floor. And then he's just standing there, gaping at me, like I'd done something terrible. It was the look you might have given someone after they had just punched your grandmother in the face. Utterly ridiculous. I'd only switched on the TV for a minute while he had gone off to make the mojitos. It had been on for ten seconds, if that. Just something to fill the time while he was occupied with the drinks. I'd barely even noticed what was on.

"What's your problem?" I ask, trying to make it sound like a joke, like it was no big deal. Because it wasn't a big deal. It was the History channel.

"I'm sorry. Please, just…".

He looked to have calmed down a little, like he'd realised he had overstepped the mark, said something he shouldn't. He stretches out a hand to me, a pleading gesture.

"Just turn it off."

I look at the TV, shrug, then back to him. I genuinely couldn't see the problem.

"It's the Secrets of the Nazis," I reply.

"I know. I just don't want it on."

He steps forward, into the room, now spilling ice onto my living room floor. Little chunks of it start to roll around on the carpet. I don't think he even realised he was still holding it.

"Steady!"

I try to bring it to his attention, get him to notice what he's doing. I didn't want a soggy carpet. But he just keeps moving, shifting towards me, his free hand outstretched. It looked like he was going to make a grab for me, or a grab for the remote. It was bizarre.

"Adam, what's wrong?"

He smiles at me. Or tries to. The lips move like they're supposed to, but the rest of his face doesn't follow. There's nothing in his eyes to suggest he means it. He's grinning at me, but he looks angry. No, not angry - worried. Maybe even scared. And I can't work out why. I have no idea what I've done.

"I don't like Nazis," is all he says.

So I laugh.

"No one likes Nazis!"

"Turn it off, please. Change channel."

"You're getting ice all over the carpet…"

"Just turn it off!"

And there it was, he shouts at me. Over the History channel. Over a stupid TV show that I wasn't even watching. I don't really know what to do, what to say, so I just raise the remote, flick the button. The TV goes blank. Adam visibly relaxes. And it pisses me off. He's shouted at me, in my own home, for no reason, with no explanation. He's shouted at me for just turning on the TV. Who the hell does he think he is?

"What the fuck, Adam?"

"I'm sorry…"

"Yeah, you should be. What the hell was that about?"

He's flustered, struggling over his words. Finally he realises he's spilling chunks of ice all over my floor. He makes the effort to steady the bag, holding it tightly, almost hugging it. Then he looks up at me, tries to smile again. It still doesn't really work.

"I'll finish the drinks."

And with that, he turns away, back to the kitchen, taking his melting bag of ice with him. He retreats. And I'm just left standing there, alone in the living room, watching these little pools start to form on my floor, tiny chunks of ice melting away into my sodden carpet.

*

It's about a week later that I meet Adam's parents. Not in an official capacity. There is no formal introduction. We just happen to be in the same place at the same time, so I guess it would have been weirder if we'd all just ignored each other.

Adam had apologised for the TV thing a lot. And I mean, *a lot*. He'd apologised and apologised to the point where, if I'm honest, the apologies had started to annoy me even more than the actual argument. I did mention to him that he didn't need to say sorry any more. It doesn't matter, I don't hold grudges. Let's just move on, forget about it. To which he had nodded, smiled at me, held my hand, and apologised all over again.

But other than all that, the week had actually been pretty good. We'd more or less got back to normal. We all have our quirks, and if Adam's only one is that he aggressively hates the History Channel then, to be honest, I've dated worse. It had also helped that his mojitos had been excellent. Obviously I wasn't going to tell him that. I had just sat there, sipping angrily on the cocktail, giving him the evil eye until the rum kicked in. At which point I just called him a dickhead and asked for another one. They were really rather delicious.

And so it's the following weekend that he tells me that his parents are coming over Sunday morning. No pressure, he understands it's pretty early on in the relationship (that word again), but he's meeting them for breakfast, and did I want to come along?

"They'll be near the flat anyway," he says.

I nod.

"OK."

"So I just thought you might…"

"Yeah, sure."

"But you don't have to if…"

"No, sounds good."

"They won't be offended."

"I'd like to."

"So if you don't want to go…"

"Adam," I say, grabbing him by the hand and eyeballing him in an attempt to stop him babbling on, "It's fine. I'd love to."

And so Sunday morning rolls around, and we're up and about far earlier than we've managed during the entirety of our month-long relationship. The sun is shining, the birds are singing, and here we are, pretending like we're a proper couple, walking hand in hand along the pavement. And it feels great. Sure, it's a little nerve-wracking, meeting the parents. But in a good way. Like I want it to happen, I want to meet them. Partly because I am genuinely curious as to whether they are as great as Adam says they are. But also because, well, I actually want them to like me. I find myself really hoping that they do. Because I like Adam. A lot. In fact, I possibly, kind of, don't want to get ahead of myself, but I maybe think that I might be moving towards feeling more than that.

It's a teeny-tiny little cafe, built into one of those railway arches. A few tables are laid out in front, on the cobbles, catching the morning sun. And there they are, his parents, sitting outside, smiling over at us as we approach. I wonder whether Adam will let go of my hand when he sees them. I don't know why. I think maybe it'll be weird for him. Like holding hands with me on a Sunday morning while we stroll merrily along in the sunshine is a pretty clear sign - *this is my girlfriend*. Maybe he's not ready for that yet.

But he doesn't let go. He holds on tighter. He waves his free hand, and there they are, waving back at us. And all the time he just keeps holding onto me. I know, I know, cheese alert, but it's true - my heart did actually skip a little at that. I had to force myself to hide it, make a mental note to keep it together. Do not give the game away. Not yet, anyway.

"Katie, hi, so great to meet you," his mum stands up to greet us. There's hellos and how are yous, the introductions made. My offer of a handshake is dismissed by both parents. It's hugs all round.

Lynn and Terry are exactly as lovely as Adam described them. All warm smiles and bright eyes, genuinely engaging, making the effort. Just chatting to them straight away is an absolute breeze. They ask about me, what I do, where I'm from, how long the two of us have been together. They must know all this already, Adam presumably has told them, but they ask anyway. They want to hear it from me. And they seem genuinely pleased to see me, and see me with Adam. They're such an adorable little unit, the three of them, all at ease, charming and friendly, bouncing off each other, silly little jokes at each other's expense. Terry in particular seems to thrive on little ribs at Adam, joyfully embarrassing him for my entertainment.

"Has Adam told you about the time he broke his arm? He was chasing after a frisbee, ran right into a tree. Wasn't even looking where he was going, the daft sod. I wish I'd caught it on camera."

"Has Adam told you about the time he threw up all over the roast dinner? One too many lagers the night before. Couldn't handle the sight of Lynn's glazed parsnips. Grandma Pearson was *not* impressed."

"Has Adam told you about the time he went for a job interview with the price tag still attached to his trousers? Had it dangling down his leg the whole time. And they still gave him the job! Must have been desperate…"

Each anecdote arrives with a round of raucous laughter, followed by an eye-roll from Adam. But he's smiling too. I can tell he's enjoying it. He's enjoying them telling me his story. And so we order, we eat, and the time passes easily. Before we know it, lunch is over, and we're just about ready to move on. Adam suggests a quick drink - "If you have time before the drive back?" - and Lynn and Terry are keen.

"I just need to visit the bathroom before we go," I say, pushing out my chair. I'm not sure I've ever used the phrase 'visit the bathroom' before. Go for a pee, find the bog, take a slash, sure. But 'visit the bathroom'? What is happening to me?

"Very sensible," Terry says as I stand, and then grins up at me, "Has Adam told you about the time he got caught short on that bus in Malaga?"

"Dad, not now," Adam tries. Terry waves a dismissive hand in his direction.

"Nonsense. She's got to hear that one. It's the best of the lot."

I flash a smile at Adam, who hits me with another eye roll, but I can tell he's enjoying it really. And off I go, leaving them to it, looking forward to hearing all about Malaga. I'm sure they're going to talk about me behind my back. If I had a friend here, a relative, a confidant, I'd be doing it. Who wouldn't? But I hope what they have to say is positive. It should be. I've been on my best behaviour, after all.

I head into the cafe, through the little bar area they have inside, past the counter and out through into a corridor out back. There's just a single unisex cubicle, but thankfully no queue (I've been holding it for a while, waiting for the right moment). As I head inside, I'm thinking about what I'm going to say to Adam later. I know I'll tell him how great Lynn and Terry are, how warm and friendly they've been. I'll make a joke, like I always do. Something along the lines of, seeing how perfect they are, it's amazing that he's turned out to be such an arsehole. And he'll join in on the gag, like he always does, and tell me that it wasn't easy, that they had him enrol in an evening class in Bastardry, which is why he's so good at it. And then we'll laugh, and kiss, and see where that takes us. And afterwards I'll tell him that deep down, if I'm being honest, at a stretch, he really isn't all that bad. Borderline OK. Maybe approaching likeable. Possibly even loveable…

I flush, wash my hands, wondering where that last thought came from. It's only been a month. Am I not just getting ahead of myself? This isn't like me, to fall so quickly. To fall at all. And yet here I am, imagining our evening together, our future. Imagining myself using the L word.

I shake my hands, dry them with a paper towel, and put the whole notion to the back of my mind. Let's not rush into anything. One step at a time. Who knows, maybe the drinks will turn into a disaster. Maybe Lynn will turn out to be an atrocious racist. Maybe Terry will be an outrageous letch, try and make a pass at me. Maybe I'll get drunk and make a pass at him. The possibilities are endless.

So out I go, back into the corridor, through the bustling little cafe, and back out into the sunshine. And it's then, with the light catching me by surprise, blinding me a little so I have to hold up a hand to shield my eyes, that I catch the very end of their conversation. They haven't noticed I'm back yet, they haven't seen me come out, and this is what I hear.

"No, Adam, you mustn't," from Lynn.

"Don't be an idiot, son, she doesn't need to know," from Terry.

"No one does," from Lynn.

And it's then that they see me. All three of them freeze on the spot, hush immediately. Terry grabs at his drink, taking an unnaturally huge swig. Lynn grabs at her handbag, fiddling with the wonky strap, as if fixing it right now has suddenly become the most important thing in the world. And Adam looks up to me, and he smiles. He smiles way too much. He's waiting to see if I heard. He's waiting to see if I'm going to ask any awkward questions.

But I don't. I just smile back, grab my bag, and ask them if they're good to go. Because I didn't want to hear what I just heard. I really wish I hadn't. I just want things to be perfect for once. I see the relief on each of their faces, the sheer weight lifted at the thought that they've gotten away with it. Everyone gets up to leave. And my heart sinks. That little daydream I was just having in the toilet, that corny romantic fantasy about where this was all going to lead, it's just been blown totally out of the water. Because Adam has a secret, they all have a secret, and now I know it's out there, I'm not going to be able to let it go.

*

"What don't I need to know?"

Adam looks at me blankly. The smile on his face starts to falter. He just stands there, hovering next to the door to the flat, still holding onto his jacket. I wanted to wait until we got home. Having this talk in public didn't seem fair on his parents, or him. Or me, for that matter. I didn't have the stomach for it. But waiting for two hours with all this on my mind and *not* saying anything took a herculean effort, of which I am extremely proud. Well done me. I deserve a medal.

But now we're alone, and we've got a couple of drinks swilling around inside us, and a couple of hours have passed, I suddenly realise that my question did arrive a little out of context. Adam's confusion is kind of understandable.

"I heard, Adam, when I came back from the toilet."

Still the blank face, the empty stare, that wobbly half-smile that seems to switch on and off as he desperately tries to piece it all together. No doubt for him, everything has gone incredibly well. Better than he could have hoped. His girlfriend (if that *is* who I am) and his parents getting on like a house on fire. A great day all round. But now I'm standing here, suddenly pissed off and grilling him about something he has already forgotten about. Maybe I should give him the benefit of the doubt.

"Your dad said something about me not needing to know."

"Did he? Know what?"

"That's what I'm asking you."

He shrugs, finally taking the time to lay his jacket down on the arm of the sofa. It only takes a second, but it seems suspicious to me. Like he's playing for time. Like he's realised what I'm talking about and is using that second to fabricate a believable answer. Or possibly he just wants to rest his arm. I don't really know any more. My mind is racing at a hundred miles an hour and it's hard to think.

"What is it that I don't need to know?"

I try again. But Adam just slips his hands into his pockets and continues to stare back at me. It's infuriating. If he was going to come up with a lie, he should have done it already.

"I honestly don't know what you're…"

"Adam, please. *I heard.*"

Again he just throws back a dismissive shrug. There's even a wide grin for good measure. I could punch him. But then there's a twitch. His smile falters. His eyes widen for a second - not even that - but it's enough. It's enough for me to see that he's remembered, that he's now fully aware of what I'm talking about. He knows he's been caught.

"It was probably just another one of dad's stupid stories," he says, but it sounds flat, sad, half-hearted, like he doesn't even believe it himself. He turns away, to finally shut the door behind him, again taking what seems to be far too long to perform such a simple task. The door is taking an age to close. When he finally returns to look at me, he looks awful. Everything about him just seems to have collapsed. His shoulders are hunched, his body pulling away from me. Like he wants to escape but has realised there is no hope. He has to confront me head on. And I suddenly realise that he is going to tell me, give me the answer I've been pushing him for. But that look, that guilt, that shame I can see just oozing off him, it sets off an alarm, a warning light flashing all around my head. The way he's looking at me now, I start to backtrack, I start to panic - do I really want to know this?

"Do I look familiar to you?"

That's his opening line. Not what I was expecting. It throws me a little, and I frown back at him, partly through confusion, but there's a considerable amount of frustration thrown in as well.

"When you look at me, do you see someone else?"

"What the fuck are you talking about?"

"Do I remind you of anyone?"

I snort, pretend that I don't understand the question. I'm trying to make it look like I think he's being stupid, or insane, talking complete gibberish. But of course, he isn't. I know *exactly* what he is talking about. He *does* look like someone else. I've known it all along, from the very start. I just couldn't put my finger on it. And the fact I did understand what he was getting at, well, that now starts to terrify me. Because it means what he is about to say is probably going to be worse than I had been anticipating. A lot worse. And there's nothing either of us can do about it.

Still, obviously I'm not going to tell him any of that, so I just say...

"Right now you remind me of a bit of a prick, if that's what you mean."

And he laughs. One, loud, utterly humourless "Ha!". As if I have somehow hit the nail exactly on the head. My response probably wasn't very helpful, to be fair. And I do think about apologising. I want to. I'm about to. But then he looks at me, *really* looks at me. Just starts staring at me, holding my gaze for ages. It felt like he was studying me, taking me all in, like he was trying to remember every detail, memorise me for some sort of test. That this was it, his last chance. After this, he wouldn't be able to see me any more. After this, I would be gone. I let it continue, mainly because I can't think of anything else to do. But after a while, when I just can't take it anymore, and it becomes just too uncomfortable, I move to speak. And that's when he gets in there first.

"I don't look quite like him now," he says, "But I will soon. When I'm older, in ten years or so, I think you'll know who I am."

And after that, Adam tells me his story.

A Town Underground

Well, here we are. Safe to say I wasn't lying. Quite the sight, ain't it? Still takes the breath away, after all these years. You should rest up a minute, enjoy this calm while you can. It won't last. But we've got some time before we need to make our way down. This town ain't going nowhere. It's done all the moving it's ever gonna do.

I'm told it's three miles to the other side. Got no reason to doubt it. All that dust, all that haze, you'd be forgiven for thinking we're standing on the edge of the world right now. That you could just step out into pure nothing. But on a clear day, you can see right over to the cliffs, what remains of Westview. That sad old place is dead now. Just a shell of what was. A damn shame. I always liked Westview. Plenty of folks I knew lived there. Good people. Happy people. Streets packed full of friendly faces. But then the Drop came. Mood changed pretty sharpish after that. Whole place emptied out overnight. Don't think they could stomach it no more.

Where we're at now, that patch of dirt you're scuffing those moc toes on, this all used to be my back garden. That wall right there, that was the outhouse. You wouldn't think it to look at it now. So much has changed. See right up there, that window, second from the left - that used to be my bedroom. My folks bought this house, raised three kids here, lived out two peaceful decades before the Drop. They didn't stay one second after. Can't say I'd have done different. We were the lucky ones. We got out. Most folks didn't.

You can fill your bottle from that stream there. It's clean enough, least so up here. You won't want to touch any water you find down there in the Pit. You won't want to touch much of anything. All you eat and drink from here on in, make it what you brought with you. What you find down there in the Pit, take it from me, leave well alone. Tainted ain't the half of it.

But this stream here, sure, it's safe enough. It used to run right through these yards, trickling on down from one into the next. I'm getting all nostalgic just thinking about it. Remembering how things were. What our life was like before the Drop. My sisters and me, we'd sneak down here when Ma wasn't looking, grab up any scrap we could find, make ourselves these little junk boats. Empty cans, sweet wrappers, old newspapers for sails - anything we could get our hands on. It'd all get stitched together into something that had a chance of floating, then off they'd go downstream. Course, most would sink. We had no real know-how. There's only so far enthusiasm and a handful of clutter can take you. But every now and again, against all sense, one of our little vessels would make it, sail next door into old man Mitchell's back garden. That grumpy old fool would come banging his cane on our front door, complaining to Ma about all this detritus washing ashore in his flowerbeds. All red-faced and sweaty he'd be, steam coming out of his ears. I saw his face like that again, come to think of it, the day of the Drop. There he stood, right where you are now, shaking his cane, shouting and swearing, watching on helpless as half his house slid on down into the dark.

Apologies, I lost myself a second there. Rambling's in my nature. There's just so many memories out here. All these past lives that got themselves buried deep, so desperate to be dug back up. It gets to you sometimes. But I'll try and keep the reminiscing to a minimum. I know you said you were in a hurry.

The descent is gonna take some time. It's shorter here than over by Westview. A lot shorter. I don't come here just for that trip down memory lane. We're not over this side so I can recall the good times, recount them back to you for my own satisfaction. It's this side that's the easiest way down. But I should warn you, easy is relative. Don't you forget that. Take one wrong step out over the edge, that step is likely to be your last. I've seen the Pit take even the most experienced, those poor fools who lost their concentration for just that wrong split second. It's not something you want to take lightly. But you follow my lead, do as I tell you, we've got a good chance of getting where we're heading.

Speaking of which, I gotta tell you, all these years I've been guiding folks down, countless explorers and scavengers, well, no one's ever asked to go see that old church before. Certainly a new one on me. But I guess there's a first time for everything. You can just about see it from here. What's left of it, anyhow. Right over there, where I'm pointing now, that spire sticking up out of the dust. That's our marker. It's easy enough to spot, should be easy enough to find. But it's not exactly most folks' idea of a tourist destination. They might want to go sifting through all those fancy mansions down Dean Street, or try their luck in one of the broken banks. Plenty of salvage there. Whole heap of riches. But that old church? No, can't say anyone's ever asked me to guide them there before.

You know the story, right? Sure you do. Everybody does. No? Well, that surprises me, I don't mind saying. Perhaps you'll let me tell it to you? I know, I know, you want to get going, but where it is we're heading, a little knowledge can go a long way. You say you've got a good idea what's down there, that you've done your research. Trust me, that won't matter one bit when you come face to face with the reality. You need to know what to expect down there, from someone who's seen it first hand. You gotta understand what it is we're gonna see. Surprises are best avoided, down there in the Pit. They have a nasty habit of being fatal.

So that old church, right, the night of the Drop, there was a full congregation in there. More than you'd ever expect at midnight mass. Whole entire place was packed to the rafters. Don't ask me why. Some say a higher purpose, some say just dumb luck. Depends which side of the fence you sit on. But I'm not one to pass judgement. I'll leave all that talk for those with the passion for it. But there they were, shouting and hollering out their hymns and prayers, just as the beams started creaking. As the ground got to shaking. As the whole damn place crumbled and cracked apart around them. And they just kept on singing, belting out Guide Me O Great Redeemer at the top of their lungs. They say not one person got up to run. Not a single soul. They all just sat and sang and accepted their fate, every last one of them. Almost like they saw it coming. And then they went and tumbled on down, deep into the Pit, singing their songs so loud and so proud, screaming out their praise right until the end. Then all of a sudden their voices were lost, taken by all the booming and the crashing, that deep, terrible rumbling that overwhelmed everything that ever was. The belch of the Pit as it swallowed them whole.

Some people say, on a clear night, when the moon is high and the wind low, you can still hear them singing now. That sweet old hymn drifting out of the dust lake, rising up and up, floating on out to the stars. Course, I've never heard it, and I've been down there plenty. I'd like to think my hearing ain't so bad that I couldn't hear a couple hundred ghosts serenading me. And if the rumour is true that no one made it out of that church alive, well, answer me this, how can a story escape without a mouth to tell it? Did it climb out of the Pit all by itself? Either someone escaped that church carrying it or the whole thing's just another tall tale, something to share around the campfire when the sun drops and the whole Pit turns to shadow. I know which side my money's on.

I have to say, it strikes me as odd, you wanting to visit the place but not knowing that story. It's got me to thinking. I'm curious now as to what it is exactly we're heading down there to find. I don't need specifics. The service I provide, you get your guide, protection too, and naturally you can count on discretion thrown in for good measure. No one up here will hear a peep out of me. Far as anyone but us knows, we were never even down there. And as it said on my notice, everything you salvage, it's all yours - minus my cut, of course. This is my living. And the way you're nodding right now makes me glad that you understand that. But still, it would be mighty handy to know what it is exactly that's at stake here. What we're looking for. Especially if there's likely to be any folks out there eager to get their hands on it as you are. Or - let me guess, by that look you just gave me - pretty determined for whatever's out there to stay buried just that little bit longer.

Don't look so surprised. I ain't no fool. You think I'd be doing this as long as I have if I was? There's two types want to risk their neck heading down into the Pit. Some are just in it for the fortune, the glory, out there hunting whatever treasure it is some sad soul got snatched away from them by the Drop. But the other sort, the kind filled with secrets and that look in their eye you're giving me now, they're after something far more valuable. A reason. Some kind of answer. A long-hidden truth. It's the latter that are a lot more dangerous, if you don't mind me saying. Those are the ones I need to watch out for the most.

You see, the Pit's not just some dirty great hole in the ground, a terrible freak of nature that swallowed up a whole town. That's part of it, sure. But there's so much more to the story. And I'm guessing what we're heading out there to find has some part to play in it. Yeah, I know, everyone's heard the science. We can all recount what they told us. They spoke for days, they did, all solemn and serious, talking in great detail, with their long, fancy words. They explained it time and time again, showed us all their maps and their graphs, their charts and their grids. Conjured up all the facts they could muster. There's these caverns down there, they said, these huge dark chambers, and they all used to be filled with water. Countless streams, rivers and lakes, all flowing along, under the rock, carving themselves a home. But then the water left. It got out somehow, flowed elsewhere, leaving nothing behind but a whole load of empty space. And the thing about empty space, well, it's got a wicked desire for wanting to be filled. We were just unlucky, they said. The worst luck in the world. And so one day the town was there, then the next day it wasn't.

Yeah, I see you smiling. Don't try and hide it. No need to with me. Those of us who were there, those of us who saw, we all know there's far more telling to be had with that tale. And I'm guessing, whoever you are, you've got far more in common with us who were there than with them scientists who came after. Those who told us they had no way of knowing it was coming. Gets you thinking back to that church, doesn't it? Those believers. And what they were doing there that night. Why not one of them chose to run. Or who knows, maybe one of them did. Some plucky soul who'd seen too much, knew too much, and wanted out. It's possible they even escaped with a story. And who knows, maybe there's something left behind in that church that could tell that story just a little bit more clearly.

Still, it's a dangerous business, digging around in a past as dark as this. Stepping out over the edge. Because the Pit isn't just that crater you see before you. Not to us. Not to those who witnessed the Drop first hand. It took our town, swallowed it whole, ripped away all that we had and hurled it deep down into the dark. And if we're going in, that's what you gotta understand. Venture into the Pit, it's not just those cliffs out to get you, or the rubble, or those mountains of dust. You're up against a whole entire town that knows it's been wronged, that wants some justice for being wiped from the map. It's a bitter resting place for a thousand smashed lives. You go sifting through what's down there, poking around in all those broken memories, well, I can't say for certain there's not gonna be something down there that might just want to poke back.

But hey, if you don't want to tell me exactly what it is we're after, I'm not gonna push no further. Your money, your call. That's how this deal works. And I don't blame you for keeping your secrets neither. Everybody's got them, me included. And for good reason, round these parts.

Anyhow, I guess we've stalled long enough. Grab that pack there, fill up your water bottle. It's time to move. I'll go over first, you follow my lead. And you do what I say, when I say it, every step of the way. If I say stop, you stop. If I say run, you don't think, you go. I give you that call, you move without hesitation. You don't want to take no chances when dealing with the Pit. But step where I step, do as I do, and everything might just work out fine. Or as close to fine as we're likely to get.

So, here, take hold of this rope. And hold on tight. No matter what happens, you keep your hands clasped firm around it. That rope's the only thing keeping you alive right now. Move yourself forward, that's it. One step after the other. Nice and slow. And take one last look at the world you're leaving behind. Drink it all in. Savour it. You'll be missing it soon enough. OK, you ready? You better be. One, two, three…

And drop.

Bugs in the Machine

"Gary, wake up!"

Louise shook Gary by the shoulder. Gary didn't move. Louse started to panic. Gary wasn't waking up fast enough. Louise thought about giving him a slap. She raised her hand at the ready, preparing to swing. Gary opened an eye.

"Don't call me Gary," he said.

Louise groaned, and again thought about giving him a slap. Gary did not appreciate her negative attitude.

"Protocol," he told her.

Louise sighed.

"Fine," she said, "Professor Stevick, wake up!"

And then she slapped him anyway.

Gary jumped off the bed, incensed at the outrageous lack of respect he had been shown. Louise was pushing her luck. He thought it might finally be time to let her go. But then he saw her expression. She looked scared.

"What is it?" Gary asked.

"You should come and see for yourself," she replied.

Gary huffed, making it clear that he was not impressed.

"I was sleeping," Gary said.

Louise nodded.

"That's why I slapped you."

Gary shook his head.

"I was awake when you slapped me."

Louise shrugged.

"I had to make sure."

*

Gary followed Louise down to the viewing platform. It didn't take long. Inside the laboratory there was The Machine, the canteen, the toilets, a makeshift bedroom and the viewing platform. Outside the laboratory there was everything else.

"This better be important," Gary said, as they made their approach. Louise gulped. Her face was pale. She pointed towards the observation window.

"Look," she said.

Gary looked.

Outside the window Gary saw a spider the size of a house. It was holding a drinking glass in its hand. Gary knew spiders didn't have hands. It was impossible. And yet that was what he was seeing. Beside the spider, a man in a bright red jacket was running and screaming. He was waving his hands wildly in the air. The spider moved above him and then lowered the glass, trapping the screaming man inside. The man continued to run around inside the glass, bouncing off the sides. He looked surprised each time it happened. It was almost as though he did not know the glass was there.

Gary then watched as the spider produced a single sheet of paper and slid it under the glass. It seemed to be concentrating hard on what it was doing. It lifted up the glass and the man, holding him in place with the piece of paper. The spider then walked away. The man in the bright red jacket was still screaming.

"This is bad, isn't it?" asked Louise.

Gary agreed that it was.

Next came a thunk. It made Gary jump. A woman in jogging gear had collided with the outside of the observation window. Her face was bloody. She appeared to be missing her front teeth. She was screaming too, just like the man in the red jacket. She headbutted the window. Gary thought he saw something pop in her nose. Blood splattered up against the observation window. She headbutted it again, flinging herself at it.

Gary put his hand up to the window, waved it in front of her. She just kept banging herself into the glass, inches from his hand. He shook his head.

"I don't think she can see us," he said.

Louise nodded.

"I don't think any of them can," she replied.

Then they heard the buzzing. It shook the room, it was that loud. A shadow moved across the woman outside. Something big had arrived. Gary leaned forward, looking up. Above the woman he now saw a wasp the size of an articulated lorry. It was hovering above her, its wings flapping like crazy. The gust of wind it produced almost knocked the woman off her feet. Gary could see the wasp's stinger waving around in the air. It was as big as he was. Gary gave a little whimper.

"What did you *do*?" Gary croaked at Louise.

She shook her head. She didn't really want to speak any more. Gary asked her again. When she replied, she did it with a whisper.

"We turned it on," she said, "We turned on The Machine."

The wasp was holding something. Gary wondered again how what he was seeing was possible. The spider held a glass, then a sheet of paper. Now the wasp was holding something too. It shouldn't be happening. But that was what he could see. He gulped, leaning forward against his better judgement. He tried to focus on what was in the wasp's hand. It was a magazine. The wasp was holding onto a rolled-up magazine. It started to raise it, high above itself, way up into the air. The screaming woman was still out there, banging herself against the observation window. Still trying to get through. Her blood was now smeared all across the glass. Gary watched as the wasp held the magazine high above its enormous head. Gary then realised what was about to happen. He almost choked.

"Oh, shit," said Louise.

Gary didn't feel like saying anything.

The magazine came down with such force that the observation window shuddered. There was a very loud thunk, accompanied by a very damp splat. Gary was impressed and extremely thankful that the window didn't shatter. The screaming woman had completely disappeared. She had been replaced by a woman-sized splodge of red and purple that was now spreading slowly out across the observation window. Louise gagged, turning away. The wasp then lifted the magazine away from the window, and a significant portion of the woman-splodge went with it.

Gary threw up.

*

After he had cleaned himself up, Gary turned to Louise.

"Why haven't you turned it off?"

Louise just stared at the red splodge covering the observation window. Quite a lot of it had dropped to the bottom of the window and was forming a little gooey pile on the floor outside. The wasp had flown away, taking its magazine with it.

"Louise!" Gary shouted.

"Huh?"

"The Machine. Turn it off. Now."

"I tried that. Nothing happened."

Gary glanced to the exit, wondering whether he should go and try it himself. Louise knew what she was doing. It was unlikely she had missed something. But even so, given what was going on outside, maybe he should go and take a look.

Gary looked back to the observation window, just in time to see a small group of people running around in the distance. They were all waving their arms in the air, flapping around wildly. And behind them, stomping along quite merrily, was an ant the size of a double-decker bus. It was holding a magnifying glass between its antennae, manoeuvring it from side to side. It was trying to catch the light. The small group of people weaved this way and that, trying to escape. The ant finally got into position, towering above them, and a beam of sunlight shot out from the magnifying glass. Gary didn't bother looking after that. He just heard screaming, and something that sounded like crackling.

"I'd better go and check on The Machine," he croaked.

Louise wasn't really listening.

*

Gary ran down the corridor. He was trying to keep his mind on the job, not on what he had just seen through the observation window. If he could fix The Machine, maybe it wouldn't be so bad. He worried what the shareholders would do to him if he couldn't. Then he realised the shareholders were outside, and considering what was going on outside, they probably had bigger problems to deal with right now.

Gary arrived at the machine. Lights were flashing, dials were ticking, needles were flicking from side to side. It looked like it was supposed to. He scanned all the switches and buttons. Gary could barely remember what half of them did. He panicked. Given what The Machine was doing, he wasn't too keen on the idea of messing around with it. But he had to do something. Somebody had to fix this mess. The fate of the world depended on it.

Gary tried the Off switch. That seemed like a safe bet. But the lights kept flashing, the dials kept ticking, and the needles kept flicking from side to side. The whole contraption just kept whirring away quite happily. His hand hovered over

Reverse Flow. The Machine was leaking out into the world. Reversing it would suck everything back in. Or it could simply make it start leaking out into the lab instead. He didn't want that. He didn't want what was happening out there to start happening in here too. But if that was the only way…

Louise shouted something down the corridor. Gary took his hand away from the button. It was best not to rush into anything. Steer clear of rash decisions. He would see what she was shouting about first.

*

"It's Phillip," said Louise. She nodded towards the observation window.

"What about him?" Gary asked, stepping into the room.

Louise gulped.

"He's outside."

Phillip was the chef. He worked in the canteen. He would have finished his shift by now, Gary realised. He would have left the building, headed for home. He would not have thought to check the observation window before leaving. He would not have bothered to check in with Gary or Louise first. In normal circumstances, there would be no need.

Gary peered around Louise to get a better view of the window. He wasn't really sure he wanted to look out there, but it was too late now. There was Phillip. He was careering around like a madman. His arms were flapping around in the air, like all the others. He was running next to a pile of something burning. Gary wondered what it could be. Then he remembered that was where the ant had been pointing its magnifying glass. He now realised he could see arms and legs poking out of the flames.

Phillip was running around and around the pile. Every now and again he would dart towards it, then jump back, revert to his circular jog. As he ran, he kept looking over to the fire, flicking his head towards it, looking extremely confused.

"What's he doing?" Gary asked.

"Like moths to a flame…" Louise whispered.

Phillip darted at the fire, almost sticking half his body into it, before dragging himself away. His trousers were burning now. But he just kept on running, around and around the human bonfire.

"We have to stop him," Louise said.

"How?" Gary replied.

There was no way they could go out there. If they did, they would end up just like everybody else.

"But we have to do *something*!" Louise cried, "Look at him!"

Phillip's top half had now started to burn. He kept running, jumping in and out of the flames. It was unlikely he would be able to keep running for much longer. Most of him was now on fire. Gary nodded. Louise was right. He had to do something. And there was only one thing he could do.

*

Gary ran back down the corridor. Louise followed.

"What are you going to do?" she asked him.

"I think we can reverse it," he replied.

"And that will stop it?"

"Yes," Gary lied.

He had no idea what was going to happen. He just didn't have any other options. But he didn't want to tell Louise that. She would only shout at him.

The Machine was waiting for them when they arrived. Its lights still flashed, its dials still ticked, and its needles still flicked from side to side. It was still transmitting its signal out into the world. God knows what madness was happening out there now.

Gary moved his focus towards the Reverse Flow button. He was sweating heavily. He wiped his forehead, then wiped his sweaty palm on his trousers. Then he stepped forward. Louise let slip a little moan, like she wanted him to hurry up. If she knew what could happen to them after he pressed the button, Gary thought, she might not be so eager for him to press it. But still, The Machine, *his* machine, had inflicted this insanity on the world. He had to stop it, regardless of the consequences. Gary gulped. He steadied himself. He reached for the button. Louise gasped.

Gary held his breath, closed his eyes, and pushed...

*

The man in the bright red jacket stood still, holding the glass in his hand. He blinked once, twice, curious as to how he had managed to get outside. He didn't remember leaving the house. Then he saw the spider. It was quite large, maybe two inches across. It was propping its front legs up against the inside of the glass, trying to feel for a way out. The man in the bright red jacket thought he must have come outside to release it. Strange that he couldn't remember catching it.

He knelt to the floor, removed the sheet of paper, and wiggled the glass. The spider dropped out onto the floor. It scurried away into the bushes. The man looked up and saw the laboratory. It was fairly new in town. No one really knew what they did there. He had heard rumours of strange experiments, but he didn't really believe any of it. Just small town gossip. People getting carried away over nothing.

But from where he was crouched, next to the bushes, he could see the strange red smudge on the outside of the window. That hadn't been there yesterday. And now he was looking at it, he thought he could see something else there too. Something on the other side of the glass. Something moving. He couldn't make out what it was.

The man in the bright red jacket stood up, still holding the empty glass. He walked towards the laboratory. Perhaps he could catch a glimpse of what was going on inside, see what all the fuss was about. Maybe put some of those crazy rumours to bed, once and for all.

He stepped towards the window. The strange red smudge came into focus. A lumpy smear down the glass, a pile of red gooey matter below it. Flies buzzing around. He didn't know what it was. A dead animal, perhaps? Then he looked to the window itself. There was something there, on the other side, moving around inside the laboratory. The sun was too bright, reflecting off the window, so he peered in closer. He formed a little shelter with his hands, a barrier against the light. He stuck his face up against the glass.

Inside the laboratory, just a few feet away, he saw a naked woman. She was crouched on the floor with her back up against the wall. She was wiggling from side to side, rubbing herself up against what appeared to be a potted plant. She was backing into it, pressing her legs up against the flowers. It looked like she was trying to rub them all over herself. Next to her, backed into a corner, he saw the top half of a naked man. Only the top half, because the bottom half was encased in something, some sort of green sludge. It looked like a kind of casing. The naked man was vomiting the sludge onto himself, spewing out green bile, and then forming it around his bottom half. He was covering himself in the stuff.

The man in the bright red jacket didn't know what was wrong with these people. It didn't look good. He decided he would go and get some help.

*

Gary looked up from his chrysalis. He made eye contact with the man peering through the window. Gary shook his head. He wished he had left a note, something on the entrance to the lab to warn people. Danger. Do not enter. *Never open this door.*

But there was so much going on, so much to think about, that it had simply slipped his mind. Beside him Louise continued to buzz. Her legs were now covered in pollen. Gary coughed up more sticky silk. Despite fighting the urge with everything he had, he could not stop his hands from smearing it all over his chest. His body was not his to control any more. And soon his cocoon would be finished.

The man in the bright red jacket rushed away from the observation window. He was waving his arms, shouting for help. He was heading in the direction of the entrance to the lab. Gary's last thought as a human was of wondering what he would turn into.

Stitches

It all starts as you would expect - a man walks into a bar. He is a mystery, a complete and total stranger. No one inside the bar has ever seen him before. No one outside of the bar has ever seen him before either. He walks with purpose, gliding between tables, sliding past chairs. He is clearly on a mission. The mysterious stranger gives the barman a nod, flashes him a wide, toothy grin. A wink is thrown in for good measure. A low rumble of a chuckle. The stranger obviously sees himself as something of a comedian. A drink is ordered. The barman, having no clue as to who this guy is, and absolutely no idea what is about to happen, simply serves the drink and moves on.

Our comedian takes up a stool at the bar, sipping his drink. He glances around the room, taking in his surroundings. It's quiet in this bar. No one is shouting or laughing too loudly, no voices raucous enough to drown out the classic rock drifting from the vintage jukebox in the corner. This is perfect, the comedian thinks. Early evening, things haven't really kicked off yet. This is exactly how I want it.

He smiles to himself. It's a smile that says, I know something no one else here does. It's a smile that would tell all the other patrons that their pleasant evening is about to come to an abrupt end, if only they were paying attention. But they're lost in their own little worlds, oblivious to what is about to unfold. Our comedian clears his throat, and begins.

"Knock, knock," he says to the room.

Most in the bar don't hear. The rest of them don't care. The nearby customers glance over, shrug, go back to their conversations. The barman pauses, looks up briefly from stacking glasses. There is a moment's glance at this strange comedian, sitting alone on his barstool. The barman shrugs, returns to his duties, thinking nothing of it. Our comedian shakes his head. This won't do.

"Knock, *knock*!" he screams at the top of his lungs, slamming his glass down as he does. His drink spills out, splashing out onto the newly-polished bar. The nearby patrons jump in shock, their attention now flashing over to this potential madman. The bar hushes, the chatter fading away. The barman carefully places the glass in his hand onto the shelf above. He turns to the comedian at the end of the bar, who is now grinning to the room with his arms stretched wide.

"Who wants to hear a joke?" the comedian calls out. No one replies, the room now silent except for the jukebox. Everyone is watching and waiting in nervous anticipation to see how the situation unfolds.

"It's a good one," the comedian tries again. Still silence, the room not quite sure how to respond. There is the occasional hushed whisper, a few awkward coughs. One or two glance towards the door, wondering if this might be a good time to head home. Later they would wish that they had.

"No one?" the comedian asks, overplaying his disappointment. The barman slowly moves over, cursing under his breath that the weirdos always seem to pick his shift to make a name for themselves. Here we go again, he thinks.

"You OK there, buddy?" the barman tries, keeping things casual. The comedian turns, flashing the barman another smile. It stops the barman dead in his tracks. This is not a jolly smile that puts the barman at ease. It is quite the opposite. It makes the barman's blood run cold. It makes the hairs on the back of his neck stand up. It's a smile the cartoon cat might give, the barman considers, when it has finally cornered the plucky mouse.

Our comedian turns back to the room, safe in the knowledge he has the barman exactly where he wants him. He raises a solitary bony finger to the roof, and then aims it in turn in the direction of every single person there. One by one by one. They all get a turn.

"I am going to tell my joke," the comedian declares as he points, "And *you* are all going to listen."

And the comedian speaks. He tells his joke. And his delivery is superb, his timing immaculate. The punchline lands with perfection. And he is correct, it *is* a good joke. The best joke any of these people have ever heard. The barman starts to laugh. The people sitting nearby start to laugh. Those at the tables in the middle of the room, their eyes fixed on this strange individual telling his joke, they all start to laugh too. The joke flows through the room, making its way right to the back, and all the people sitting there start to laugh along heartily. A woman returning from the toilet walks straight into this wall of laughter and suddenly finds herself helplessly joining in too, giggling away where she stands. And she never even *heard* the joke. That's how good it is.

The barman starts to lose his footing. He is laughing so hard he is forced to lean back against the wall to steady himself. His lips are flapping away, his face turning red, his chest heaving. The laughter is infecting his entire body. If you caught a glimpse of him, you would assume that he was having the time of his life. But if you took the time to gaze a little deeper, look a little closer, you'd see something entirely different. You'd see his eyes widen, start to dart around the room, searching in desperation for a solution. Because the barman has realised he is laughing so much he is going to run out of air. He hasn't been able to breathe for a good thirty seconds now. He is laughing so hard it is beginning to hurt.

Our comedian at the bar leans back on his stool, chuckles to himself. The joke has gone down a treat. He takes up his glass, leans over the bar, and refills it himself. The barman slumps and stumbles nearby. The comedian sits up straight, relaxed, sipping on his drink, as the whole room falls apart around him.

The barman lands with a thud on the floor, crumples into a ball, his chest on fire. The laughter has now turned his face purple. All he can hear are the hysterical squeals from all around the room, laughter so loud and high-pitched that anyone hearing it from a distance might not even think of it as laughter at all. To them it might sound a lot like screaming.

Other sounds begin to circle the room - people dropping their glasses, falling through tables, smashing to the floor. The barman convulses, the blood rushing into his skin, turning his whole body red. The agony overcomes him but still he can't stop laughing, not for one second, not to take in that deep hit of oxygen that he so desperately needs. He can feel his body shutting down. He knows the laughter is killing him but he just can't stop. The pressure in his chest is immense. It feels like his heart is about to burst. And then it does.

The last thing the barman sees as the laughter drains his life completely is the comedian leaning over the side of the bar, looking down to him, grinning down to him. So many teeth. *Too many teeth.* So bright and white. It's the grin of a shark looming out of the depths, a predator who has cornered its prey.

Our comedian leans back, takes another casual sip from his drink. He glances around the room, admiring his handiwork - a room full of spasming bodies, blood soaked faces, wide, fearful eyes. A room full of the recently or about to be deceased.

The comedian downs the rest of his drink and gently lays the empty glass back on the bar. He calmly gets to his feet and heads for the door, carefully stepping over the still shaking bodies lying around him, avoiding all the smashed glass and tipped-over chairs. Those who have not yet expired stare up at him. Some clutch at their chests, trying to hold the life in. Others stretch out their arms to this comedian, in one last-ditch attempt to secure rescue that they know deep down is never going to come.

And all the while, they just keep on laughing.

As he leaves the bar, the comedian makes sure to leave the door slightly ajar, so that the sound can escape, so that any passerby might hear the laughter coming from within. Hopefully that passerby will be intrigued, be curious enough to go and investigate what could possibly be so funny as to bring an entire room of people crashing to the floor. And then that passer by might well catch the giggling bug, find themselves laughing along too. They might find themselves falling to the floor, guffawing so much that it begins to hurt.

And so our comedian heads off into the night, hands in pockets, a joyous skip in his step. He smiles to himself. It really is a good joke.

*

I signal for Nelson to pass me the needle. In all the commotion he misses the message, too busy concentrating on holding down the feet. I have to keep reminding myself that he hasn't been doing this for as long as I have, that my first time I was a wreck too. No matter how detailed and in depth the briefing, nothing can prepare you for the real thing. Being new to this, he is bound to make mistakes. I just have to accept that. But knowing all this doesn't make it any less frustrating. We all have a job to do here and, to put it simply, Nelson isn't doing his properly.

I try again, lifting my right hand away from the writhing body beneath me, and then holding my thumb down against my flat fingers. I tip the whole hand towards me, gesturing the sign for "give me". Then the sign for "sewing", holding my thumb and forefinger against one another, gliding them through the air before me like a boat skipping across waves. All of this is utterly pointless, of course, because Nelson still hasn't looked up. His eyes are stuck on the legs he is still trying desperately to hold in place. He's so focused on keeping them from kicking out, he's not taking in anything else around him. And now it is starting to get to me, because just minutes ago I specifically mentioned this. We work as a team and we must communicate as a team. Those were my exact words. And yet Nelson is stuck inside his own head. I know deep down he'll learn - a kick can be painful but it isn't going to kill you - but right now it's really hard to remain diplomatic. He should know better.

Luckily for both of us, Serena is paying attention. Serena is always paying attention. I wish everyone I was handed was like Serena. Serena knows the steps, she doesn't get distracted, and she is an excellent communicator. She is everything you'd want when performing the procedure. She gives Nelson a nudge. Finally, his eyes flash up from the feet and meet mine. My anger subsides slightly when I see how terrified he is. And again, I have to remind myself that what we are doing is terrifying, that the way Nelson is reacting is perfectly normal.

I raise my free hand, palm facing the floor, and wave it gently up and down through the air - "Calm down." Nelson puffs out his cheeks, clearly trying his best. The poor man is drenched in sweat and it isn't even that hot in here. It's panic sweat. No doubt if it wasn't for the smells coming off the operating table, Nelson's body odour would be stinking the place out. Luckily for him, this thing below us smells a hell of a lot worse than he does.

I again signal for Nelson to pass over the needle. This time he does as instructed. I smile and mouth as clearly as I can - "Good job" - as I take the needle from him. He's not done a good job at all. He's done a fucking terrible job, and I will let him know all about it when we are finally out of theatre. But we need to get this thing done and done quickly, and so getting Nelson all riled up right now isn't going to help anyone. So I lie, like a professional, and even throw in a little smile as well, as inside my head I put a big black mark against his name.

Serena takes her cue and moves over to the upper chest, forcing her hands down to keep it in place. The mouth below is wide open. From my position, over the head, I can see right down the throat, beyond the grey, shrivelled up tongue that still flaps around wildly. It's not really an image on which you'd want to dwell, so I move on, instead focusing on the top of the head, forcing my palm down onto the forehead and pushing the whole thing back into the vice. Without hesitation, Serena leans over, grabs hold of the lever and spins it as quickly as she can, closing it shut. It clamps down solidly onto the sides of the temple, holding the head firmly in place. The move is so synchronised, so perfect, that it goes off completely without a hitch. Not for the first time, I thank God that Serena is here with us.

When I'm certain the head isn't going anywhere, I signal for Nelson to move up. It doesn't really matter what the legs are doing now, this thing isn't going anywhere. Nelson seems to be getting the hang of it, or at least pretending he is. There appears to be considerably less panic in his expression, anyway. I don't really care if he's calmed down or if he's simply faking it. At least faking it shows initiative. It shows you know what is expected of you. You are at least pretending to be capable, even if deep down you know that you're not.

Nelson places one hand below the chin, the other on the top of the head, and pushes. The legs flap around wildly, but again, they're not a concern right now. Serena has control of the upper body, the head is contained, and I have the needle prepped and ready to go. We're doing OK.

Now the thing is secure, I take the opportunity to check my music. We're on the home stretch now, and the last thing I need at this point is a flat battery. Nope, three bars, we're all good. I couldn't even tell you what song this is. It's not like I listen to this shit for enjoyment. Would anyone admit to enjoying a best-of-the-90s ultimate house megamix? But it's repetitive, has no words, and more importantly, has absolutely no song breaks. That's one of the key instructions I always make sure I beat into the first-timers. Whatever you want to listen to, make it as loud as possible and, whatever it is, make sure there aren't any silences. A good hour of solid noise. Whether you like it or not is irrelevant. Just make sure it drowns out everything else.

Nelson grimaces, forcing the mouth closed, and finally the lips come together. I can't see the tongue any more. There's something about a dead tongue that gets to me, even now. The colour is one thing - ash grey, drained of life, like the whole inside of the mouth has somehow escaped from some black and white movie. It always looks otherworldly and off-putting, no matter how many times you see it. But it's also completely devoid of moisture. The mouth has been open since death, chin flapping away constantly, so all the liquid has slowly evaporated, leaving behind just a bone-dry hole. If you look closely you can see the damage where the dry flesh has simply given up and ripped itself in two. The tongue seems to have taken the brunt of it. It looks mummified, like some centuries-old dead animal that someone has jammed into this poor creature's orifice. I imagine having one of these in *my* mouth and am suddenly thankful that whoever this person was is now long gone. They won't ever have to see what I'm seeing now.

The cold, grey lips finally come together. I get to work, bunching them up with thumb and forefinger of my left hand, before moving the needle into position with my right. I lean in, focus firmly on the target area. Nelson looks away as I make the first incision. I can't really blame him. This is not a pleasant thing to look at. Clear white dust puffs out of the hole as I force the needle up and out of the top lip. I pull it all the way through, the thread with it, and then twirl the whole thing around, plunging back down. The thing's eyes stare up at me as I go. I know they're not looking at me - they're not looking at anything - but it's still unnerving. You can get lost in the eyes sometimes. You can think you see something alive in there. But there never is. That's another thing I always make sure to drill into the newbies. This is not a person. Never think of it in those terms. This is a thing, a threat, a deadly time-bomb, and we are simply here to diffuse it.

I begin to find my rhythm and lose myself in the repetitive beats pounding out of my headphones. Within seconds I'm not even seeing lips any more, seeing eyes, or a face. I'm just seeing my hands, calmly moving up and down, the needle and thread working their way through time and time again, the mouth slowly starting to seal shut. The needle slides through easily - there's not much resistance in dead flesh - and in a possible all-time personal record, I finish the job super fast, tying off the loose end of thread.

I stand back, nod to Nelson, who cautiously removes his hands before edging away. The mouth remains shut, that grey, dead-animal tongue sealed away forever. The creature still writhes away, but with considerably less enthusiasm than before. Whatever power it had has now been cut off. Soon it'll tire itself out and stop moving altogether. They always do.

Nelson moves a hand to his own headphones and Serena stops him, grabbing hold before he can get close enough to do any damage. She makes sure he sees her clearly before giving him a firm shake of the head. This isn't done yet. She nods down to the creature and holds her hands up to her side, wiggles her fingers slightly - "Wait".

With almost perfect comedy timing, the creature kicks out, one final act of defiance that rounds a square kick firmly on Nelson's sizeable rump. He staggers forward and, although I can't hear it myself, I'm fairly sure he must have let out a little yelp. More out of surprise than of any sort of pain. The creature on the operating table finally stops shaking. Nelson turns, shocked but unharmed, to watch our patient die for the second time. I try to suppress a smile. I don't really feel like shouting at him any more. A swift kick up the arse from a dead man should be all the motivation he needs to improve his performance.

*

We called it Stitches. I have no clue as to who came up with that name. A disease that spreads through laughter and can only be combated by sewing up the victim's mouth, well, the name seemed appropriate. A little gallows humour. Maybe not the best joke in the world, but by that stage we were happy to take whatever we could get.

Everyone has their own take as to how it got started. Names and places differ, but they all involve the same basic ingredients - a comedian shows up, he tells his joke, everyone starts laughing and then everyone dies. Sometimes it's a friend of a friend who witnessed it, sometimes a distant cousin, or someone they vaguely knew in the next town over. I guess claiming some connection to the outbreak gives people a twisted sense of pride. "I have a part to play in all this, don't you know. I was there when it all began." For my part, well, I don't have a story. I don't know how it all started. I really don't care. I just know that it happened and it'll keep on happening unless we can get in there as quickly as possible and perform the procedure. And so that's what I do.

What we *do* know is that in its most basic form it's an auditory virus, passed along the frequency, or within the frequency itself. It burrows itself into the brain and corrupts the motor functions, causing the victim to start laughing uncontrollably. As far as we can tell, the victim has no idea as to why they are doing it. They just can't help themselves. I say as far as we can tell because it is simply impossible to determine. We haven't been able to stop it, once it takes hold, so we can't ask people what it is they're laughing at. They are unable to tell us what's so funny. Once the laughing starts, that's it. The victims can't talk. They can't communicate in any way. They just start giggling, fall to the floor, and essentially suffocate.

When you see someone go through this, it's not something you forget in a hurry. I've seen enough people expire in my time on the wards and, while I'm not saying there is a good way to go, there are definitely bad ways to go. Stitches is most certainly a bad way to go. Once the giggles get you, all other bodily functions begin to shut down. You can't talk, you can't move, you can't breathe. You just fall to the floor and start convulsing, cackling away to yourself at God knows what. Your eyes bulge out of your head, in some cases popping right out of the skull. The tongue almost detaches itself, straining to get free, desperately reaching for that hit of oxygen that'll never come. There can be a lot of blood. I've seen people's skin change colour at the strain of it all. They actually turn purple. After a few minutes of all this, death comes as some relief, at least for the victims. For them it's all over. But sadly not for the rest of us. Not by a long shot. Because this dead body, this recently expired human being, just keeps on chuckling away to themselves, post mortem. This joke is apparently so funny, you see, that you keep on laughing at it even after you die.

And that's how you catch it. That's how it spreads. If you are unfortunate enough to be in the vicinity of one of the giggling dead, if you happen to hear them cackling away to themselves, well, that's it, you've got it too. You've caught Stitches. Pretty soon you'll be guffawing along to whatever sick joke this whole thing is. You'll fall to the floor, your eyes will bulge out, your skin will go purple, and you'll die desperately where you lay. And of course, you keep on laughing afterwards, and then someone else hears it, and they start chuckling away, and so on and so on until…

It didn't take long for people to cotton on that if a sound was going to kill you, the first thing you had to do was try not to hear it. Plug up your ears like your life depended on it. Industrial-grade ear defenders were suddenly all the rage. If you couldn't get your hands on some of those, some basic headphones playing very loud music would do the trick. It wasn't a long term solution, but it at least allowed us to stem the tide. Take stock. Attempt a strategy.

Entire towns were cordoned off, labelled no-go zones. If there was even the slightest chance there was Stitches there, if the place hadn't been fully investigated by the Silent Squads, wandering through with their guns and their military issue ear muffs, then it was simply sealed off. Signs erected. Stitches - Stay Away. We lost thousands, millions in the first few days, but after the initial retreat we at least managed to keep things isolated. It wasn't getting any worse. We could hold up in our laughter-free outposts to try and formulate a way of fighting back.

The procedure itself was the result of a happy accident, if you can call it that. Our first port of call was to experiment. We didn't really have anything else to go on.

We had to get some idea of what we were dealing with close up. So in went the Silent Squads to an infected area, they picked up a body, dumped it in a soundproof booth, and then called in the medical professionals. We were shipped in, suited and booted in the finest gear the military could get their hands on, and thrown in to try anything and everything we could to get these things to shut the hell up.

Our first theory was that some part of the brain must still be active. It must still somehow be passing along signals to the vocal cords, the lungs, the mouth, and if we could just get in there and remove the rogue tissue, then maybe we could simply switch the thing off. After several extremely messy tries, we quickly learned that this was not the case. The brain was most definitely dead. Removing some of it didn't work. Removing all of it didn't work. You could literally rip out the entire thing and throw it against the wall in frustration (believe me, I know) and the dead body would just keep on laughing away. Like it was laughing at you. Laughing at your complete failure to comprehend what was happening and your embarrassing inability to find a solution. So I can fully understand what happened next.

The story goes that, at the end of a very long and unproductive shift cutting up too many dead and giggling bodies, some end-of-their-tether surgeon simply flipped, thought to themselves, "I don't care how crazy this looks, I'm going to shut you up", grabbed a needle and thread, and sewed up the dead thing's lips. And by some miracle, lo and behold, it had worked. Deprived of the ability to project their killer sense of humour, the dead finally gave up the ghost. They shut down completely. A few violent spasms and that was that, they finally stopped laughing. We had our answer. Seal up the mouth. That was the cure.

Unfortunately, the victims were all long dead before anyone could get them still enough to perform the procedure. A few attempts were made to try it out on those still living but, as you can imagine, that didn't turn out to be a very pleasant experience for anyone. But sealing up the lips post-mortem at least meant they couldn't infect anyone else. And so the word was spread, the message put out there. That's the key, stitch up the lips. That was the answer. We had our weapon.

So out went the army, into all the no-go zones, armed with their "state-of-the-art" Stitches protective gear (ear plugs) to identify where all the infected still were. Once a source had been confirmed, specialist sound-proofed clinics would be air-lifted in, along with any available surgeons in the area who had been specifically trained to operate completely without sound. In the early days, those silent surgeons were in pretty short supply. Which is exactly why I was so enthusiastic about bringing Serena in from the off. In a world where sound had become deadly, not being able to hear a thing suddenly became a distinct advantage.

*

I find Serena sitting on her own on a bench just outside the complex. From a distance she looks relaxed, hands in her lap, staring serenely out into the silent woods that surround us. This has been one of the most isolated spots we've visited. Usually Stitches confines itself to populated areas. Being as the only way we've discovered that the disease can spread is from mouth to ear, you'd expect the victims to be fairly close to each other. Close enough to hear each other laughing, anyway. But every now and again a report will come in from somewhere a little more out of the way - a small village or detached farming community - and the mystery deepens. How the hell did it get all the way out here? This particular site, a few holiday cottages deep into a forest, has no identifiable point of contact with the outside world. Our best guess is someone had become infected while taking a phone call, immediately pinging the disease via satellite to the unfortunate soul holidaying in these picturesque cottages. Seeing as we can never ask anyone how they became infected, it's impossible to tell for sure, but that seems like the most likely scenario.

As I approach Serena, before she notices me coming, I see her lean her head back against the outer wall of the complex and run her hands through her hair, no doubt in an attempt to wipe away the stress of the day. That sort of simple action would be impossible for me, and nearly everyone else here, as removing the clunky head gear while on duty is punishable by death. Harsh, you might say, but when you see the consequences of removing it at the wrong time, you can kind of see the reasoning behind it. It just isn't worth taking the risk. So when I see Serena pull off this move, I must confess, the first emotion I experience is envy. To be covered in all this equipment feels constantly restrictive. I can't help getting a little jealous at this point that Serena is able to move so freely.

I take a seat next to her on the bench and she looks over and smiles. Then comes a roll of the eyes together with a puffing out of the cheeks. The message is clear - a tough one. I shrug back to her - we've had worse.

I lean back against the wall, mirroring her pose, and gaze out into the woods ahead of us. It's beautiful here - trees swaying in the breeze, golden brown leaves cluttering up the floor of the forest, scattered all around the clusters of ferns. Looking at it now - this calm, perfect, picturesque scene - you'd never have guessed that two families recently expired here.

The patrol says this should be the last of them, that we'll be moving on soon. I sign this to Serena and she raises half a smile, but doesn't seem overly enthusiastic about it. I can't say I blame her. We're being told that we're winning, that after the initial panic and the multitude of deaths, we're now finally on top of things. But it doesn't feel like that. From our point of view, all we see is the same thing, day in, day out. We fly somewhere, we stitch up the dead, and then move on, do the same thing all over again. From our point of view, it just doesn't feel like it's ending. Stitches just keeps on coming. There's always more gigglers to find out here.

Serena turns to me and raises a flat palm, before running her index finger from the opposite hand along it - "What". The flat palm then becomes a fist, and she rotates her finger around it, like a planet orbiting a star - "About." I can guess the next word that's coming, but she spells it out anyway - "Nelson?". I shake my head enthusiastically, rolling my eyes, then think for a second about how best to describe him. One word immediately pops into my head. I raise both index fingers into the air, pointing to the sky, bring them together, and then throw both arms wide, imitating an explosion - "Disaster".

Serena pushes me gently on the arm, pulls a face to indicate I'm being cruel. But I don't think I am. Nelson can't keep on making mistakes like this. Mistakes in this environment can get people killed. It would be irresponsible to pretend otherwise.

Serena's hands glide through the air before her, signing out her response to my review of Nelson. It's not really what I expected - "But he's *our* disaster. You should talk to him."

I shake my head again, pointing a finger to Serena, trying to make it as clear as possible that if anyone is going to talk to him, it should be her. I'm in charge here, I tell her, and I don't have time for employee feedback. Serena then points out that we're both sitting on a bench staring out into the woods, and so my argument of not having the time immediately falls flat. He won't get any better unless you help him, Serena tells me. I screw my face up, over-egging my distaste at her suggestion.

But she's right, of course. Nelson volunteered for this. Most people don't. Most people choose to stay as far away from this madness as possible. They stick to the clean-zones, where sound doesn't kill. Most people have the right idea. But Nelson signed up because he wanted to help, and now he's part of the team. Like it or lump it, the army tracks Stitches down, and the three of us step in to fix it. That's how this works. Disaster or not, Nelson is one of us, and I'm going to have to find a way to make that work.

*

It had initially been hoped that the search and clean-up teams could operate using radio contact. It didn't take long to learn that when you have a network of linked signals, and one of them then becomes infected, things turn bad pretty quickly. I think you can imagine the consequences of a helicopter pilot being infected with Stitches while flying at 5,000 feet. We lost two entire units this way. So fairly early on, sign language became a pretty essential tool of the trade. Those who already knew it were brought in, often against their will, to train up those who didn't. It actually didn't take that long to get most people up to speed. You'd be amazed how quickly someone can learn a new language when their life might literally depend on it. Unfortunately, "quickly" does tend to mean different things to different people, and I was reminded of this while glaring at Nelson, and wishing not for the first time that day that I could simply rip off his headphones and shout crystal clear instructions directly into his chubby little ears.

We'd found ourselves a nice, quiet spot out of the way (quiet in this instance being simply free of soldiers or dead bodies - nowhere is ever really quiet when you have white noise or happy hardcore constantly blasting in your ears) in what looked to be an old laundry room for one of the holiday homes. The house itself had been set up as a basic base of operations for the military, but out back was this tiny little shed with a washing machine and dryer taking up most of the floor space. It was grotty and grimy but it would do. I just wanted to find somewhere I could talk to Nelson where he couldn't get distracted.

I asked him how he thought the job had gone. He replied, in a roundabout way, that it wasn't what he had expected. I suppose it doesn't really help the fight if the recruitment teams in the clear-zones are actually honest with the folks joining up.

No one would be here if they knew exactly what they were letting themselves in for. They're telling these kids that we have state-of-the-art facilities, exciting new-fangled equipment and an unlimited budget to get the job done safely and efficiently. When they get here, they see what basically amounts to a pop up tent for the operating theatre, outfitted with whatever cobbled-together equipment we can get our hands on. It's not exactly Grey's Anatomy. We literally use a carpenter's clamp to ram the giggler's head into and hold them in place for the sewing.

I ask how Nelson's bum is. He rubs a hand against it, looking like he's still in a little bit of pain from the kick. To be honest, I don't really care. I only asked to try and set him at ease before I criticise him for losing focus. Win their trust and then hit them with the big guns, that's my management style. I don't want Nelson despising me, that won't help either of us in the long run. If I can make him like me, then I can make him feel terrible for letting me down. Guilt and shame are powerful tools, and far more effective than anger. If he gets angry, he might well end up taking it out on me.

I explain to Nelson that he's seen it now, first hand, with his own two eyes. The stories back home don't really do it justice. This is what we have to deal with, and if you let go for just one second, if your mind wanders, that's when the mistakes happen. Nelson nods along. I have no idea if he can understand any of this, but I guess it makes me feel better. I'm covering my back. If it all goes wrong at least I won't get the blame. He makes some gestures that I interpret as him being taken aback when he saw the man's face. When he looked into the eyes, he thought about what might still be in there. What semblance of humanity might still remain. I sigh and do by best to explain the situation as I see it.

I need you 100% focused, I tell him. Mind on the job at all times. You can't think of them as people. They're not people. If they had a soul, if you believe in that sort of thing, then that soul departed a long time ago. What is left behind is simply a very dangerous and highly infectious lump of rotting meat. If you stare too long into the face of this decomposing animal, you might get lost in it. You might start to think you can see a person in there. Trust me, you can't. It is simply a poor imitation of humanity. Let those feelings go and just get on with the job. When you are trying to pin something down and sew its mouth shut, the last thing you want to be doing is thinking of that thing as a living, breathing, conscious human being.

Nelson nods again. I've been mouthing at him and waving my arms in his direction for a good few minutes now. God knows if any of it got through. I won't really be able to find out for sure until we make it back to the city. Or when we next get into theatre, I suppose. If it all goes horribly wrong, I'll know then that he had absolutely no clue about what I was talking about.

*

Serena lost her hearing in a car accident. While waiting at traffic lights on her way to work, a car ploughed into the back of her, the driver distracted by a phone call or a text message. Or maybe he was just checking the time. No one ever found out as he died before they got him out of the car. Serena's own car was shunted forward, hit the car in front, and off went the air bag. Her body's forward momentum was suddenly halted by the expanding airbag, and the extreme whiplash effect resulted in severe inner ear concussion. It pretty much stopped her hearing on the spot. After coming round in hospital, there was a brief period where she could hear ringing in her ears. But once that faded, that was that. All sound departed, the world suddenly silent.

I can't imagine what it must be like to lose that ability to hear, or see, or smell, or feel. To have your capacity to interact with the world stolen away from you in such a brutal way. One second you have it, the next second you don't. And there's absolutely nothing you can do about it. It must have been heartbreaking.

And yet, as I sit here in the helicopter looking across at her, I can't help feel just a tiny bit envious of Serena. It's ridiculous, I know. Selfish, even. But she's immune to all this. She can sit there head-phone free, not having to worry about the consequences of a wire coming loose or her music stopping dead. That terrible laughter breaking through. She doesn't have to fear a flailing arm from one of the gigglers knocking her protection off during the procedure, which has happened to a few unfortunate souls. Perhaps she would say I was being an idiot. Perhaps she would hate me for feeling like this. But right now, as she signs angrily at me from the other side of the helicopter, I can't help but get a little jealous that, without the restriction of all our equipment, she is able to move so freely.

Serena is annoyed with how I handled things with Nelson. I have no idea why. I thought I'd gone easy on him. But apparently, after our little debrief, she had caught him shedding a tear or two on his own out in the woods. He'd been worried about what I said, about distancing himself from the things these giggling terrors used to be, whether he'd ever fully be able to do it. Serena, being Serena, had been sympathetic. But me, being me, had been anything but when she'd passed on the message. Don't get me wrong, I don't mind people getting overwhelmed by all this, having a good cry about it. Jesus, if you can't cry about the horrors that we have to witness on a daily basis, then what can you cry about? But if you are feeling that way, I certainly don't need to know about it. And I'm certainly not going to change my feelings on the matter just because it makes you feel bad. What I'd told Nelson was the truth. A hard truth, maybe, but it needed to be said and understood before we can continue. I have no regrets over that.

Serena shakes her head at me, signs over that just because that is the way I think, it doesn't mean that is how everyone else does as well. I scoff, tell her we'll see who has the right attitude next time Nelson gets all sentimental in theatre and accidentally knocks off his own headphones. Serena gives me the finger and looks out of the window.

I don't know, maybe Serena has a point. But the fact is there is a chain of command here, and I'm at the top of it. She shouldn't really be going behind my back to console Nelson, tell him he did OK, when I've already explained to him otherwise. And she certainly shouldn't be having a go at me about it in such a forthright manner. We've been through a lot, Serena and I, and in normal circumstances you would probably say that we were friends. But that shouldn't distract her from the fact that I'm her boss. I'll have to remind her of who's in charge once we land.

The helicopter takes a turn, dips to the side. I look away from Serena, out of the window, to the big wide world beyond. Not too far away, maybe half a mile, our next target is approaching. A small collection of rough stone houses, their roofs just about visible between all the reds and browns of the woodland below. Sunlight glints off a small river running to the side of the town, which then winds itself away off into the hills beyond. I have to admit, the whole scene looks idyllic. A picture-postcard view of a perfect rural autumnal scene. At least until we get close enough to see all the dead bodies lying on the ground.

Even from up here, you can make out the legs twitching, the spasms in the chest. As we approach the makeshift landing pad, you can even see wide open mouths and bulging eyes, the dead lying on their back, laughing and glaring up into the sky. I adjust my headphones, making sure they haven't slipped out of place on the flight. Time to queue up the next available playlist. I pull out my MP3 and scroll through, select Oldskool Trance MegaMix. The booming beats clatter into my ears as I again tighten the headphones. The music is awful, and the headphones pinch my ears so much that it hurts but, as always, it is better than the alternative.

We land and seconds later the door is pulled open. I glance across at Serena, who runs her hands through her hair before trying it back in a ponytail. My own head itches like a bastard, but for now I'll just have to ignore it. She glances over at me and I try a smile. She doesn't respond. It's difficult to tell what she's thinking. I briefly think about apologising, but then swifty decide I don't have anything to apologise for. If anything, she should be apologising to me for undermining my authority.

Finally, Serena nods over, points to the ground, and then waves a finger between the two of us. She flattens out her hand, her palm facing towards the floor, and wiggles it towards the open door - "Here we go". She's doing the right thing, being professional, and not letting our argument get in the way of the job we now have to do.

I move to the doorway as Serena hops down and scrambles away, ducking below the blades, her hair and clothes flapping wildly in the wind. As I watch her go I can't shake that sharp pang of frustration, that niggling feeling that our conversation isn't over. That I still have more things to say. I hop down from the helicopter and try to forget about it, force my thoughts onto other things. To the job at hand. Let's leave all this for later.

I make a run for one of the nearby buildings as the next Oldskool Classic kicks in and, not for the first time, I wonder how anyone can tolerate this shit when their life doesn't literally depend on it.

*

Before arrival we are forewarned that there are several families in this town. They don't really mean "families" when they tell us this. They mean children. It's a heads up that we're going to be dealing with kids.

The one they bring in first, I'd put her at maybe eight or nine. Nelson and I lift her up and throw her down onto the operating table. It's certainly less hassle getting her into place than it would be with an adult. Or ex-adult, I have to remind myself.

Not children, not adults, just gigglers - large, medium or small. The small dead thing still flails around wildly, of course, but there's less movement to contain, less weight behind the punches. Even Nelson can hold her in place without too much trouble.

If he or Serena are harbouring any resentment towards me, they are doing a fine job of hiding it. Credit to them for that. After the quick debrief from the military personnel about what we were dealing with - how many, what age, how long they've been dead - we whip up our operating theatre and get to work. There's no point hanging around to admire the scenery. With the children involved, I think everyone is of the same mind on this one - the quicker we can get this done, the quicker we can all try to forget about it and go home.

The gigglers' eyes are dark, its lips grey. The tongue does its thing, drained of life and colour, flapping around in that dried up hole that used to be a mouth. There's some mud and leaves in there, which seem to be clogging up the throat. I can only imagine she must have fallen face down, laughed herself to death, and gobbled up all that grime and dirt in the process. In the past we would have had a coroner examine her to determine the exact cause of death. Did she asphyxiate on the dirt, or was it Stitches that got her? We don't really bother with that any more. The girl is dead. How she went doesn't really matter. We just need to make her safe for everyone else.

I catch Nelson staring at the mouth full of mud and snap my fingers in his face, grabbing his attention. I shake my head - "Don't think about it" - and then form my hands into fists, tapping one against the other - "Get to work". Nelson nods back, wipes possibly a tear from his eye, possibly a bead of sweat, and focuses back on holding the thing down. I catch Serena's eye and roll mine, doing my best to show my displeasure with Nelson again. But she just shakes her head, shrugs. As if what he's doing is normal, understandable. As if his behaviour isn't going to screw things up for all of us. And again, I feel that sense of irritation. Here she is, defending him, when she should really have my back at all times. I'm in charge here. She must know that Nelson's turning out to be a liability and yet she refuses to acknowledge it.

Maybe the terrible trance is getting to me, maybe these headphones are too tight, maybe it's just been a long day, but I'm finding it hard to look at her without getting annoyed. There she is, comfortable and headphone-free, able to let her head breathe. Able to run her fingers through her hair at any moment. And then here I am, restricted by my headgear, in a claustrophobic world of insane music blasting in my ears non-stop, just so I can stay alive.

I can feel my temperature rising, my skin turning red. The frustration is beginning to show. So I look away, to the thing on the table below us. Nelson is holding it in place while Serena moves to gather the needle and thread. With the size and relative strength of the girl, I'm able to force the shoulders down and bring the vice forward myself, one hand for each. It's then a fairly easy task to tighten it around the girl's head, to hold her - it - in place.

And that's when she looks at me.

She's not looking past me, she's not looking around me, she's staring *right at me*. The girl on the table covered in mud and dirt with her head trapped in a vice is looking up at me. Her lips still moving, her tongue still waggling, but she no longer looks like a giggler, a victim of Stitches. She looks like what she is - a terrified young girl being held down by three strangers, who are about to seal her mouth shut with a needle and thread. What the hell are we doing?

And suddenly I don't know what to do. Serena moves back to the table, needle in hand, and goes to pass it over to me. But I'm lost. I'm away, just staring into this girl's eyes, wondering what on earth I'm doing here. And so I completely miss the needle itself. It moves towards my hands, but I'm not looking, and so it pierces through the base of my thumb.

I scream, yanking my hand away, causing Serena to jump back in shock. The needle remains stuck in my flesh, wobbling comically at the end of my arm. Serena just stands there staring at me, wide eyed and static. And it's at that moment I catch a glimpse of the girl on the table. But she's not a girl. She - it - is just a giggler. Just a muddy, rotting, grey dead thing that needs fixing. The dark eyes are just glazed over, not even looking in the same direction. She can't have been looking at me. I must have imagined it.

I pull the needle from my hand and glare over at Serena. It's not her fault. I know it's not her fault. I'm the one who lost it. I'm the one who made the mistake. But I can't admit that right now. After all that big talk about being in the zone, staying focused, making sure you do your job, I did exactly the opposite. I got distracted, and ended up with a needle in my thumb for my troubles. I'm embarrassed, and I take that embarrassment out on Serena.

I rant and I shout. All the frustration and jealousy and rage comes flying out in a torrent of unjustified abuse. I know she can't hear a thing - I can't even hear it myself - but out it flies anyway. She can see the look on my face. She can see my arms flying around wildly. I presume she can get the gist of it. How could you be so stupid. Watch what you're fucking doing. So unprofessional. Blah, blah, blah. Get the fuck out of my theatre. The classic trance blasts in my ears and my face glows red and my throat burns and all this venom just flies out at her.

And Nelson, bless him, moves to her rescue. He moves in to diffuse the situation. He moves away from the dead girl on the table. He raises his hands to me, palms out, a universal gesture to signal that we all need to calm down, back up, take a deep breath. And of course he's right. I know he's right. But in the moment, knowing I'm in the wrong, knowing I'm the bad guy, just makes things worse.

So I keep going. I turn on him, ready to vent in his direction. And that's what causes him to lose sight of what the dead girl is doing. Nelson is concentrating so hard on me, and my hissy fit, that he doesn't see the giggler's leg shoot up until it's far too late.

The dead girl's foot catches him hard on the side of the face. The strength of the kick is impressive, given the size of the leg producing it. He loses his footing. Nelson slips, his feet go from under him, and down he goes. His head slams against the corner of the operating table. Hard. I can almost feel the impact myself. He then drops further, disappearing behind the table, out of view. I can only presume he's crashed to the floor in a heap. The dead girl's legs are still flailing around, and so I jump forward, pinning them back in place, thinking to myself that it's OK. It's not a disaster, not yet. We can still fix this. We still have time to rescue the situation. We can still finish the job.

Until I see Serena, that is, and realise something is very wrong.

She is crouched on the floor, next to Nelson, her mouth wide open. It takes a while to register, to understand, because obviously I can't hear anything. I waste a second wondering to myself why she's doing that, pulling that face. And then all of a sudden it clicks. She's screaming. I peer over the side of the operating table, presuming that Nelson's head must be in a bad way from the impact, from the fall. Thinking to myself as I look that he'll have a cut, a bruise. Maybe a concussion. It won't be that bad. Hopefully it won't.

Nelson lies on his back, his body jerking and spasming, and his face contorted into that all-too-familiar agonising grin.

Because Nelson is not wearing his headphones.

Somehow they must have got stuck on the girl's leg - the thing's leg - as he went down. It tore them right off. They spin almost comically around the foot as all four of its limbs just continue to wave around madly in the air. The giggler's expression remains the same as always - mouth wide open, lips flapping, tongue waggling. It seems to take an age for my brain to get there, for my thoughts to catch up. But finally it hits. The girl is laughing and Nelson no longer has his headphones on. The girl is laughing and Nelson can hear.

I scramble around to the other side of the operating table and join Serena in trying to hold Nelson in place, trying to pin him down, trying to stop him from injuring himself from all the spasms. He convulses, hard, and his eyes bulge up at us as his tongue reaches out, searching desperately for air. Serena grabs the headphones off the dead girl's foot, forces them over Nelson's big, fat, purple head. But obviously it does nothing. I knew it wasn't going to work. So did Serena. And so, sadly, did Nelson. But I guess at that point you just try it anyway. You try anything. In desperation, you reach for the impossible.

Nelson dies on the floor of the operating theatre. His body keeps on shaking, his lips keep on flapping, and he keeps on laughing. Serena slumps against the wall, her hand going to her mouth. She shakes too. I can only imagine the sounds she must be making. I'm glad for the headphones now. I'm glad I can't hear her. I'm thankful for the terrible trance megamix. Because it dawns on me then exactly what has just happened. It hits hard like a punch to the gut. After all my big talk, after all my lectures, it was me who made the mistake. I'm the one that lost it. I'm the one that fucked up. And now Nelson is gone. The poor kid is dead, and it's all because of me. If I could hear Serena now, I don't think I'd be able to stand.

*

The helicopter pulls away and the village slowly shrinks below us. I lean my head against the window, peering down at the tiny stone cottages that become dollhouses, the cars parked beside them that become toys. The entirety of the past few days becomes visible. There's the building where they found the young girl.

There's the worn down patch of grass where the operating theatre stood. There's the place where I killed Nelson. None of it looks real from this height. It looks like a model, something a child would play with. I try to think of it like that, I try to forget, as the whole sorry place sinks away amongst the reds and browns of the treetops.

Before Stitches, there would probably have been a disciplinary procedure. There would certainly have been a hearing. I'd have been brought before a panel to explain myself. Serena would have given evidence. She would have told the truth and I would have been punished. A suspension at the very least. People would have questioned whether that was harsh enough. After all, my unprofessional actions had resulted in the death of a colleague. His family would no doubt have wanted to press charges, see me behind bars. They had lost a son and all I get is a slap on the wrist - where is the justice in that? Maybe they would have a point.

Of course, none of that happens these days. If anybody fucks up, on any level, the only real options are to tell them not to do it again or simply go ahead and shoot them. No one really bothers with the middle ground any more. We just don't have the manpower for it. We don't have the time.

Serena and I were pulled out of theatre shortly after the accident, with the reserve team sent in to deal with Nelson and the girl. Without all the screaming and shouting they had managed to stitch them both up fairly quickly. In less time than it took Serena and I to be debriefed, anyway. We explained what happened to the soldiers and they decided not to shoot me. To be honest, I am not sure my execution was ever really up for discussion. The fact of the matter is, my skills and expertise are too useful a resource to throw away over the death of an underling. Maybe if I had managed to kill someone more senior, a general perhaps, they would have been forced into making an example of me. But not for a newbie like Nelson. He was just about the lowest rung of the ladder. Possibly even expendable. And so I am allowed to get away with it.

Serena sits across from me in the helicopter. It's noticeable that she is avoiding eye contact. She just stares out the opposite window, looking down at the forest, the rivers and streams, all the little stone cottages. She looks anywhere and everywhere but me. When we get back, I presume she will ask to be transferred. She will say that she wants a change of scenery, to try something new. I will tell her that I understand and I will see what I can do. And we will both skirt around the real issue that she can't stand the sight of me and desperately wants to leave.

I watch her as she brushes a loose strand of hair away from her face, tucking it behind her ear. An ear that remains free, open to the world, not hidden away behind industrial size headphones and subjected to hour upon hour of teeth-grindingly awful music. An ear that I have become increasingly jealous of after suffering with the constant sweaty heat of my own. With the sounds of the world shut out, I feel trapped, imprisoned inside my own head. I am stuck in here, alone, with my grim thoughts, my terrible memories of the past few days. There's the girl with her mouth full of leaves. There's the needle, sticking into my flesh. And there's Nelson, keeling over, his face slowly turning purple. And this slide show of horror is at all times accompanied by the constant duff, duff, duff of my insane playlist, repeatedly bashing my brain into submission. I am really not sure how much more of this I can take.

Procedure dictates that we never remove headphones while out in the field. Removal of headphones while on duty is punishable by death. Of course, you would soon die anyway, giggling yourself into an early grave, but being immediately shot in the head after taking off your protective headgear does send a pretty clear message to anyone who might have been thinking of doing the same.

It's this thought I find rolling around my head as I slowly start to raise my arms. The movement is almost instinctual, out of my control. I barely even notice it is happening. It is as if my limbs are acting independently from the rest of my body. Although, I note to myself, as my hands move their way slowly towards my head, the rest of my body appears to be doing precious little to stop them. And I suddenly realise - I'm going to do it. I'm going to take my headphones off. I'm going to let the world into my head and I'm going to let all this guilt and trauma out. And then I'm going to be shot. I'm going to escape. I'm going to be free of all of this madness. Realising all this is about to happen is actually the most relaxed I've felt all day.

But then Serana looks over at me. Right at that moment, as my fingers creep up towards my ears, she snaps her attention away from the window, from the world zipping by outside. She is all of a sudden focused firmly on me. She stares at me. She *glares* at me. Her eyes widen. They start to bulge. Her face begins to turn red. She must have worked it out. It's obvious. She must know exactly what I am thinking of doing. And she does not look happy about it.

So I wait for a second. I wait to see if she's going to say something, sign something, *do anything*. I pause just long enough to see if she is doing to stop me.

73

And that pause is all it takes. Those few seconds are all I need. Because what I see in Serena's face, staring back at me across the helicopter, it isn't sadness, or sympathy, or even any particular desire to prevent the action that I seem intent on taking. She doesn't launch herself across the helicopter at me, pin me down, physically restrain me. She just keeps on glaring across at me. And it's in those eyes of hers, in that stare, that I see so much fury, a whole well of anger and disappointment. I witness in that moment exactly what it is Serena thinks of me and what I am about to do. And I realise, with supreme clarity, that this is not the last thing I want to see. I do not want my final moments to be accompanied by that seering image of Serena's pure rage aimed in my direction. My final vision cannot be of Serena hating me *that* much. Like she wants to beat me to a pulp, rip my throat out. To kill me herself. Seeing all that, it's no way to exit this world, cruel and devastating and terribly soundtracked that it may be. I don't want to go out now, here, like this. What was I even thinking?

And so slowly, ever so slowly, I allow my arms to relax. They are back under my control now. I force my hands away from my headphones and down into my lap, where they can't do any harm.

The soldiers around us don't appear to have noticed a thing throughout this whole interaction. Or if they did, they certainly don't seem to care. Maybe they've seen it all before. Maybe they're even a little annoyed that I didn't go through with it, so they could see a little bit of action. Who knows. But if they are disappointed, they don't show it. They haven't moved at all.

And as for Serena, now that she sees I've changed my mind, that I've backed down, turned a corner, she just turns slowly away. Her attention goes right back out of that window. She doesn't bother to sign anything, say anything, send any message out to me whatsoever. There is no need. Her work here is done. That look was all it took.

*

The helicopter lands, the door slides open, and we all file out. Once free of the zip of the blades I am able to stand up straight, stretch my back, breathe in clean and clear air that doesn't taste of dead bodies and rotten leaves. We are in a cobbled courtyard surrounded by empty bars and restaurants. Where once tables and chairs had been laid out under colourful little gazebos, now there are dark piles of bags and crates, all overflowing with weapons and armour and sound proofing equipment, covered in grubby plastic sheets. Military tents scatter the perimeter, sealing us off from the rest of the city. Checkpoints must be passed before our job is completed. That much-appreciated R&R is tantalisingly close but there is still quarantine to go through. We are not home yet. But, still, we are officially out of the field now, back in the safe zone. And that can only mean one thing.

I cannot describe the sheer joy that accompanies lifting the headphones away from my sweaty temples. The cool breeze gently glides against my ears, the wind lapping against the side of my head. All this time, days on end, locked away inside my own brain - to finally be free of it, to let the glorious cacophony of the world come crashing in, it feels like I have escaped from prison. There's the light chatter of the soldiers behind me, the clunk and the clang as they unload all their equipment. There's the rustle of a nearby tarpaulin, laid out over a series of crates to protect them from the rain. It crinkles and creaks beside me, the cool air pushing its corners back and forth. There's the sound of dead brown leaves crackling under my boot as I take my next step. I just close my eyes and stand there, letting it all in. And I remember there is more to life than the world outside these walls. It isn't just gigglers and death and non-stop happy hardcore. There are things here I actually enjoy. And I am so very glad to still be alive.

I hear footsteps clip-clapping on the cobbles behind me, another overwhelming auditory sensation. I can't help but grin as I open my eyes and turn, to see who it is making all that beautiful noise.

My smile swiftly retreats when I see Serena marching up to me, her face still like thunder. For a second I wonder what it is that she can be so pissed off about, when all I feel is freedom and relief. And then I remember. She hasn't escaped from the prison of her headphones. Her world hasn't just suddenly come alive with the removal of some sweaty headgear. For her, nothing much has really changed at all. She is just staring at the same man who shouted at her, who got Nelson killed, and who then tried to escape it all by doing something dumb and short sighted in the helicopter. To her, I am not a changed man set free by the relief of returning home after a terrible and traumatic tour of duty. She just sees the same person I was twenty minutes ago. To Serena, I am still just a bit of an arsehole.

"Hey…" I try, a little startled at the sound of my own voice, but desperate to deploy it to get in there first. To stop Serena from telling me the things I probably need to hear. And so, as she continues to stare daggers at me, I try to sign to her that I'm sorry, that I know I did wrong. Nelson was my fault and it won't happen again. I shouldn't have shouted at him. I shouldn't have shouted at *her*. I did wrong. I *am* an arsehole. But I can do better.

All these words keep spilling out of me. So much so that at times I'm not even paying attention to what I'm saying. It just becomes one big blur of regrets and remorse. Which is possibly why, as I enter my third or fourth round of apologies, Serena reaches both her hands up into the air, palms facing out at me, and then snaps them closed into fists.

Stop.

Serena sighs. She looks up at me and I can see that she is totally exhausted. With me or the job, I can't really tell. I suppose I can't really blame her either way. And so I do stop. I gulp loudly, letting my arms slip to my side. My act of repentance has failed. Serena did not believe me. I'm not even sure that *I* believed me. I just didn't want her to shout at me. To attack me. To hate me. To run off to another safe zone, find a home in another giggler squad. To leave me behind. I just don't want to go out there again without her.

I hold my breath, preparing myself for the worst. Ever so slowly, Serena begins to sign. She nods seriously to me as she goes. She has my full attention. Nelson was out of his depth, she says. You are not an arsehole for thinking that, but you *are* an arsehole for thinking that you are any different. We are all out of our depth. Each and every one of us. That's just what the world is now. Do not think you are above it.

I can now see her welling up as she goes. I even find myself following suit. My stomach lurches as she spells out his name once again. N-E-L-S-O-N. There is an actual lump in my throat as her fingers tap against one another in sequence. I swallow hard, trying to force all the guilt back down. I wish that she would stop. But Serena doesn't stop. She just battles on through. Like always.

Nelson died, she tells me, and perhaps that was your fault. Perhaps you should be blaming yourself. Beat yourself up about it if you want. Feel terrible about it if you must. Deal with it in whatever way seems best to you. But don't you *dare* attempt anything like you just did on that helicopter. Don't even think about giving up like that again. You can't just bow out. You can't just quit. Because if you do, you're just killing Nelson all over again. You're killing me. You're letting each and every one one of us die just because you can't deal with yourself. And if you do that, if you leave us behind like that to clear up your mess, then you really *are* an arsehole. You have to stick around. You have to stay with us. You can't run, because you still have a job to do.

And that's when Serena looks up and actually smiles at me, an act of warmth that I was not at all expecting and almost certainly did not at all deserve. She looks up at me, tears in her eyes, and signs the final few words that end up breaking me completely.

And that's why I'm sticking around too.

It's that final sentence that sends me over the edge. I whimper and I squeal. I start to shake uncontrollably. The tears burst forth and the snot streams from my nose and I collapse into a gibbering emotional mess. I don't think anything like this has happened to me since I was a child. It is not a pretty sight.

And Serena, bless her, Serena steps forward, wraps her arms around me, and lets me bury my head into her neck. She does what needs to be done. She lets me fall apart without another word. She holds me close, pats me on the back, and just lets me get on with it. Lets me cry it all out. And strangely, for some reason I can't quite fathom, even though I am bawling my eyes out and basically a complete wreck, I start to feel better than I have done since this whole sorry Stitches mess started. For the very first time since that very first case, I actually begin to feel like everything might just be OK.

*

It's later that night that I have the dream. As far as I know, it's the first time I've ever had it. And yet, when I try to recall it the next morning, something about it seems all too familiar.

I walk into a bar. That's how it starts. I walk into a bar and I look over at the barman. I look at the barman, give him a nod, and order a drink. The barman serves me my drink, takes my money, and moves on. And so I take up a stool at the bar, begin to sip my drink, while taking a glance around my surroundings. It's nice and quiet in this bar. No one is shouting or laughing too loudly, no voices are raucous enough to drown out the classic rock drifting across the room from the vintage jukebox in the corner. This is perfect, I think to myself. So calm and relaxed. This is exactly how I want it.

But it's then, at that exact moment, that the comedian appears. I swear, a second ago he was nowhere, and now he is there. Sitting next to me on a stool, cosying up to the bar just like I am. And he is also surveying the room, taking in the surroundings. And he is also looking extremely pleased with what he is seeing.

No one else in the bar seems to have noticed him except for me. No one else seems to care. But now I've seen him, now I know he's there, I can't take my eyes off him. I stare on, almost helpless, almost dumbstruck, as I see the comedian's face contort into what appears to be a smile. But it doesn't look right. It's far too wide. There are way too many teeth in there. It doesn't appear possible to keep that smug, self-satisfied and all too hungry smile on the comedian's face, given how huge it appears to be. But somehow he seems to manage it.

The comedian moves to speak. And just like that, the bar appears darker. Shadows creep from the corners and clamber up the walls, wrap themselves around table legs, slide silently over chairs. They slither across the floor unnoticed towards all the soon-to-be unhappy patrons. The jukebox fades. The classic rock drifts away to silence. It is all in preparation for what the comedian is about to say.

And I find my mouth has run dry, my body frozen, my throat closed and unable to shout out and warn everyone of what is about to happen. Of what the comedian is about to do. Because terrifyingly, I don't know how, I know exactly what the comedian is about to say.

"Knock, knock."

Most of the bar doesn't hear, the rest of the bar doesn't care. The nearby customers glance over, shrug, go back to the conversations. And I want to scream at them. I want to tell them to get up, get out, drop their drinks and run, run as fast as they can for the door. Don't look back. Run far from here before it's all too late.

"Knock, *knock*!"

The comedian screams it this time, at the top of his lungs. And still I can't get my lips to move, my mouth to form anything approaching a word of warning. I am a prisoner in my own body, watching this whole sorry scene unfold.

"Who wants to hear a joke?"

Not this. Please not this. My eyes which can no longer move just stare out across the bar, watching on helplessly as the comedian takes the attention of the entire room and gathers it up tightly in his grasp, never to let it go. He has them now. I know it. He knows it. There is no escape.

"I am going to tell my joke," the comedian declares calmly, "And you are going to listen."

I want to close my eyes. I want to shut my ears. I want my legs to suddenly spring into action and bolt towards the door, taking the rest of me with them. I want to run out into the night and never see this comedian ever again. I want to be free of his terrible joke and all that comes along with it. I just want all this to end.

And so the comedian speaks. He tells his joke. And the delivery is perfect, his timing immaculate. It's probably the best joke I have ever heard. I start to laugh. The barman starts to laugh. Everyone across the room, from the stools to the front tables and all the way to the booths at the back, they all start to laugh too. It catches and it spreads and pretty soon everyone in sight is in stitches, struck down with the giggling disease.

Next to me, the barman slips to the floor. His lips are flapping away, his face turning red. The other patrons follow suit. One by one they slide from their chairs and crash to the floor. They shake and they spasm as the stitches take hold. Their faces turn purple.

And I know it's only a matter of time before I do the same. There's a fire in my chest beginning to build, a desperate desire for air that will not come. I am giggling uncontrollably. I am laughing so hard it feels like my heart is about to burst. And there before me, there at his stool, the comedian sits, chuckling to himself and sipping at his drink.

And slowly, ever so slowly, the comedian turns to look at me. His whole body seems to turn at once, or maybe even the whole bar. He's right there now, this comedian, facing me, staring right at me. I'm coughing and I'm crying and I'm about to expire and all he is doing is grinning his horrible grin right in my direction. That impossible smile that just grows wider than wider. A shark looming out of the darkness. A predator that has cornered its prey.

But then, at that precise moment, a flicker in his eye. A moment of hesitation. A slight downturn in the corners of his mouth. The ever-so-slight emergence of doubt in that grin of his that somehow seems to stretch across the entire room. His focus shifts slightly, away from me - as I feel my face burning and my lungs about to explode - to whatever is behind me. To the person who has just stepped into view and placed their hand upon my shoulder. To the one person in the room who his joke is powerless against. To the only human being the comedian is afraid of. To the only one of us who knows how to fight back.

Serena steps before me, placing herself between my violently shaking body and the wall of teeth. She just stands there, a barrier between the comedian and me. My saviour. My protector. And as my eyes begin to bulge out of their sockets, one last attempt to locate the oxygen my body so badly needs, I see the comedian's mouth begin to move, the words begin to flow. The joke beginning to form once again. But his confidence is shaken. His delivery is poor. His timing is awful. He completely fumbles the punchline. His eyes are as wide as mine now, his body shaking almost as much. It's as obvious to him as it is to me and to everyone else in the room. The joke is falling flat. Serena just isn't listening.

There is no smile on the comedian's face now. The only expression I can see is panic. His eyes dart from side to side. Sweat begins to form on his brow. Now it is the comedian looking towards the doorway, for a way out, for a way to escape. He needs to run. He needs to head for the door, to never look back. He's completely lost the audience.

And slowly, ever so slowly, Serena turns back towards me. My body is still convulsing and my chest is still burning, but I feel strangely at peace. Even though I know I'm dying, it seems so much easier to accept now Serena is with me. It doesn't matter any more. Serena is here. And it's at that moment, just as Serena turns and our eyes make contact, just as I see Serena smiling and reaching out towards me, that I realise I can breathe again. And that's when I wake up.

One Last Party

Olivia didn't like parties. They were too noisy, too crowded, too full of forced conversations. There was always that threat of being trapped in a corner with people you don't want to be trapped in a corner with. No, parties were not her thing at all. She'd only gone along because she hadn't wanted to be on her own, when the time came. Facing all of that alone was a far more terrifying prospect than anything the party could throw at her. At least, that was the theory.

Sam was attending the event with friends. They had all been left behind, for one reason or another. Their escape routes cut off. And so, when news started to spread that someone was throwing a party, they didn't hesitate. They were relieved. They were excited. One last chance to let loose, blow off some steam. A chance to forget. That was all Sam wanted to do, really. Forget everything. Forget it all. Distract himself for long enough so that reality didn't seem quite so scary. He wasn't hoping for anything more than that. And he certainly wasn't expecting to meet anyone.

Olivia heard the celebrations from all the way down the street. So many people making so much noise, drowning out the rest of the world. When she arrived, the front garden was lit up with glowing lamps hanging from trees, all flanking the path and guiding her in. The front door was wide open, revellers spilling out onto the lawn. They were everywhere. It immediately put her off. For a second, she considered running. But then she thought about the alternative to the party and decided the alternative was not worth thinking about. She would brave it, fight her way inside, find a quiet corner - if there was a quiet corner - and work things out from there.

Sam lost his friends almost immediately. Stacey went first, kicking off her shoes and running upstairs, without even saying goodbye. The noises coming from the first floor suggested she wouldn't have to wait long to find what she was looking for. Next went Mike, who just would not stop crying. He hadn't stopped all day. It was understandable, given the circumstances, but was hardly getting Sam in the party mood. This was supposed to be a distraction, after all. Mike's tears were not helping. So Sam told him to wait - "I'll get us some drinks" - and fought his way off to the kitchen.

Olivia found her quiet corner in the living room. It wasn't exactly a picture of calmness and solitude, but it was at least a close approximation. Getting there had been a struggle. The hallway had been one horrible, packed out, sweaty mess of bodies. She'd managed to avoid the chuggers, drinking god-knows-what through a hosepipe. She had fended off a girl with insanely large pupils, who was loudly proclaiming that "this place is amazing!" because you could "literally get away with anything!". She had sidestepped the vomit on the carpet, which no one was bothering to clean up. The living room was her solace. All the furniture had been removed, most likely being burned out in the back garden. People sat around on the floor, in tight little circles, clinking glasses over flickering candles. Compared to what was happening in the rest of the house - especially what was going on upstairs - it was all relatively civilised.

Sam returned with the drinks to find Mike missing. In his place, leaning up against the living room wall, was a woman standing alone, arms crossed, silently surveying the room. Sam hesitated. He probably ought to go looking for Mike. That was definitely the right thing to do. He looked to the beers in his hands, counted them - one, two - and then looked back to the woman, standing in Mike's place. Sam nodded. Mike could look after himself.

*

Olivia found herself warming to Sam the longer the conversation went on. At first he had seemed more preoccupied with the whereabouts of some guy called Mike than he was with her. Yes, she had told him, she *had* seen people crying. There was a lot of that going on. Whether she had seen this *particular* man crying, she had no idea.

"He was standing *right there*," Sam insisted.

"Well, I haven't moved him," Olivia replied, somewhat snappy, to which Sam puffed out his cheeks, shrugged, and then offered Olivia one of his beers. Olivia took it. It wasn't as if hangovers were going to be much of an issue.

Sam felt bad about Mike. He really did. But the longer the conversation went on with Olivia, the less bad he started to feel. Mike was a grown man. He'd be fine. And if not, well, Stacey would be there for him, after she had finished… whatever it was she was doing upstairs. He didn't need to worry about Mike. And this girl he was talking to, she was interesting, she was different, and she had a story to tell. Like Sam, her family lived abroad, and she had missed the travel deadline. She hadn't really wanted to talk about it - "I've said all I needed to say" - and Sam was happy to leave it at that. They had both accepted what was coming. There was no need to dwell on what could no longer be avoided.

It was Olivia who moved the conversation on to missed opportunities. It felt pointless to hold back. The time for embarrassment had passed. And so she let fly. A long, sad list of everything she had never gotten around to. Various drugs, sexual experiments, wild adventures for which she had never plucked up the courage. Bungee jumping, skydiving, climbing mountains, galloping a horse along a sandy beach, surfing all the biggest waves. Countries she'd never visited, cities she'd never seen. A whole, wide world of regrets. Sam listened intently, not interrupting, having the good grace to keep his judgements to himself. She liked that. When she finished, she asked him in turn for his list. After some deliberation, he replied with a single word.

"Quesadillas."

Sam had actually been telling the truth, but after Olivia burst out laughing, he pretended it had been a joke all along. It was simply the first thing that had come to mind. He explained to Olivia that he'd always seen them on menus, on boards outside cafes, but for some reason never ordered them. And since no one was likely to be delivering tonight - who would be working *tonight?* - he had probably missed his chance.

"Maybe we can find the ingredients in the kitchen?" Olivia suggested. Without hesitation, she took his hand, leading them both out of the room. And all of a sudden, Sam had an additional item to add to his list of missed opportunities, a brand new searing regret - that he hadn't met this girl sooner.

*

It came as no real surprise to either of them that the kitchen could not provide what they were looking for. But it didn't really matter. The throng occupying the room had thoroughly enjoyed the search, shouting and cheering as each cupboard was wrenched open to reveal nothing inside. The kitchen had been stripped days ago, nearly all the contents thrown onto the bonfire. With no gas, no electricity, no water, why would anyone need any appliances? But through the search, Olivia and Sam made a name for themselves - The Quesadilla Couple. And as they were searching together, often linked hand in hand, people just assumed they were an item. Neither Olivia nor Sam felt the need to correct anyone.

Suddenly a cheer went up from out in the dining room. Olivia suggested they went to investigate. What they discovered when they arrived was a huge TV screen hooked up to an exercise bike, on which a red-faced man was peddling full throttle. Encouraging yelps and whoops from the gathering crowd accompanied his efforts. And there, next to the screen, stood Mike, gripping hold of a microphone.

"It's working, keep going!" somebody shouted. The man on the bike peddled even harder, as the lyrics to some almost-forgotten song popped up on the screen. And then Mike, followed swiftly by the rest of the room, started singing.

Sam shook his head.

"Mike hates karaoke," he said, to no one in particular.

Olivia's smile beamed.

"I love this song," she shouted in Sam's ear, leaning in close to drown out the singing. Sam turned his head to hear her better and that was all it took. Their eyes met, their faces touched. It just seemed obvious, to both of them, what the next move should be.

As they kissed, and as the crowd belted out their joyful tune, a deep rumbling began far off in the distance. Those outside the party heard it and started to prepare, knowing what was coming. Some shouted, some screamed, some fell down and cried. Some stood in silence, making their peace. But back at the party, the karaoke continued. Mike belted out the lyrics and the room kept crooning along. And as Olivia kissed Sam, and Sam kissed her back, they both had exactly the same thought, at exactly the same time. They both wished, both begged, that maybe, just maybe, they could all be given just a little more time.

Interview With Michael Hector Baumann

At the time of Michael Hector Baumann's arrest, Sarah Milton's body had not been found. The area of Neary Forest where Baumann was suspected to have taken Milton had been searched thoroughly. No items of clothing had been discovered, no hair or blood samples recovered. She had been missing for over 72 hours. It was considered unlikely that Milton was still alive. The Murder Investigation Team were operating under the theory that Baumann had taken her remains elsewhere for disposal.

*

DCI Barker leaned forward, resting her arms on the table. Her eyes did not move from the suspect. Baumann himself was static. He sat upright, his back straight. His hands were placed neatly before him, palms face down. His focus was firmly on DCI Barker, his expression blank. There was no obvious sign of emotion. The way his hair was parted, pulled back to the left, revealed enough of his receding hairline to reflect the flickering light above back towards DCI Barker. At times, it even caused her to squint.

"For the purposes of the DIR, can you please confirm your name?"

Michael Hector Baumann did not respond. There was no obvious sign of movement. He had remained in this exact position ever since DCI Barker and DS Richards had entered the interview room. Baumann had not responded when they had read him his rights, said nothing when offered a solicitor, and even remained silent when presented with the customary glass of water. Not one word had been uttered. Not one muscle moved. If not for the gradual rise and fall of his chest as he breathed, DCI Barker would have struggled to convince herself that he was actually still alive.

Beside her, DS Richards sat slumped back in his chair. He held a ballpoint pen in his right hand and was spinning it nonchalantly between his fingers. He had been doing so ever since he had sat down, continuously twirling it between thumb and forefinger. His notepad, which sat before him on the desk, remained unopened. The lid had not been removed from the pen.

"The property at which you were arrested…"

As she spoke, DCI Barker glanced down at her own folder. It lay open on the table before her - a file full of notes, all beautifully organised, colour coded and bullet-pointed where appropriate. Tabs had been placed neatly throughout to highlight all the relevant sections. DCI Barker was extremely proud of it. She scanned a finger down the page before returning her attention to Baumann.

"..84 Lacombe Terrace. Can you confirm that this is your current residence?"

Baumann said nothing. DS Richards snorted loudly.

"For the purposes of the DIR, the suspect is not responding."

DCI Barker glanced to her side, catching a glimpse of DS Richards rolling his eyes and clicking his tongue. He had not stopped spinning his pen. It was not immediately obvious to DCI Barker whether his display of frustration had been aimed towards Baumann or was in response to her line of questioning. Prior to entering the interview room, DS Richards had expressed his opinion that the interrogation process was largely a pointless formality. A box-ticking exercise. Baumann was almost certainly guilty, he had declared. He was able to reach this conclusion simply because of the way the suspect looked and the way he was acting.

"Gut instinct," DS Richards had explained to DCI Barker, as they had stood outside the interview room, observing Baumann through the window, "Nine times out of ten, that's all you need."

DCI Barker took a second to study the man opposite her. Baumann continued to sit there silently. His beady little eyes poked out from under his crooked brow, his eyebrows noticeably jutting free from his rather clammy forehead. His nose and chin were slightly pointed. His whole face was remarkably angular, like it had been constructed using origami. "Goblin-esque" had been how the arresting officer had described him. DCI Barker felt that this was not an entirely inaccurate description. She returned to her notes.

"Your wife, Mr Baumann," DCI Barker began, "a Mrs Catherine Baumann, has provided us with a statement. She confirmed that she was unaware of your whereabouts for almost four days prior to your arrest."

It had been Mrs Baumann who had first contacted the police. She had previously notified them that her husband was missing and then called again when he had returned. When the arresting officers arrived at 84 Lacombe Terrace, Baumann had been found sitting in the driver's seat of the family car, parked on the driveway. The engine was still running. He had been seated much as he was now - back straight, head upright, hands placed neatly before him in his lap. When asked to exit the vehicle, Baumann had been silent but compliant. When the arresting officers had handcuffed him, Baumman had not questioned why he was being taken into custody. He had made no protests of any kind.

During the arrest, Mrs Baumann had been standing at the top of the driveway in her dressing gown, directing what was described in the report as a "fair amount of abuse" in the direction of Michael Hector Baumann. Hidden amongst the expletives and rather personal insults were notable expressions of annoyance that Baumann had been absent for several days. He also appeared to have taken the family car without permission. Mrs Baumann had been unable to attend her monthly bridge club as a result. Upon witnessing that the vehicle was now almost entirely coated in mud, dirt and various samples of foliage, Mrs Baumann had threatened repeatedly to remove rather specific parts of Mr Baumann's anatomy.

It had only been upon Baumann's removal from the vehicle that his wife's anger had dissipated somewhat. Indeed, it was noted by the arresting officers that, as Mr Baumann had been escorted away from the property and taken into police custody, Mrs Baumann's response had become increasingly agitated. Her tirade of abuse switched from Baumann himself and towards the arresting officers. She had repeated to them, at great volume, "Why does he look like that?" and "What have you done to him?". The arresting officers had been unable to ascertain exactly what it was about her husband that had been causing Mrs Baumann so much distress.

DCI Barker glanced up from her notes. Baumann sat opposite, motionless and silent. His eyes had not moved from her for some time. DCI Barker found it slightly unnerving. Her anxiety was heightened somewhat by DS Richards' continued pen spinning. The ballpoint was just about visible out of the corner of her eye and remained a constant distraction. DCI Barker tried her best to ignore it. DS Richads let out a loud sign and glanced up at the clock.

"Are you able to explain what you were doing during those 72 hours?"

DCI Barker gave Baumann a few seconds to respond. She studied his reaction. Or, more accurately, lack of one. He gave no clear indication he was even listening to her. DCI Barker waited, tolerating the repetitive tap-tap-tap coming from the direction of DS Richards, who continued to express his impatience through a series of audible sighs. Baumann himself just stared back across the table.

"What happened in those three days, Mr Baumann?" DCI Barker asked again.

Baumann held her gaze but said nothing. DCI Barker nodded slowly. She returned to her notes and opened up the next page.

"For the purposes of the DIR," she said, "The suspect is not responding."

*

The disappearance of Sarah Milton - young, popular, attractive - had garnered a fair amount of attention in the local press. Sarah was well-liked in her community. People knew her. She was a regular participant in fundraising bake sales, volunteer supervisor for the under-13s athletics team and was also chair of her village monthly book club. She had a good-looking husband and two extremely photogenic children. National news channels had begun increasing their interest in the case. Progress was being monitored on an hourly basis. Her disappearance was being described as a tragedy.

This all made the Commissioner of the local police force extremely nervous. No longer was this simply another run-of-the-mill missing persons investigation. People were watching. And so orders were passed down through the chain of command. The matter was to be dealt with delicately. Justice must be served and it must be seen to be served as quickly as humanly possible. Get your best men on it.

DS Richards had initially taken point on the investigation. Unfortunately for him and for the department as a whole, DS Richards was no one's idea of a best man. If people were being polite, they would have said he was a little too green behind the ears, lacking experience where it mattered. Off the record, they would say that DS Richards was a liability. His investigatory style was known to be rather rough around the edges. It was not uncommon for a suspect to take the odd unfortunate fall while in DS Richards' custody, or accidentally walk into a wall at high speed. This simply could not happen on the Sarah Milton case. A more reliable presence was required to keep him in line.

"Mr Baumann, are you able to confirm the exact nature of your relationship with Sarah Milton?"

DCI Barker paused. Her eyes remained fixed on Michael Hector Baumann. And his beady little eyes continued to stare right back at her. It was a strange expression he wore on his face, one that DCI Barker couldn't quite place. He certainly didn't look angry, or scared, or seemingly even slightly concerned to be in this situation. If anything, DCI Barker would have said that he simply looked curious

"Colleagues? Friends?"

DCI Barker took the moment to glance briefly in the direction of DS Richards. His stern eyes were targeting Baumann. He wore a slight sneer on his lips, aimed squarely in the direction of the suspect. He had stopped spinning his pen at least, but his notepad remained unopened. DS Richards now sat back, arms aggressively crossed, looking anything but pleased to be there.

DCI Barker could not help but find her colleague's expression slightly amusing. So much visible contempt aimed towards a man who wasn't even looking at him. DCI Barker considered for a second whether she should confirm for the DIR just how mean DS Richards was attempting to look. It seemed a shame to let all that hard work go to waste.

DS Richards had not responded well to his enforced partnership with DCI Barker. He had complained loudly to her, and anyone else within the vicinity who would listen, that he didn't need some "out-of-towner" to hold his hand and that he was perfectly capable of "busting this shit wide open" on his own. DCI Barker had considered explaining to DS Richards that she was not exactly thrilled with the prospect of working with him either. Within ten minutes of meeting him, DCI Barker had formed the opinion that being partnered with the now defunct coffee machine in the station canteen would have been preferable. It certainly seemed to have been cleaned more recently and she suspected probably held a higher level of investigatory intelligence. However, DCI Barker felt that informing DS Richards of these opinions would not have been beneficial to the investigation. Instead, she had told him that the decision was out of her hands.

Following their first exchange, DCI Barker had then headed swiftly for the nearest toilet cubicle, locked herself inside, and leaned her head up against the wall for a good five minutes. The Sarah Milton investigation had been sold to her as a great career opportunity, a high profile case to show the powers that be exactly what she could do. A chance to show off her meticulous attention to detail, her ability to spot things others failed to see. It would get her noticed. After her initial meeting with

DS Richards, reality dawned. DCI Barker had been called in simply because she was of significantly senior rank that blame could land squarely in her lap should anything go wrong.

"Were you lovers?" DCI Barker asked, looking up from her notes. If Baumann had been rattled by the question, he certainly showed no signs of it. His expression remained blank, his entire body still. DCI Barker shook her head and sighed. Whatever was going on in that head of his, he was doing an almost admirable job of keeping it hidden from herself and DS Richards.

The working theory - DS Richards' theory - was that Sarah Milton and Michael Hector Baumann had been having an affair. Something must have gone wrong, an argument got out of hand. Perhaps Milton had threatened to expose their relationship. Perhaps she had threatened to end it. Whatever it was, Baumann had reacted badly, responded violently. Whether intentional or not, Milton had been killed.

The issue DCI Barker had with this theory - other than it in no way explained what they were doing out in the woods - was that she found the idea of a physical relationship between Michael Hector Baumann and Sarah Milton so outlandishly implausible. And she was not the only one. When Mrs Baumann had been informed of the suggestion that an affair had taken place, she had laughed heartily, expressing some disbelief that Michael had managed to persuade any other woman to sleep with him.

DCI Barker took the time to study her suspect. His pale skin showed no sign of any scratching or bruising, no evidence of a victim defending themselves or fighting back. There was a red mark just above his left wrist, around the size of a golf ball. Mrs Baumann had mentioned it as an identifiable feature, a "grotesque and unsightly" birthmark that Baumann had never felt any need or desire to hide. But other than that, not one obvious blemish of any kind to suggest that a struggle had taken place. He looked clean. DCI Barker sighed.

"Mr Baumann, I shouldn't have to tell you that you are in quite a lot of trouble."

Baumann continued to appear completely relaxed. His brow remained unfurrowed, his entire demeanour that of utter serenity. His eyes stared calmly ahead, without even blinking, waiting for DCI Barker to continue.

"It would be in your best interests to answer some of our questions. Help us clear up any misunderstandings. What happened out in the woods?"

Baumann said nothing. DS Richards' groaned loudly, glanced over to the clock on the wall, and then back to the suspect.

"Just answer the question, prick," he snarled.

DCI Barker raised a hand between herself and her colleague. The last thing she needed right now was DS Richards losing patience and bringing his customary sledgehammer approach to the table. DS Richards clocked her gesture and rolled his eyes, muttering something insulting under his breath. Perhaps DCI Barker would use the DIR later to identify the remark and have him disciplined. The idea appealed to her. If the interview went nowhere, she might as well try and get some satisfaction out of the day. But not yet. For now, there was still policework to be done.

"Where is Sarah?" DCI Barker tried.

And there it was. Baumann's focus slipped away from her. For the first time, a reaction. He moved his attention down to the table. Perhaps the sound of Sarah's name had finally rattled him.

"What happened to her?"

Baumann's hand reached out slowly across the table. It was not an aggressive move. DCI Barker felt no threat, and so allowed the action to continue. DS Richards sat up sharply, ready to pounce. Again, DCI Barker raised a hand in an attempt to calm her partner. She wanted to see how this all played out.

Baumann continued to reach forward, seemingly oblivious to the pair of them. His fingers slid across the table and closed gently around DS Richards' pen, pulling it slowly back into his palm. The entire movement was fascinating to DCI Barker. There was something oddly deliberate about the whole performance. It was as though Baumann was having to concentrate on each and every movement his hand was making, planning all sequential actions well in advance. The stretching out of his fingers, wrapping them neatly around the ballpoint - none of it seemed to come naturally to him.

Of course, DS Richards did not notice any of this. He was just extremely angry that someone was trying to steal his pen.

"Hey, leave that alone, you fu…"

DCI Barker pushed past him, grabbing at DS Richards' unblemished notepad. Her partner's rage increased. First the pen, now this. It was an outrage.

Baumann picked up the pen as DCI Barker pushed the notepad towards him. This was it. He was going to explain, reveal his secrets, tell them everything. He just needed to write it down.

DCI Barker smiled gently to Baumann, laying the notepad neatly before him on the table. Baumann looked up to her, paused, and then began twisting his face into a rather curious arrangement. His cheeks rose and his lips curled. His chin waggled. His bottom row of teeth pushed themselves out of his mouth. Baumann seemed to be having some trouble performing the act of smiling. In the end, he seemed to give up, leaving this half-grin, half-grimace where it was. DCI Barker gulped. DS Richards swore under his breath. It was not a facial expression either of them had ever seen before.

And then, with this bizarre gurn seemingly there to stay, Baumann slowly raised the pen up to head height and began to spin it. The notepad was completely ignored. He rolled the pen effortlessly from finger to finger, watching with great curiosity as it glided silently over his knuckles. It was a perfect re-enactment of the skill DS Richards had demonstrated earlier. DCI Barker watched on, transfixed. Other than his hand, and his waggling fingers, Baumann's whole body remained completely still. It really was a remarkable display.

DCI Barker blinked slowly, bringing herself back to the present.

"What happened out there, Mr Baumann?"

The question came out as a croak, a clear nervousness in her voice. Something definitely was not right about the man sitting opposite her. DCI Barker cleared her throat, not taking her eyes away from Baumann. She worried slightly about looking away from him, his party trick and his utterly unnerving smile.

"What happened to Sarah?"

But Baumann did not answer. He continued to stare down at the pen, dancing back and forth along his knuckles. He didn't say a word. He didn't even look up at her to acknowledge a question had been asked. He didn't even blink.

*

Everyone liked Sarah Milton. When interviewed, not one work colleague had a single bad word to say about her. This in itself was not unusual. In DCI Barker's experience, people would rarely use openly negative language to describe missing persons, especially missing persons who were suspected to have been murdered and dumped out in the woods. In death, people would often become saints in the eyes of those around them. For some, this was done out of respect, a belief in not speaking ill of the dead. For others, it was simply done out of self-preservation. If the MIT come sniffing around, it is probably unwise to inform them of your hatred of the victim, as that might well lead them to start sniffing around you.

In order to gauge an interviewee's true feelings, for DCI Barker it was often a case of reading between the lines. Were they short, sharp and precise with their answers, designed specifically to convey the minimum information required in the shortest amount of time? Or were they long and overflowing, unable to contain the emotion held within and bursting at the seams with unnecessary detail? When it came to the friends and colleagues of Sarah Milton, it was definitely a case of the latter. When DCI Barker read between the lines, all she found there was an abundance of love, loss and respect.

Sarah was regarded by all as a genuine good egg. She was regularly described as an "absolute sweetheart", a "friend to the entire office" who was "always willing to lend a hand." Half of her work colleagues appeared to be in love with her. The rest were simply in awe of her. DCI Barker had identified several members of staff who Sarah had gone out of her way to help personally with out-of-work issues. She was always willing to go the extra mile, for anyone, at any time.

Baumann, on the other hand, was not so popular. No one interviewed seemed to actively dislike him, but not one interviewee seemed altogether surprised he was the suspect in a murder investigation either. Most questioned responded by saying that they didn't really know him because he largely kept himself to himself. Those willing to go into further detail described him as an avid mint tea drinker who spent most of his time in the office chewing on his pen while struggling with crosswords or just staring out of the window.

Only after a little more digging was DCI Barker able to squeeze out from some of the more talkative members of the team that Baumann was not shy of a few unusual beliefs. A couple of "pretty out there" ideas. "Not quite one of those conspiracy nuts," she was told, but, "you know, not far off." His internet search history showed more than a passing interest in simulation theory, supernatural sightings and alien abduction. The unwashed mug on his desk displayed an aged and faded photograph of bigfoot. He had once owned an American bobtail called

Mulder before Mrs Baumann had requested it be rehomed as a condition of their marriage. All this had been noted down and underlined in DCI Barker's extensive notepad. DS Richards had dismissed it all as "nerdy saddo bullshit" and moved on.

"We don't have time for these games, Mr Baumann," DCI Barker said, as calmly as she could, eyes still transfixed by the spinning pen. Baumann's peculiar smile had at least departed but her suspect was still sat opposite, rolling a pen around his fingers for no apparent reason. And he still had not responded with a single word to any of DCI Barker's questions.

"Oi, dickhead, give me back my fucking pen," DS Richards tried, somewhat more aggressively. Baumann paused for a second, glancing absently between the two of them, before returning to the spinning. DCI Barker felt it was only a matter of time before DS Richards' tether snapped completely and he dived across the table to retrieve his property. She hoped to get *something* out of Baumann before this happened. The way the interview had been going, this seemed increasingly unlikely. In an attempt to placate her partner and buy some time, DCI Barker took a spare pen from her folder and pushed in gently in DS Richards' direction. She did not bother to look over at DS Richards' reaction to this gift. She doubted very much he would have been particularly impressed.

"If Sarah is out there, if she is still alive…" DCI Barker began, before she was interrupted by a loud derisory snort coming from the direction of DS Richards. DCI Barker closed her eyes, took in a deep breath, and tried to pretend she hadn't heard it.

"If she is still alive, Mr Baumann, you need to tell us as soon as possible so that we can help her."

Baumann did not respond. DCI Barker sighed, looking back down to her folder. DS Richards ignored the new pen he had been given, instead reaching out for his coffee cup. He took hold of it, lifted it to his lips and began slurping abrasively. The noise was infuriating. Again, DCI Barker found herself closing her eyes and taking a deep breath. She was beginning to lose patience with DS Richards and was seriously considering asking for him to leave the room. She would deal with the consequences later. The only thing that was really stopping her was Baumann himself. DCI Barker did not get the impression that the man sitting opposite her twirling a pen between his fingers was a cold-hearted killer, or even particularly likely to have committed a spontaneous crime of passion. Baumann did not strike her as a murderer. But she was beginning to grow increasingly uncomfortable in his presence, for reasons she could not quite put her finger on. Something was definitely off about him. The continued silences, those bizarre hand movements, and the way he had tried and failed to smile at them… Yes, she would keep DS Richards around for the time being, no matter how annoying the man was proving himself to be. It certainly seemed preferable to being left in the room with Baumann alone.

"Let me tell you what we have, Mr Baumann."

DCI Barker looked up from her folder, to the suspect, and then slowly began to lay out some photographs before him. Baumann did not look down. DS Richards continued to slurp away, muttering something under his breath that almost certainly contained the words "waste of time." DCI Barker didn't care. She had enough evidence to place Michael Hector Baumann firmly at the scene of Sarah Milton's disappearance. Perhaps if she presented it to him now, he would be more forthcoming with his information. At the very least, DCI Barker hoped this new distraction would stop him from spinning that stupid pen.

"For the purposes of the DIR, I am showing the suspect item references MB-11, MB-12 and MB-13."

The images placed before Baumann had all been labelled accordingly. DCI Barker went through them one by one, piecing together the evening of Sarah's disappearance. First, a still from the security footage taken from the office car park, showing both Baumann and Milton leaving the building together. Next, a slightly blurred but still identifiable Baumann and Milton driving along the north side of the Dreyfuss Overpass, taken from the nearby traffic camera. Baumann could be seen driving the vehicle, Milton seated beside him on the passenger side. They were heading towards the woods. In both images, there seemed no obvious animosity between the pair. In fact, Milton could be seen quite clearly smiling as they drove across the bridge. In the security footage taken outside the office, it was also obviously apparent that she had been wearing trainers. Milton had changed from her work attire into more suitable footwear for the terrain. She had known where it was Baumann was taking her. And in the third picture, the final photograph, Baumann could be seen driving the same vehicle, back across the same overpass, three days later. There was no other passenger in the vehicle. Whatever had happened to Milton, it had happened in that three day window.

DCI Barker kept her focus on Baumann as she asked the next question.

"What were you doing out in the woods?"

Baumann did not respond.

"Why were you there? What were you looking for?"

At that, DS Richards snorted loudly. DCI Barker looked across to see his face twisting into a comical smirk. Baumann glanced between the two of them, studying DS Richards' expression in great detail, but did not say a word. DCI Barker couldn't help herself. Enough was enough. She was going to have to respond to her partner's unprofessional behaviour.

"Something to say, DS Richards?"

DS Richards slurped loudly at his coffee.

"Anything you wish to add?"

DS Richards swallowed, gulping with as much force as was humanly possible. It almost seemed to echo through his oesophagus, like a large rock bouncing around inside a soggy cave. DCI Barker would no doubt have to explain the noise for the DIR later. DS Richards then smacked his lips, looked to Baumann, looked back to DCI Barker, and shrugged.

"Pretty obvious what he was looking for, I'd say."

DCI Barker raised her eyebrows, prompting him to continue. DS Richards nodded, clearly pleased that he was finally being given his time to shine. He reached forward and placed his coffee mug down on the table. He coughed, clearing his throat. Out of the corner of her eye, DCI Barker spotted Baumann, looking on with great interest at what DS Richards was doing. A look not dissimilar, DCI Barker found herself thinking, to that of observers studying animals at the zoo. A curiosity without judgement as to what these strange creatures were going to do next.

Knowing he had his audience gripped, DS Richards then slowly raised his left hand, forming a ring with his thumb and index finger. He then raised his right hand, outstretched a single finger, and proceeded to poke it through the middle of the ring repeatedly. DS Richards grinned suggestively. He even gave Baumann a wink.

DCI Barker let out a long sigh, closing her eyes and massaging her forehead, just wishing the day would end. Beside her, DS Richards then began to make little squeaking noises, presumably to give the impression of creaking bedsprings.

"For the purposes of the DIR," DCI Barker groaned, "DS Richards is reenacting sexual intercourse with his fingers."

DS Richards nodded.

"The international symbol for shagging," he declared proudly.

Opening one eye to look at Baumann, DCI Barker did at least see that her suspect appeared fascinated with what DS Richards was doing. Not unnerved, not embarrassed, just... interested. And to DCI Barker's surprise - not to mention relief - he had finally stopped spinning the pen between his fingers. Baumann's left hand had frozen still, still hanging in the air, but the pen had dropped from his knuckles and bounced onto the floor.

"That got your attention, didn't it, Mike?" DS Richards proclaimed.

Reluctantly, DCI Barker had to admit that it almost certainly did. Whatever it was that DS Richards was doing, Baumann seemed fascinated. More so than he had appeared throughout the entirety of the interview so far. This reaction of Baumann's, wherever it led, was at least something new. And so DCI Barker sat back, opened both her eyes, and waited. She doubted that DS Richards' method was going to be drastically more productive than her own, but it would at least give her the opportunity to see how Baumann reacted to a new style of questioning. DCI Barker decided then and there to let DS Richards have his moment.

"I mean, that's why you went out there, wasn't it?"

Baumann said nothing, but continued to stare down at DS Richards' fingers.

"We've all been there," DS Richards continued, finally ceasing his crude gesture and sitting back in his chair. He then crossed his arms. The action didn't seem to phase Baumann one bit. He continued to stare at DS Richards across the table, watching on with great interest.

"Back seat fumbles and cheap hotel rooms can only do it for you for so long," DS Richards said confidently, clearly pleased with himself that he was finally getting his chance to shine.

"So when the opportunity arose, I bet you jumped at the chance for a little al fresco loving, didn't you, Mike? A change of scenery to really get the blood pumping."

DCI Barker watched on as Baumann slowly slid back in his chair. DS Richards grinned, satisfied that his little story was clearly getting to the suspect. He was onto something.

"So you drive out there, out into the woods, all eager and excited for that little slice of outdoor nookie..."

Baumann crossed his arms, not taking his eyes from DS Richards for a second. And as DS Richards talked, slowly but surely, Baumann's face began to contort itself into a little grin of its own. But not like his previous failed experiment, DCI Barker observed. There were no misplaced lips or strange, angular chin movements. Gone was the awkward and frankly disturbing attempt at a smile he had performed earlier. This time, it looked totally natural.

"But when you get out there, what happens? Sarah has second thoughts, right? I guess those dark, damp, creepy woods weren't quite as romantic as she was hoping for. And so… she wants to back out."

DS Richards' grin widened. Baumann's followed suit. DS Richards looked across the table and saw a suspect being rattled, a fake smile to cover up his unease at being found out. Finally, a bit of direct policework was getting the job done. None of DCI Barker's pussyfooting around, this was how you open up a suspect - you go straight for the jugular. Baumann was about to crack.

"Sarah asked you to drive her back, didn't she? She'd had enough. She wanted to go home."

But when DCI Barker looked across the table, she saw something entirely different. She saw Baumann - the grin, the slouched back, the crossed arms - and she saw someone observing, studying, and now recreating what they were seeing before them. A game of imitation. The first failed pass at a smile, that had been a dry run. But now, with DS Richards' constantly smirking across the table towards him, Baumann had a lot more information to work with. Everything was right there in front of him. He could simply copy what he was seeing. Baumann wasn't reacting to the story at all. He was reacting to DS Richards.

"But you didn't want to go home. You were in the mood now. All fired up. You'd gone through all that effort. Sarah couldn't back out now. It wasn't fair."

DS Richards' grin widened.

"There was all this anticipation, all this frustration, just built up inside with nowhere to go. And now Sarah wasn't playing ball. You just couldn't help yourself."

Baumann's grin widened as well.

"That's what happened, wasn't it, Mike? Out in the woods. That's what went down. Sarah rejected you. She screamed. She fought back."

Not one scratch, not one mark, DCI Barker thought to herself.

"And so you killed her. You had to. It was all you had left. You killed Sarah and you buried her, left her out there in the woods. You murdered her and dumped her and ran back to wifey, hoping the whole damn thing would just disappear."

And no sign of Milton anywhere, DCI Barker reflected. Just this strange man before her, who won't say a word, who went to the woods with a colleague but came back all alone. A man who appears to now be copying her partner, his each and every gesture, learning it all as he goes. A man who smiles at the world like he has never seen it before.

DS Richards nodded slowly, pleased with his day's work. And Baumann nodded in return, a clear confession if ever there was one. DCI Barker wanted to ask DS Richards to wave, or put his hand on his head, to see if Baumann would copy that too. She tried to ask but she found her mouth was dry. She couldn't get the words out. Her mind was racing almost as fast as her heart.

"You killed her."

DS Richards glared across the table now, towards his cornered suspect. He had Baumann exactly where he wanted him. Perhaps the story he had told was true, perhaps it wasn't. But it had garnered a reaction. That's all he needed, really. Some sign that the suspect had been wrongfooted. Then he would go in for the kill.

Baumann sat there in silence, arms crossed, an exact replica of DS Richards' grin writ large on his face. DCI Barker gulped, waiting to see what was going to happen next. Baumann did not disappoint. He held DS Richards' gaze and then, with almost perfect comic timing, let out a long, loud derisory snort, firing it off in DS Richards' direction. Much to DS Richards' surprise and condemnation, Baumann laughed right in his face.

DCI Barker recognised it immediately as another performance, a like-for-like reenactment of the childlike petulance that DS Richards' had displayed throughout the interview. Even the sound of the snort, a perfect imitation of the one DS Richards' had given prior to performing his inappropriate hand gesture. It was simply another act on Baumann's part. A copy. DCI Barker saw this quite clearly.

DS Richards, on the other hand, saw something quite different.

"You pisstaking little fuck!"

DS Richards' arm shot out, snatched up his mug of coffee, and flung the steaming drink in the direction of Michael Hector Baumann. DCI Barker shouted, trying to stop him, but it was too late. The piping-hot liquid arched through the air and splattered squarely over Baumann's chest, arms, neck and face. DCI Barker froze. DS Richards almost roared with anger, jumping to his feet, ready for action.

But Michael Hector Baumman did nothing. He did not react at all. He simply sat there, still smiling, still smirking, with all that scalding coffee dripping down his face, burning little red marks all over his pale skin. He didn't move a muscle. He didn't say a word. He didn't even blink.

"What the hell?" DS Richards croaked, staring down at the now soggy suspect. The man should be screaming in pain, but was in fact just staring back at him, seemingly quite content to be there. DS Richards did not know how to react. It just didn't make any sense. And for the first time that day, DCI Barker felt that her and her partner were on exactly the same page.

*

Mr Milton had been understandably shaken by the disappearance of his wife. During his interview, he had been welcoming and polite, forthcoming with whatever information he had to give, but rather reluctant to go into any great detail regarding his marriage to Sarah. DCI Barker had felt rather uncomfortable herself, asking such unsympathetic questions to a husband and father whose partner had been missing for several days. But the questions needed to be asked. Every possibility had to be explored, every angle covered.

No, there was no ill-feeling between him and his wife and no, there was no trouble at home. Their marriage had its ups and downs, of course, but was generally considered to be happy and healthy. There certainly hadn't been any serious arguments, nothing that he was aware of that might have pushed Sarah away. As far as Mr Milton had been concerned, all had been well in their perfect little family unit. He could think of no logical reason why she would have left him and the children deliberately. Foul play had to have been involved.

Had Mr Milton ever met Michael Hector Baumann? Only in passing. Occasionally Mr Milton had visited his wife at the office, to drop something off that she might have forgotten, or to pick her up if she was finishing early. Very rarely, if a colleague of Sarah's had been retiring, switching jobs or throwing a significant birthday party, they would be invited along to the event as a couple. Mr Milton would always stand to the side of the room, drink in hand, politely interacting with anyone who came by, but not going out of his way to socialise. He never really felt part of the team. He wasn't like Sarah in that way, he told DCI Barker. Sarah was always happy to meet and greet. She liked getting to know people. If there was a team to be part of, Sarah was always first in line to be part of it.

Mr Milton had met Baumann at one of these events. He could not remember exactly when, but he was sure it had happened. He knew what he looked like, enough to recognise him. But Mr Milton could not say for sure if he had ever shared a conversation with the man. Certainly nothing that he could recall right now.

However, Sarah had been talking a lot about Baumann recently, Mr Milton had gone out of his way to add. DCI Barker probed further, careful to skirt around the issue of a potential affair. But Milton had cut her off on that tangent before she had even come close. That wasn't who Sarah was, he had said.

No, Sarah liked projects, Mr Milton had told DCI Barker. Things that she could work on and fix. She loved completing puzzles and solving riddles. Deciphering codes. Mr Milton had not said so to his wife, for fear of upsetting her, but he had begun to suspect that she viewed Baumann as her latest mystery to be investigated. There was no malice involved, Mr Milton was keen to stress. Sarah did it all out of love. She simply wanted to mend things she saw as broken, to help out wherever she could.

And what had Sarah told him about Michael Hector Baumann? What about the man needed fixing? Mr Milton had shrugged apologetically, confessing that, for the most part, he had not taken any of it in. He was happy for Sarah, that she had a new passion project to work on, but Mr Milton personally had very little interest in it. The only thing that had really stuck had been what Sarah had told him about Baumann's childhood. Something about him running away from home when he was very young. DCI Barker had nodded along, jotting down all the details in her notebook. She was not sure how useful any of it was going to be, but she was experienced enough to know that nothing could be dismissed entirely. No matter how minute or seemingly insignificant, no detail was so unimportant as to not potentially become useful further down the line.

Has Sarah mentioned anything further regarding Baumann's disappearance? Yes, Mr Milton had replied. Sarah had explained to him that Michael Hector Baumann had run away from home when he was around ten years old. However, upon his return, the young Baumann could not recount a single detail or where he had been, who he had been with, or what he had done. For the child Baumann, the entire two week period was a complete blank.

Doctors had examined him and found Baumann to be slightly malnourished and dehydrated but otherwise completely unharmed. There were no obvious signs of assault or physical trauma, no clear marks or bruises except for one unusual blemish. A small red mark, like a birthmark, had appeared just above Baumann's left wrist. Almost perfectly circular, around the size of a golf ball. It did not appear to be causing him any pain or discomfort, and so the doctors at the time had not been particularly concerned by it. Perhaps it will fade over time. Come back if the situation changes. The whole experience remained a mystery, one that Baumann himself had never managed to solve. Sarah had been fascinated.

Mr Milton had apologised after that. He couldn't recall any further details. DCI Barker had thanked him for his time and reassured him that they were doing all they could to locate Sarah and bring her back safely. They had exchanged numbers. Should Mr Milton remember anything else, he should not hesitate to contact her, at any time, day or night. DCI Barker had stood, tucked her notepad into her bag, and headed for the door. It was at that moment that Mr Milton had called after her, remembering one more tiny, probably insignificant detail. Sarah had mentioned something about the forest, he said. DCI Barker took out her notepad and pen once more. After Baumann had gone missing as a child, Mr Milton had said, that was where he had been found. The same place he had taken Sarah, all these years later. Out to Neary Forest. Mr Milton explained to DCI Barker that the child Baumann had been found wandering around out there, not wearing a thing. That was where the police had picked him up - bewildered and disorientated and totally naked, not able to recall the events of the past two weeks. Just all by himself, stumbling along, out there alone in the woods...

Back in the interview room, DCI Barker jumped to her feet, pulling her notepad away from the slowly spreading pool of hot coffee. It had escaped relatively unscathed. The evidence photographs had not been so lucky. DCI Barker grabbed them up swiftly, shaking off the liquid as best she could, speckling the floor and table with little spots of brown. All the while, Baumann looked on curiously, not moving a muscle, not saying a word.

DCI Barker turned to DS Richards, fire in her eyes.

"That was extremely unhelpful. What were you thinking?"

DS Richards shrugged.

"Waste of a good coffee."

DCI Barker turned away, resisting the urge to fire anything more insulting in her partner's direction. Instead, DCI Barker turned back to Baumann and the mess now all over the table. She sighed.

"For the purposes of the DIR," DCI Barker barked, "DS Richards has acted in a highly unprofessional manner and thrown his drink all over the suspect."

"For the purposes of the DIR," DS Richards retorted, "The suspect was acting like a right little bitch and totally deserved it."

DCI Barker glared back at her colleague.

"Oh, come on," DS Richards replied, "This isn't an interview, it's a freak show. He's wasting our time."

DCI Barker had to admit that there was some truth in DS Richards' last statement. Whether intentional or not, Baumann was giving them absolutely nothing. Her line of questioning had led them nowhere, her evidence had been ruined, Baumann was drenched head to toe in coffee, and she probably had more questions now about what had happened out in Neary Forest than she did when they had started the interview. Perhaps it was time for a break.

"Interview terminated at 11:34am," DCI Barker said, "To be resumed at a later date."

She reached forward and clicked off the tape. Beside her, DS Richards sighed with some relief and made his way towards the door. Unexpectedly, DCI Barker felt a sudden pang of panic shoot through her entire body.

DCI Barker had been in worse situations than this, with worse people. She had confronted career criminals, serial offenders, violent killers and not been fazed. And yet the thought of being left alone in the interview room with this strange little man covered in coffee filled her with dread. Even though he had done nothing really but pull a few odd faces and perform a couple of party tricks, the latest of which involved not reacting in the slightest to a face full of hot coffee. DCI Barker didn't find herself feeling particularly threatened by him but she certainly found herself unnerved. Something was off about him, something which she couldn't quite put her finger on.

"Where are you going?" she asked her colleague.

DS Richards shrugged back at her, clearly unimpressed with the question.

"I need a piss," he said, reaching for the door handle.

"Wait!"

DS Richards paused, rolling his eyes yet again. DCI Barker paused, not really sure what she was going to say. She looked to Baumann, whose attention now seemed to have shifted to the table before him. Little droplets of brown liquid were edging down his pointy nose and dripping into the pool of coffee below him, which for some reason he seemed to find fascinating. DCI Barker turned back to her colleague.

"He'll need a towel," was the best she could come up with.

DS Richards stared blankly at her, shook his head, and then pulled open the door.

"I'll get him a fucking towel, then. Jesus…" he grumbled, before stepping through and slamming the door shut behind him.

DCI Barker gulped.

The interview room fell silent. The light on the ceiling flickered slightly, crackling once or twice. The extractor fan rattled loudly in the corner. DCI Barker felt her heart beat faster. She became very aware of the sound of her own breathing. It seemed far too loud. She tried to calm her nerves, convince herself that she was panicking over nothing. There was no need to be so scared. DS Richards would be back soon. Baumann was of no real threat to her. What was she even scared of?

Michael Hector Baumann's hands began to lift from his sides. DCI Barker froze. She considered shouting out, bolting for the door. If she had had her firearm, she might well have been tempted to draw it. But she remained still. She stood and watched. DCI Barker waited.

Baumann lifted his hands, all the while staring down at the pool of coffee, and then ever so slowly lowered them into the mess before him. They landed palms down on the table, both at exactly the same time. He then began to edge them around clockwise, sliding both hands around before him in tight little circles, making two little brown circuits of coffee over the table. And as he did so, he watched both his hands glide through the pool with great interest, totally entranced by the movement. He didn't show any particular signs of enjoying the performance. It did not appear to be a playful or mischievous act. Baumann simply seemed fascinated, watching on intently as he drifted each hand through the lukewarm brown liquid. It was not the behaviour of a grown man, DCI Barker considered. More like a child - a newborn baby, experimenting with their surroundings. Baumann was simply learning how the world works.

Except, as DCI Barker knew all too well, the man before her was a middle-aged, married, slightly eccentric office worker. He was not a child. He had several decades experience of knowing how the world works. So why on earth would he be acting otherwise?

It was at that moment that DCI Barker realised she had been holding her breath. The light flickered again. Had it been doing so throughout the entire interview? DCI Barker couldn't remember. The extractor fan thudded around in the corner of the room, at a greater volume than she had noticed before. Had it always been that loud? DCI Barker wasn't sure. Something about the situation, about Baumann, this unusual little man with his mysterious past and his strange not-quite birthmark, had heightened her senses. She was on high alert. She noticed everything around her, every little noise or movement, keeping a keen eye out for any potential threat. Ready to act if necessary. Not because DCI Barker thought Baumann was a murderer. She didn't at this stage. She knew there was more to the story. She did not believe he was a killer. DCI Barker believed he was something else.

The door to the interview room clicked open. DCI Barker almost screamed. She stumbled back and clattered into the wall. Baumann momentarily stopped toying with the coffee stain to glance up at her to see what she was doing, seemed to decide it was nothing worth concerning himself about, and promptly went back to his business. DCI Barker's attention shot over to the doorway. There stood DS Richards. There was a flash of relief, a momentary reprieve from the tension. It lasted around a second before DCI Barker clocked the look on DS Richards' face. He was white as a sheet. His eyeballs almost bulged out of his head. He looked terrified. And he was looking not at her, but staring straight down at Baumann.

"DS Richards?"

Her colleague did not reply. The man sitting at the table below them raised his palms in front of his face. He appeared to study them in great detail, taking in every crease of skin and tiny blemish, cataloguing every bruise and scar.

DS Richards reached out an arm towards DCI Barker. She noticed immediately that his hand was shaking. Under normal circumstances, from what she had come to know regarding DS Richards' personality, she would have batted the arm away without a second thought. But the fear he was displaying made her hesitate. Her instinct was not to back away from DS Richards' outstretched arm but instead retreat from Baumann. She still was not entirely sure why she felt this way. DCI Barker allowed DS Richards to grab hold of her shirt and pull her towards the doorway. The man still sitting at the table seemed to care little about any of this. He was far too interested in studying his own extremities to care about the strange dance the two police officers were currently performing.

"What?" DCI Barker snapped in a whisper.

DS Richards shook his head, glanced at Baumann, and then pulled his partner again towards the doorway. DCI Barker saw quite clearly the anxiety in her colleague's expression. Obviously he had been told something upon his return from the toilet. New evidence had come to light.

DCI Barker paused. She eyeballed DS Richards and pursed her lips, deciding firmly that answers were required before another step was to be taken. DS Richards looked almost like he was about to cry.

"DS Richards…"

"They found a body."

DS Richards flung the words at her as if he were desperate to be rid of them. DCI Barker's stomach dropped. A lump began to form in her throat. Sarah. The news did not come as a particular shock to DCI Barker - sadly, this was how these cases usually resolved themselves - but that did not make the news any less devastating. She couldn't help but imagine the conversation she was going to have to have with Mr Milton. She couldn't help but imagine the look on his face when she explained to him that his wife's remains had been discovered.

DS Richards looked to her with a curious expression. DCI Barker found it hard to place. It was as if her colleague was surprised with her reaction, that she had not responded appropriately to the information he had provided. The discovery of Sarah's body was indeed a tragedy, but the look DS Richards was giving her now suggested he was more alarmed that DCI Barker was not as terrified as he was. There had to be more to the story. DCI Barker proceeded with caution, feeling very much like the only sane person in the room.

"Where was she?"

DS Richards frowned. Again, that difficult to place confusion.

"She?"

"Milton."

Her colleague's expression remained uncertain.

"Sarah. Sarah Milton. Where did they find the body?" DCI Barker tried, laying the words down in as clear and precise an order as she could think of to alleviate any further confusion on DS Richards' part.

DS Richards' shook his head.

"They haven't found Sarah's body," he replied with a hissed whisper. He appeared to be attempting to keep the information between himself and DCI Barker, almost as if he did not want the man sitting at the table toying with the coffee stains to overhear. He appeared afraid of what that might result in.

"Well, whose body is it?" DCI Barker replied, also in a hushed tone, as if she were now in on the conspiracy. Had a third party been involved that she had been unaware of? As far as she knew, only two people had gone out into the woods that night, Milton and Baumann. If Milton's body had not been discovered, then who could it possibly be that the team had found?

And then DS Richards replied. DCI Barker felt her stomach lurch. The name he gave seemed both impossible to her and yet also made more sense to her the more she let it sink in. It was the only obvious answer. The light above continued to flicker. The extractor fan continued to thud. And DCI Barker knew now what her instincts had been trying to tell her all along. She understood why she was right to be afraid of the man that was sitting down at the interview table. It all made an inconceivable kind of sense. Baumann had gone out into Neary Forest that night, looking for answers. Milton had followed him, hoping to help. They had found what they were looking for. Milton had not returned. Perhaps she would one day, with a similar golf ball-sized birthmark. An identifiable feature that would make her easier to track. Like Baumann had been tracked. Some sort of calling card, drawing him back to the woods to be catalogued and then disposed of. Because DCI Barker now recognised what she saw sitting at the table. She understood. What had come back out of the woods was not Baumann at all. It was simply pretending to be. And it was learning.

DCI Barker found herself edging towards the open doorway. She took hold of DS Richard's outstretched arm. She held onto him tighter than she could remember holding onto anything in her life. And as she made her escape, she glanced back to the table. The thing pretending to be Baumann continued to stare at its palms, observing them with great interest, as if they were the most captivating objects in the entire universe. DCI Barker almost felt some sympathy for it. It must be confusing, she thought, as she fled the interview room. No wonder it is so fascinated with its own hands. It probably hasn't had them for very long.

The Sceptic

What I saw cannot be a ghost, for ghosts do not exist. This statement shall form the foundations of my investigation. It shall be my guiding light. When fear threatens to cloud my judgement, at the moment I am tempted from the path of reason by thoughts of nightmarish fantasy, I shall retreat to the refuge of those 12 words. They shall be my safe haven, my liferaft in an ocean of superstition. I shall repeat them as a mantra. What I saw cannot be a ghost, for ghosts do not exist.

Before my encounter, I would have passionately denied the existence of the supernatural. I would have scoffed at any evidence put forward in its favour, for all evidence put forward relies heavily on folk tales, hearsay and unsubstantiated claims. I would have refuted accounts of spiritual encounters, demonstrating quite clearly and precisely how the human mind can be so readily swayed, how an indoctrination to ancient beliefs and naive wishful thinking can so easily cloud one's judgement. Put simply, when we gaze deep into the abyss, we glimpse nothing but our own soul peering back at us. The darkness within contains only what we have been conditioned to see.

It is true that what I witnessed last night in my bedchamber cannot be immediately explained. But this does not - nor should not - grant me free reign to reach wildly for the outlandish in order to explain it. There must be a rational interpretation. I simply have to search for it.

And so throughout this investigation I shall examine the facts and nothing more, drawing my conclusions from the evidence presented. I cannot allow the bizarre and downright horrifying events of last night to send me running and screaming from the notion of rationality. I must remain focused and calm. For the above statement remains as true now as it did before my encounter. Nothing has changed. What I saw cannot be a ghost, because ghosts do not exist. That remains a scientific fact.

*

It is a peculiar thing, how the mind finds form in the chaos. The eyes may perceive an unidentifiable shadow, the ears identify an inexplicable sound, and yet the brain takes this confused barrage of information and moulds it into an altogether identifiable and recognisable outcome. The unexplained becomes explainable simply through interpretation. It is this miraculous process I find myself contemplating as I recall waking into the grim darkness of my bedchamber, at some unholy hour in the dead of night.

A sound had raised me from my slumber. A sound that was at once unnerving and altogether familiar. I hear it every day, I know it off by heart. And yet still, it had caused my heart to race immediately upon waking. I emerged from my dreamstate unnerved. For it was a noise that can be made by one thing, and one thing only, and should certainly not be occurring during the middle of the night. Something out there in the dark was amiss, a potential danger lurking in the shadows.

I attempted to blink myself awake, peering over the lip of my bedsheets. It was almost completely dark in my bedchamber, bar a slither of silver moonlight breaking through the gap in the curtains. It was this illuminated pathway I attempted to follow, scanning it across the wider room until it collided with the western wall, hoping it would provide some clue as to the source of the noise. There it was again. The same sound. A subtle creaking, a muffled squeak. Beyond the pathway, further into the gloom. I squinted out into the shadows, looking directly towards where I assumed the noise was coming from. I saw nothing but darkness. It was then a chillness began to overwhelm my body, a shivering down my spine. Something was out there. I was certain of it.

Beyond the moonlit passage breaching my bedchamber lay my leather wingback armchair. I could not see it at this juncture, sleep and shadow forcing a grogginess upon my senses, but I knew it was out there. It always was. Not simply because I always leave the wingback facing into the room as I remove myself from a daily stint at my writing desk, but also, more pressingly at that moment, the sound I heard - was still hearing - was the unmistakable sound of someone - or *something* - relaxing down into it. Of that I was certain. The chair did not creak and squeak of its own accord. It had an occupant. There could be no other explanation.

My voice croaked as I attempted to find speech. No words came to me. My body stiffened as I searched for the outline of the chair, out there beyond the light. It took some seconds for my vision to adjust. Perhaps my imagination had beaten it to the punch, forming images from the shadows that my eyesight had yet to fully discern. It was a moot point. For whether imagined or not, what I saw appeared all too real to me at the time. The outline of the wingback began to form - the legs, the arms, the arched leather back. But it was not alone. There was the clear image of a figure as well, a shadowy being occupying it. It was enough to confirm my suspicions. I had awoken into unusual and frightful circumstances. My bedchamber was sanctuary no more.

The shape sitting in my wingback had no obvious features. There were no eyes to reflect the moonlight back at me, no nose or mouth or thick head of hair to add description to the form out there in the dark. Nevertheless, in my now heightened sense of alarm, I was able to roughly identify the shape of a head, of shoulders, of an upper torso. Of something sitting there silently in my wingback, facing toward me from out of the murk. A jet-black shadow in human form.

My already disturbed mind became overwhelmed by a whirlwind of possibilities. Had I invited a guest to stay and simply forgotten? That would seem to be a stretch. And even if I had, it would be quite remiss of me to force them to reside in my wingback while I slept comfortably and soundly (until this point, at least) in my own bed. Was there an intruder in the house? A criminal? A robber? This at least appeared to be within the realms of possibility. Apart from the obvious fact this intruder appeared to not be robbing at all. They were not taking from me, only watching, simply waiting. If some miscreant had broken into my residence to rid me of what meagre possessions were to be found there, they would surely not take the time to relax down into my armchair midway through their criminal escapade. No, this visitor, this stranger, was not in my bedchamber to conduct an act of larceny. There appeared a darker mystery here, a more nefarious purpose. This was no run of the mill ransacking. This was something worse.

Fear rose within me. I found my heart racing, my palms sweating profusely. Almost without thinking, I began to draw my feet up and away from the stranger, dragging them silently towards me under the covers. Nightmarish visions began to course through my mind. A cold grip around the ankle, nails digging deep, and then being dragged squealing and screaming from my bed. I considered addressing my invader, calling out to them, but found myself paralysed by the grim possibilities of what such direct contact could bring. Perhaps the stranger thought I were still asleep. If they knew different, would they not be forced into action? And who knows

111

where that would lead. I looked to the doorway, so distant and dark, out there in the midnight gloom at the far end of the bedchamber. The being in the wingback sat directly between me and my escape. Could I move swiftly enough to reach the door before they were upon me? And even if I did, where would I go? The house was empty. I was totally alone. There was no respite for me beyond my bedchamber. My shadowy visitor had me trapped. And all the while they just would not stop looking towards me. Despite being unable to make out any features out there in the darkness, I knew without doubt that I was being watched. It was all too much.

I looked away. I wished almost immediately that I hadn't. For what I saw when I glanced down from the chair, to the rug below and the slither of moonlight that danced across it, merely heightened my terror. A pair of human feet, almost unnaturally pale, sticking out from the base of the wingback. They were the only part of my assailant that were clearly visible to me and provided an immediate clue as to who or what it was I was dealing with. The information I garnered from them was not promising.

The feet themselves were as white as bone. The toenails appeared rugged and uneven, clearly untrimmed, and coated in what appeared to be jet black dirt and soot. From the heels all the way to the tip of the largest toe, I could make out tiny little scratches and blemishes along the skin. There appeared to be lesions. The possibility immediately sprung to mind that they were the result of bite marks, of repeated attack by some small rodent. The dirt under the toenails suggested the feet had spent some time in or around the earth. They had been immersed in soil. And the colour of the extremities themselves - or, more precisely, the complete lack of it - led me to swiftly conclude that the owner of said feet was not in exactly tip-top medical condition. If anything, one could have said that the feet appeared to be completely devoid of life. They were repulsive to me, wholly unnatural, absent of colour or even a hint of warmth. It became quite apparent in that moment that what I was faced with was not from the world of the living.

I attempted a whimper. No sound came. I tried desperately to shut my eyes, wishing the apparition away. Almost cruelly it seemed to me, my lids refused to close. This creature, this monstrosity, sat there opposite my bed, seemingly gazing directly at me (I had to assume, for I could see no facial features of any kind) and I appeared helpless to prevent it. It remained there, lifeless and unmoving, while I continued to cower under the covers. My only plan for salvation was that, if I simply ignored the beast, pretended to still be asleep, then perhaps my otherworldly guest would depart the scene. Whatever reason it had for this visitation, whatever dark purpose it had in mind, if I gave it no cause to interact with me further, then hopefully it would creep back away to whichever nightmarish realm from whence it came. It should surely come as no surprise to learn that this was extremely wishful thinking indeed.

I cannot say for certain whether the choice to remain frozen in place was mine or chosen for me by the phantom. In any case, it took several seconds of cowering for reality to dawn. A horrible truth became rapidly apparent. I was unable to move. Whereas before I had sensed the ability to drag my legs up and away from my supernatural assailant, to pull the blanket up over my face, it appeared now my entire body had chosen a rather inopportune moment to remain entirely unresponsive to my commands. I was unable to wiggle a finger, to jiggle a toe. I could not even attempt to blink. The blanket had positioned itself just above my chin, leaving my nose and eyes exposed. I could see the creature but the rest of my body remained hidden. And yet I could not move a muscle. I was at once detached from my own physical form and at the same time trapped within it. The creature had me paralysed from head to toe. I was utterly helpless.

I prayed for rescue. Perhaps this may come as a surprise, perhaps not, that a proud man of science and reason reached deep into the spiritual realm in a moment of extreme trepidation, asking for forgiveness and redemption from an unseen force he had no previous cause to believe in. In truth, I had no real clue as to who or what it was I was praying to. It is as unclear to me now as it was then. And yet still, I prayed. It was my last recourse. While the ability to speak and move had been taken from me, my consciousness had not, and I was still able quite clearly to articulate through my own thoughts what it was I required. And so, I am ashamed to say, I screamed quite passionately within my own mind. I cried out internally, promising a lifetime of devotion and worship to whoever it was who answered my call. Save me from my nightmare, release me from its grip. Force the morning sun to rise, crashing through the curtains, burning away the darkness and the beast with it. Let the whole sorry affair come to an end. I could bear it no more.

It pains me to think of it now, the depths of despair I plunged to. But I was, at that point, a truly hopeless and desperate creature indeed. And with good reason.

For no such salvation came. My prayers were answered in the worst possible manner. The apparition began to move.

Ever so slowly, as if being birthed by the very darkness itself, the grim menace rose to its feet. It moved in silence, the only sound being the accompanying creak of the wingback. And that of my poor heart pounding in my ears. The monster seemed to flow through the gloom, bleed in and out of it, like water grazing along a riverbed, capturing rocks and soil from along the shoreline and dragging them along with the current. At times it was hard to tell exactly where the shadows ended and the form of the creature began. But I knew it was there. It stood facing me, mere feet from the bed. As it rose, moonlight struck the knees, the thighs, the entire midsection. Like the feet before them, the areas of the spectre that entered the light turned a bright white, the clammy skin now clearly visible. Those tiny blotches and scars ran all the way up to the lower torso. It was obvious to me then that the body I was seeing illuminated in the moonlight had begun to decompose. It could not possibly be alive. But there it was, standing before me, in my very own bedchamber. And there I was, eyes wide, heart racing, in complete paralysis, dreading what now seemed to be grimly inevitable. The beast was coming for me.

The phantom stepped forward. I attempted a scream but only managed a pathetic dry wheeze. Despite increasingly desperate attempts at persuasion, my limbs remained immobile and lifeless. I called out to my legs, my arms, my feet, my hands. I begged and I pleaded. Not one limb responded. I remained trapped. And the demon out there in the shadows, that nightmarish vision, began to make its approach.

A silent step forward. I screamed inside. The moonlight slid up its chest, revealing deep scars, jet black divots in the skin. As it encroached, the light slithered up its neck, the lower body returning to the shadow. Only the sections of the creature that were struck by moonbeam revealed themselves fully to me. Once the light had passed, that pale, blotched, gruesome dead skin returned to the dark. It became black and formless again, a mere outline against the colourless backdrop of the room.

And so it dawned on me - as the apparition made its creeping approach to my bedside, all too soon the face would become visible. The nightmare's true nature would be revealed. I dreaded that more than anything. To see the mouth, the nose, to look into its eyes - the anticipation of what I was about to witness gripped me with

114

a cold dread, pulling my waking thoughts into a domain of terror that I had not thought previously could even exist. There was a terrible inevitability to my fate. The impending horror was unavoidable. And while the face was only revealed to me for mere seconds, seconds were all that it took.

A gaunt and cadaverous chin, flesh almost hanging from the bone. It led up to a lifeless, lipless grin. The skin had been drawn back through decomposition, the gums receding through desiccation. All that remained were crooked yellow teeth, jagged and sharp, built for ripping and tearing. Beyond the mouth, a deep crevice where a nose once stood. Tattered ashen skin skirted the edges, grey bone jutted out from the gaunt skull underneath. It was the grim image of death that I was looking upon, sheer hopelessness in human form.

And then the moonlight drifted up to the eyes. Oh, to think of them now is to contemplate horrors unimaginable, a revulsion I can barely comprehend. As best as I can describe, what was revealed to me at that moment were two patches of shadow so dark as to be almost unrecognisable. An altogether unnatural emptiness beyond reason. They appeared to absorb the light, drink it all in, steal it away from the living world and draw it back into the creature's head, deep down into the netherworld. The sheer blackness of those eyes, the cruel expanse held within, seemed to drain the very life out of the room. To gaze into them was to experience despair in its purest form. It was to witness the end of all things.

But as the moonlight drifted on by, all of a sudden the face was gone. It once again slipped back into the shadow. And yet, having seen it, having witnessed the true horror of that face mere seconds before, I found no comfort in its sudden departure. For I knew then that the spectre was coming for me. And although I could not see them, those terrible eyes were still out there in the gloom and were edging ever closer.

The weight on my chest seemed immense. I could not move. I could barely breathe. An unseen force was pushing me down into the mattress, preventing my escape. I wanted to close my eyes, to look away. My body prevented me from doing so. It was locked rigid with fear. And so I was forced to watch on as the beast slid up onto the bed, clambering forward across the sheets. That face, that monstrous visage with its rotting features and jet black, soulless eyes, would soon be upon me. I could not know what it had in store for me. All I knew was that it would be an experience too terrible to imagine. The monster was here. It was above me. There it hovered, directly atop my body, primed and ready to enact whatever evil it had in store. Up there, in that black outline of purest darkness, was all I had ever feared come true. Never have I felt such desperation and despair. Never have I suffered such hopelessness. I was utterly done for.

*

I suppose it must, at this point, be difficult to take this account seriously. As monstrous as the events described may appear to be, one inescapable fact remains - this story is being told by an individual who remains alive to tell it. The demon did not take me. My life was spared. In fact, not only did I survive the encounter, but I was well enough to jump out of bed the following morning and scribble down these notes while they were still fresh in the memory. Perhaps this will come as an anticlimax, a thirst for blood denied. For that, I must apologise. But I cannot exaggerate the facts in order to augment the narrative. This is a study in science, after all. An attempt to understand what happened to me using only accepted knowledge and established reason. Spirits cannot communicate with the living. Ghosts do not exist.

So what then happened? How did my ghoulish encounter arrive at its conclusion? In truth, I cannot say with any certainty. All I can describe is what I remember. When the creature climbed on top of me, pinned me to the bed, I became lost in a veil of absolute terror. There was nothing but fear. My ability to interact with my surroundings deserted me. I could not see, hear or feel. It was all-consuming. The only truth that existed in the entire universe was pure horror, and I was lost to it forever.

But then I awoke. I found myself lying still in my bed, drenched in a layer of sweat, the covers drawn down to my clammy thighs. Somehow, I was still breathing. My end had not arrived at the hands of the monstrosity. There to my side I witnessed the first welcome signs of daylight, penetrating through a gap in the curtains. The night was at an end, the darkness defeated. Morning was its conqueror once more. Before I could even look around the room, I could feel that the evil presence had departed. The air appeared clearer, tasted sweeter, the world feeling instantly less bleak. And so I knew with absolute certainty that the apparition was no more. The room was empty. I had been saved.

And I could move. I could wiggle my fingers, jiggle my toes, raise my arms and legs to the ceiling in triumphant celebration. I could leap around atop the bedsheets and shout out my praise and my thanks that the nightmare was at an end, the beast defeated.

I cannot fully describe to you the euphoria I felt in that moment. A literal and metaphorical awakening, to a new dawn free of desperation and misery. I had made it through the night. That dreadful creature - whatever it was and wherever it had come from - had not caused my untimely demise. I had faced death in its most hideous and horrifying form and escaped unscathed. The joy was overwhelming. I cried out in delight. I thanked the universe for allowing me to live. I wept tears of sheer elation.

And it was at this point that I hauled myself from my bed, rushed over to my writing desk and flung my body down into the wingback (with accompanying squeak). I was so very eager to document my experience as soon as possible, while it was still fresh in the memory. Others must learn from my encounter. It was my duty to tell them. To tell everyone. Whatever had happened to me was too important a discovery to not share with the world immediately. Actual documented evidence of the supernatural. An encounter with the beyond. It could change everything.

But before my pen made a single stroke, I paused. Before I began to write my story, it was important to decipher exactly what story it was I intended to tell. It was my duty to mull over the encounter in its entirety, try to draw some sense from it. To break it apart into a neatly identifiable sequence and not rush to any conclusions. To determine if I might have missed something. I went into the encounter possessing a fully rational mind and a fiercely determined - some would say stubborn - scepticism in relation to all things supernatural. Could I say with absolute clarity that my experience provided enough evidence to deviate drastically from this position? What exactly had I encountered? What had I discovered? What, indeed, had actually happened to me? There was only one thing for it. In the cold light of day, it was my duty to return to the horrors of the previous night, viewed through the prism of clarity that a new dawn can bring.

*

To begin, as one tends to, at the beginning, let us first consider the time and place in which the encounter occurred. I was in my bedchamber, in my own home, in the early hours of the morning of January 12th. Unsurprisingly at this time, I was deep in slumber, regretfully unaccompanied and tucked up cosily under the covers. A familiar and comforting setting but also one that conjures up a sense of isolation, of being separated from the wider world. The house itself would have been empty, with the darkness beyond the sanctuary of my bedchamber adding to that overall sense of solitude. I am all alone in the dead of night. It is not uncommon for anxiety to spring up from this set of circumstances alone.

I was awoken by a strange noise, a sound at once familiar to me and deeply unsettling. It is a sound I immediately sense should not be occurring at that time. My anxiety is heightened. And yet, let us return for a moment to a not insignificant detail from the above paragraph - "deep in slumber." For that is how this whole experience began, after all. I was asleep. The noise woke me. But can I be wholly certain that the creaking sound made by the wingback was not already playing some part in the narrative of my dream? The lines between conscious thought and subconscious fantasy can often become blurred when slipping in and out of the dreamstate. Can I be sure the sound was not simply a figment of my imagination? Do I know, with absolute clarity, there was even any noise at all? The truth is, I cannot. It therefore remains a possibility - in fact, a likelihood - that the whole encounter may have been sparked by nothing more than my own playful subconscious.

Regardless of the origin of the noise, I was nevertheless now awake. I had emerged from a deep sleep into an almost entirely darkened room, entirely alone, in the very early hours of the morning. My senses had been heightened by a noise that I perceived to be emanating from out of the gloom. It had me on high alert. I knew immediately upon waking that something was amiss. Fear had me in its grip, staunchly on the lookout for any potential threat, searching the shadows for signs of danger. And there it was, mere feet away. A dark figure, a shadowy outline of a mysterious character, an unknown stranger, some nefarious being unidentifiable in both form and purpose. I had expected to find something unpleasant and my expectations had been immediately met.

But if the squeaking wingback had escaped my dreams and followed me into waking life, could I be certain that the figure I saw before me had not emerged from my nightmares as well? And let us also consider the other great trick the senses

118

play. Or, more accurately, the brain's interpretation of them. Information is received through sight, sound and smell, and then a picture constructed by the mind of the world around us. But that process is not infallible. The eyes, the ears, even the nose can be fooled. They can be thrown off course. What we see before us is not always a wholly accurate portrait of our environment. It is an interpretation. It is the brain's best guess. At no point in life do we truly witness the world around us in all its glory, we simply perceive it as best as our mind allows.

Therefore, returning to the outline of the dark figure sitting beyond that slither of moonlight, facing towards me from out of the night, let us also consider what I now know to be present on the wingback at that time - my silk coated dressing gown. For the chair itself was sat in the same position it forever occupies when it is not supporting my ample rump - facing towards the foot of the bed, its back to the doorway at the far end of the bedchamber. After each and every session sat at my writing desk, I slide the chair back, turn it to one side, and face it out into the room. A force of habit. The chair swivels as I push it away from the desk. It remains in that position as I head for the wardrobe, to prepare myself as best I can for what remains of the day. And it is right there, onto the back edge of the wingback, that I fling my dressing gown with unflinching regularity. I cannot think of a single instance where I have tossed the item elsewhere. And so, in summary, if I am not to be found nestled back into my armchair, hurriedly scribbling away at my desk, then the chair itself will be left facing towards the bed, with my dressing gown lain strewn across it.

And, sure enough, this is what I can see, just about, as I wake to find myself groggily blinking across the bedchamber in the dead of night. In those initial waking moments I focus as best I can towards my writing desk, towards the wingback, to ascertain the source of the possibly-imagined noise. And it is there I witness the outline of the chair, with the gown draped across it. Now, what do we know about the shape of a regularly sized dressing gown? Could it not be described as fairly similar in overall shape to that of a grown man, especially when viewed through extremely dim lighting after emerging from a deep dreamstate? And is it not far more likely, when examined in the cold light of day, that it was simply the gown I saw, ruffled up by its haphazard placement on the back of the chair, staring back at me from out of the shadows? My mind, in its waking confusion, created from those vague outlines something instantly recognisable - a humanoid shape. But what I truly observed was simply an item of clothing. That is the far more logical conclusion.

Of course, this hypothesis does not adequately explain the feet. For while I can dismiss the squeaking of the wingback as merely an escapee from my nightmare, and the presence of a dark figure sitting in the chair as a confused construct of my failing senses, I can recall with absolute clarity, and with no little sense of dread, those two monstrous appendages stretching out into the moonlight. I saw them. They were there. I am wholly certain of it.

And yet, let us pause for a moment to again consider the evidence available. It is not without precedent for visions from the subconscious mind to find their way into waking life, especially in moments of great confusion or high anxiety. While it is true to say that I had been awake for several seconds, become accustomed to the darkness and gained a clarity of focus that had been all too absent in my initial waking moments, it would remain speculative to assert that I was in full control of my faculties. I was afraid. And as has been well documented, fear can have a strange and rather detrimental effect on one's clarity of vision. It can cloud the senses and heighten paranoia. It can create threats that a relaxed mind would dismiss in a heartbeat. And let us not forget one simple and unavoidable truth - the possibility of hallucination is far more likely than the existence of the supernatural. Knowing this, would it not be foolish to get carried away with one's own personal experience when there is countless evidence presented by the scientific community to explain or contradict it? In short - if what I see before me is unbelievable, the most sensible course of action would be not to believe it.

Now morning has come, and the warm glow through my window has banished the shadows and my anxieties along with them, I find myself ever more leaning towards the conclusion that what was out there below the wingback was simply a slither of moonlight across my rug and nothing more. After seeing an outline of a figure, I had most likely placed the feet there all by myself. And after believing in the presence of the feet, and the dark figure that sat above them, there really was only one path down which my mind was going to tread - that there was an evil presence in the room.

And now, inevitably, we come to the most traumatic segment of the encounter, what I can only describe as "the attack." The creature rose into the light, illuminating its terribly decomposed body, while using its demonic powers to pin me to the bed. I became paralysed, totally helpless. And then - it still forces a shiver down my spine to think of it, even with the warm morning sun caressing the back of my neck - the monster slid to my bedside, climbed on top of me, and sent my mind tumbling on down into a state of pure hopelessness and terror. I have never felt anything like it. I hope to never again. I witnessed my total and utter demise. It was a truly and uniquely terrifying experience.

So how, you may ask, can this sceptical mind dismiss all this as imagined? How can a hallucination perform such a heinous, soul-destroying act? It was so visceral, so horribly real. It must have been a supernatural encounter. What else could it possibly be? Well, dear reader, if you know your history, you will no doubt already be reaching towards the same conclusion I have come to. Because upon recounting my experience, writing it down, mulling over the finer points and examining the various steps in great detail, I could not shake the realisation that what I was attempting to document had an eerie sense of familiarity. Not to me, thankfully, but certainly to many others before me. I have read about it, I have heard tell of it, as I'm sure you have too. My terrible story had been told before, by people the world over, repeated several times throughout many cultures and all with a similar outcome. The incubus, the jinn, the night hag of folklore, the shadow people of wicked horror tales. Night-time visitors who torment and torture, pinning their victims in place to enact their terrible deeds. Notable tales from classic literature deal with the subject, not to mention countless religious texts and teachings. What I had to document was nothing new, other than the unfortunate fact that this time it had happened to me.

And prior to my own encounter, which had been altogether terrifying, how would I have explained away these accounts? What would I have said in response to these second-hand experiences? Well, I would have dismissed them. I would have said they were the result of an imagination run wild, too full of fancy, and no more truthful than a common fairy tale or cautionary myth. I would have vehemently denied the existence of the supernatural, knowing it in my heart to be an impossibility.

To support my argument, I would have recounted evidence of a confusion of the senses, of vivid hallucination, of the phenomenon of sleep paralysis - that feeling of terror, hypnagogic visions, and a distinct feeling of being trapped inside one's own body. And while the experience can be dreadful and terrifying and feel horrifically real to the poor soul suffering from it, it can be explained and resolved quite rationally, without resorting to wild fantasy. The mind has awoken but the body has not. In its panic, the mind then creates an external presence to explain away its confusion, a focus for its anxiety. But upon waking fully, the menace departs. Clarity of vision allows reality to seep through the senses. The truth becomes apparent. There was never anything there. We know that this condition exists, is very real, so why dismiss it in favour of grand delusions which cannot be substantiated? Why would I assume that, because this time it had happened to me, that it was now all to be believed? My experience changes nothing. My position remains the same.

And so now I shall rise from my writing desk, push the wingback to the side and leave it facing out towards the bed. In the process, I will fling my dressing gown towards it, leaving it to lay lazily over the back of the chair. From there, I will bound over the wardrobe, as I always do, with a spring in my step, eager to start the day anew. For not only have I faced the terrors of the night and lived, I have set myself the challenge of explaining them fully, in a clear and rational manner, and succeeded wholeheartedly. There is nothing to be afraid of. The demons are within. With this understanding under my belt, I feel no anxiety towards the future. Should I experience something similar again, I will know there is a light at the end of the tunnel. I will survive. The troubling experience will pass. There is nothing spiritual out there that should concern me, no grim spectre that can cause me harm. What I saw cannot be a ghost, for ghosts do not exist.

Yummy

The first thing that hit her was the smell. Blood, flesh, metallic and cold. Long lost memories she couldn't quite place. Strung up limbs. Sharp, silver tools. Life brought to an end before its time. She stepped through the door, ignoring the instinct to vomit.

The specimen itself hung free, swinging slowly, its yellow mass stretching up to the roof of the laboratory. Wires jutted out at all angles. Thick, black tubes, dripping with condensation, waving gently back and forth in the breeze emitted from the fans above. They gurgled and hummed, nutrients channelled in and waste channelled out. It caused the whole structure to vibrate. Where the wires pierced the flesh, red liquid oozed forward, dripping down and pooling on the floor below. The metal arms that held it in place pierced its sides, claws digging deep.

This was it, what they had paid for. What she had built. She should feel happy, seeing it in action for the first time. She should feel proud. But the only thing she felt was repulsion.

"Is it alive?" she asked.

The scientist nodded.

"Of course."

"But is it conscious? Can it *feel*?"

He shook his head, making no attempt to hide his disappointment regarding the validity of her question. The specimen shuddered, the metal arms clunking in their holsters. The scientist responded by jotting something down on his tablet.

"Are you sure?" she asked.

"Hmm?"

"How can you be sure it's not aware?"

He sighed and took a few steps forward, towards the specimen. When she remained still, the scientist gave a nod of the head, beckoning her to follow. She sniffed, regretting it instantly. The stench was overwhelming. The scientist shrugged.

"It does take some getting used to."

She stepped forward, now almost directly below it. She could make out tiny blotches on the skin, little red marks dotted all over, seemingly at random. The yellow lump of flesh that hung above her seemed to have no identifiable form. It had no limbs or features, no bones to give it structure. She thought of how she would describe it, something short and snappy to sum it up to the board. The only stomach-churning idea that came to her now was a tumour. Yes, that was it, it looked like one huge, elephant-sized tumour. She doubted the marketing team would like that.

"There's no brain," said the scientist, his sharp voice in the sterile surroundings of the laboratory snapping her back to the present. He pointed upwards, prodding a low hanging lump just above his head, pushing his finger up into it as he talked.

"No spine, no nerve endings. It's about as self-aware as the hairs on your head."

Suddenly a shudder from the specimen, the metal arms clanking under the pressure. Her heart jumped, a thousand nightmare scenarios firing through her brain in an instant. Was it safe? Was it secure? What if it fell on her, pinned her to the ground and crushed her? The scientist seemed unconcerned by the movement, remaining in place directly below. He simply jotted more notes on his tablet.

"What was that?" she asked.

He frowned at her.

"Why did it do that?"

Another dismissive shrug.

"It's nothing we can't fix," he replied, grinning with it. No doubt the smile was an attempt to put her at ease. To her, he just appeared creepy - the insane keeper of her monstrous creation.

She reached out a hand, slowly moving it up towards the belly - if you could call it that - of the huge lump of flesh above her. An inner voice tried to convince her it was a terrible idea. Don't do it. Back away. Run. Leave this place. Pretend this never happened, pretend you never saw it. But she knew, after everything she had been through to get to this point, there was no backing out now. And if she was unwilling to take the next step, how would she convince anyone else?

She touched it, placing at first a tentative finger against the yellow, bobbled skin. And then, when nothing had ripped itself free of the specimen to attack her, when it finally felt safe, she allowed her whole palm to lay flat against it. One thing struck her as significant. Surprising, even. It was warm. She had expected cold, clammy, unpleasant. Dead. But it was anything but. Smooth and soft, almost pleasing to the touch. She stared up at the strange body hanging above her - pulsing, bleeding, without a head, arms, legs, anything. A living lump of nothing. Her life's work.

Nearby something popped, a wet squelch above her head. She stepped back. A substance thicker than blood, almost jelly-like, slipped from an open sore. It drooled down and then finally let go, tumbling towards the floor and hitting home with a damp slap. Her stomach turned. The scientist tutted, adding further notes to his tablet, before looking over to her.

"Would you like a taste?" he asked.

She stared down at the ball of red gloop now sinking into the floor. She shook her head slowly.

"No," she gasped, her face turning green, "I think I'd like a bucket."

*

She was six when she first saw a cow. There had been pictures, obviously. Tattered old children's books passed down over generations. The pig goes oink, the sheep goes baa, the cow goes moo. Her father would explain what each one was - what they looked like, how they moved, how they smelled. How they used to be everywhere, fields full of them as far as the eye could see. Were any of them still alive? He didn't know. As pets, maybe. Playthings for the rich and eccentric. He thought perhaps they still kept some in zoos. But the fields were largely empty now, those not used for sustainable crops left to their own devices, to grow back as they saw fit. To be "reclaimed by nature", he'd say with a sneer.

"Can we go, Dad? Can we go see the cows?"

She had cottoned on at an early age that he couldn't resist big brown eyes and a hopeful question, and so that had been all it took. He smiled, nodded, and promised her that, for her next birthday, he would save up and they would celebrate by going to the zoo. They would go and see the cows.

"This is more like a museum," he had grumbled as they wandered from enclosure to enclosure, her hand in his. But she had loved every second. Each animatronic animal whirred into action as they passed, stretching out a nose to imitate a sniff. For her father, it was a wholly depressing experience. He could remember news reports of whales beaching themselves to escape poison in the water. He could remember polar bears roaming into cities to rummage through bins. He could remember the headlines when the last elephant died. But for her, these animals were all myths, legends, tall tales of creatures she could barely believe had ever existed. For her, interacting with their robot replicas was nothing short of magical, no different from the real thing.

Then they came to the cow. Her tiny mind was blown. It didn't clunk and creak as it moved, its feet weren't bolted to the floor. When she reached up she could feel its breath against her skin, warm and wet and alive. A squeal of delight as it rubbed its head against her palm, desperate for some contact and affection. Their eyes had met and she had fallen in love.

"God, they were tasty," her father had said, grinning down to her.

"You won't eat *her*, will you?"

He shook his head.

"Not this one. They'd throw me in jail."

"Good."

She continued to stroke the side of the cow's face, having never felt anything quite like it. Her father reached his hand over the top of the bars, giving the cow a scratch behind the ears which it seemed to appreciate. He glanced around the enclosure, a poor recreation of a 21st century farm - imitation grassland, a trough for water, fake sunlight thrust into the tiny box room from the bulbs above. He let out a long, sad sigh.

"They were better off before."

"Before what, Dad?"

He shook his head.

"Never mind."

*

Everyone took their seats in the boardroom and then in came the plates. One in each hand, delicately handled, placed carefully before the eagerly awaiting recipients. They all leaned in, taking a sniff, and grumbles of appreciation began to circulate the room. She smiled. The meals looked the part, they *smelled* the part. The chefs had studied the archives, dug out all the old recipe books, re-watched the finest cookery programmes, and then tested and tested and re-tested until perfection. This was her big moment. She wasn't going to leave anything to chance. If this went well it wouldn't just change her world, it would change everyone's. She took her own seat and smiled to the room.

"Bon appetit."

Impatient hands shot out, scooping up the buns, lifting them up to salivating mouths. Most of these men were old enough to remember the protests, the marches, the violent reactions to the ban. She knew some of them well enough to know how much money they had thrown at the lobbyists to keep the industry going. And how much money they had then thrown at the terrorists when the legal battle had been lost. And now here they were, for the first time in so many decades, finally able to dig their teeth into real flesh, finally able to bite through something that had lived. The satisfaction was clear to see.

Mouths opened wide, taste buds were primed, before eager teeth plunged on down through soft, fluffy bun, and further still, into the juicy meat. Some closed their eyes, lost in the sensation. Others let out little orgasmic moans, chewing, nodding, groaning with delight. They couldn't help themselves. Bite after bite after bite, cramming more and more in when the last mouthful had barely been swallowed. She noticed the one closest to her had a stream of blood running from the corner of his mouth. He let it drip from his chin and onto his shirt. He didn't seem to care. She knew that for every board member she satisfied she would be handsomely rewarded. They would throw more money her way than she could count. She would finally receive recognition for all that hard work. And yet…

She looked down to her own meal, the blood-red patty jutting out from between white buns and laboratory-grown salad. She couldn't get the image of the specimen out of her head. Those lumps of pulsing yellow flesh, the dripping blood, the soggy gloop drooling down from open sores. The wet splat it made on the cold metal floor. She looked to her dinner and all she could see was the creature.

"Are you not eating that?" the man next to her said between mouthfuls, his hopeful eyes fixed on her untouched lunch.

She needed fresh air. She needed to get away from their bloody fingers, the wet crunch of each overenthusiastic bite. She thought of the cow. She thought of pulling it to the floor, plunging a knife into its side, ripping out chunks. She thought of cold, wet meat in her mouth, of blood rushing down her throat. She thought of eager

127

teeth against her own skin, clamping on, piercing through. She thought of her flesh being torn away. Of being consumed.

"Excuse me, gentlemen."

She pushed out her chair and stood. No one looked up from their food. She backed away to the door and pushed through, leaving behind all their satisfied moans and groans, the crunching and the munching, and just about managed to shut the door behind her before collapsing onto the carpet.

*

Her father had refused to go on the march.

"People don't take kindly to being told how to live their lives," was his go-to line.

"But this is about our future," she'd argued, "Mine, yours, *everybody's*."

He shook his head, went back to his newstablet, mumbled something about it not being much of a future if you weren't allowed to think for yourself. She had just laughed at him. At 15 she had no time for his outdated views. The world had moved on, he hadn't, and that was that. Just deal with it, Dad.

Small pockets of resistance had started to pop up in the last few years. People who remembered the good old days, or at least thought they did, and had begun to question the validity of the ban. Could we really trust these scientists? Whose payroll were they on, anyway? Weren't all these decisions just political, when it came down to it? For the good of humanity, the planet, or just to line the pockets of those opportunists who had got in ahead of the curve?

There were rumours of isolated communities in far off places that were breeding again, stories passed down through friends of friends of friends. For the right price you could get your hands on whatever you wanted - steak, ribs, leg on the bone, Sunday joints and blood-rich burgers. All you needed were the right contacts. Political parties began to sense an opportunity. Promises were made. The mistakes of the past would not be repeated. This time there would be stricter regulation, controlled pricing, everything in moderation. We know what we're doing. Trust us - this time everything will be fine.

She just didn't understand. Neither did any of her friends. The world had struggled so hard to quit first time around. There had been so much anger on both sides, anger that had spilled into violence, violence that had escalated to deaths. Why were people so desperate to go back to that?

And so this was her opportunity - *our* opportunity, as she saw it - to put a stop to events before they even got started. Her merry band of hopeful little protesters made their way to the city. They joined up with the millions on the streets, raised their voices and their placards, all chanting together in joyous solidarity. Let's show the powers that be that we won't stand for it. This is *our* world now, not yours, and we like it just the way it is.

The first bomb went off some distance away. She had heard it, felt it, but that wasn't what scared her. It was the quiet afterwards. A million people suddenly holding their breath, a crowd shocked into silence. And then shouts in the distance, screams passed along through the masses. Cries getting louder and louder, moving closer and closer, almost like the sound itself was hunting her down. Soon it would be on her, in her, forcing its way out of her and she would be screaming along with everyone else. She grabbed her best friend's hand, squeezed tight, her eyes wide. Looking back, that was the last thing she could remember with any clarity - holding hands.

In the hospital bed they had told her that the second bomb had detonated within just a few feet. The crowd beside her had taken the brunt. She was lucky to be alive. Her father leaned over from his chair at her bedside, took her hand in his. It triggered a memory. A smokey image popped into her head. Lying on her back, feet scrambling all around, legs running in all directions, the smoke clearing and realising she was still holding onto her friend's hand. Only her friend was no longer there. Just fingers, palm, a wrist and then bone. She had cried out but couldn't hear herself. Faces crowded over her, lips flapping, teeth chattering away but no words. No sounds at all except for the ringing in her ears. And blood. Blood in her hair, on her face, on her clothes. Blood on the pavement, on the cars, up the walls. Blood everywhere. Clumps of flesh scattered across the street. A road covered in meat.

When her ears had stopped ringing she had asked her father, "Why would they do that?"

In between the tears he had managed a sad shrug, mumbling something about people not taking kindly to being told how to live their lives.

*

The door fizzed open and she stepped though, now fully prepared for the smell. Up above the specimen hung in place, still gulping from the wires, still bleeding from the wounds. Flesh still pulsing away. Without hesitation she lifted her hand to touch it, feeling its warmth on her palm. She thought of cows in museums.

Moving in closer, she allowed her forehead to brush against it, to rest gently on its lumpy yellow skin. She thought of gnashing teeth, of deep red liquid dripping from an old man's chin. She closed her eyes and listened. Life pumped inside, channelled through veins and arteries just inches from her face. She thought of blood running down walls, of streets covered in dead meat.

She felt sorry for it. She knew it was irrational but she felt it anyway. This was supposed to be the solution. A half-way point. Something to bridge the divide, to put an end to all the anger. Alive but not. Living but unaware. A guilty pleasure with all the guilt removed. And yet right now that is exactly what she felt. Guilty. For doing this to the specimen. For making it live without its permission and then allowing them to tear it apart. For forcing it to give parts of itself away. She didn't care that it didn't know, *she* knew, and she wanted it all to stop.

"What are you doing?" the scientist asked, only now looking up from his samples.

She ignored him, reaching up and grabbing hold of one of the wires protruding from the beast above.

"Don't touch that!"

It slipped out surprisingly easily, resulting in a gush of blood colliding at some speed with a squirt of green liquid from the tube - whatever they were pumping into this thing. The force of it knocked her off her feet. The scientist rushed over but she was prepared, aiming the still gushing tube in the direction of his face. He stumbled back, frantically rubbing the nutrient-rich gloop from his eyes, screaming loudly.

"Security!"

With the scientist now out of the picture, she made her way calmly to the other side of the specimen, not caring one jot about the various stinking liquids now covering her. She removed another wire and a siren began to pulse throughout the room. In the distance, behind the blare of the alarm, she could hear rushing footsteps.

Nearby, a control panel. Life support monitors. Dials and switches galore. She flicked them all to zero. Behind her the door fizzed open. They had arrived, sooner than she had expected. Rifles were raised in her direction.

"Hands in the air, ma'am."

She turned to them, grinning, face and hair now drenched in blood. She felt suddenly clear headed. She was happy, satisfied, guilt free. She had made the right choice. Behind her the specimen continued to spew life out of itself and onto the floor, the liquid pooling around her feet as she stood to face the guards. She glanced up at the specimen, the yellow flesh gradually losing its colour, the pulsing slowly fading away.

"Let me say goodbye," she asked.

She stepped towards the enormous dying lump beside her. The guards moved closer. Radio chatter buzzed in earpieces, orders being passed down from head office. She knew she didn't have much time. She had to act. She launched herself forward, arms outstretched, and collided with the specimen as the guns opened fire.

She landed on her back at the foot of her creation, within touching distance but not quite there. Her own blood mixed with the pool on the floor, spreading further out across the laboratory. She breathed as best she could as the guards gathered around her, gun barrels pointing down. As if she was still a threat.

A buzz from a nearby radio. A man's voice.

"Can it be saved?"

The scientist frantically attacked the switches and dials. All this ranting and raving. Red faces, screwed up in anger. Heads dropping into hands. She smiled. She knew without her they would never be able to bring it back.

The sounds began to blur into one around her, the shouting and screaming fading away. She rocked her head to the side and focused towards the now dead specimen. The men upstairs didn't deserve to have it. And the creature had done nothing so bad as to deserve them. She coughed, more blood added to the lake now surrounding her. She smiled.

She thought of the breath of a cow on her palm. She thought of her friend's hand in hers. She thought of bright blue skies, crisp clear air, of golden meadows and lush green forests, stretching on forever until the end of time. She thought she had never been happier. And then she thought of nothing at all.

Lesco and The Find

Antar stood in shadow. Its people waited on black sand, shivering and cold, gazing hopefully towards the horizon. They held each other - some for comfort, others simply for warmth. They shuffled nervously from side to side. All those gathered there on the beach, the entire population of Antar, were huddled together in fear, overcome with doubt. And how could they not be? No one knew for certain that Sulla would return. Not one person could say with confidence that the Olds would send her back to them. Sulla was the greatest gift they could provide, but she was in no way guaranteed. All Antar knew this. To believe otherwise was heresy.

And so the people waited. They listened patiently to the sound of the waves, gentle and soft, rolling up against the shore. They felt the cool breeze whip up from the ocean, lapping their skin, rolling around their goosebumps. They stared out across the deep, dark water, praying to the Olds that the Great Shadow was finally coming to an end. Many feared it might not. Half a cycle of darkness can do strange things to the mind. It can make you forget the light ever even existed. It brings forth terrible fears that the shadow might prevail. The notion takes hold. This could be the final turn. We are in The End Cycle. The Olds have forsaken us. Sulla has perished.

Grand Mother stood at the head of her congregation, her bony toes tickling the surf. She sensed the apprehension in her people. The dread hung above them like a stormcloud. She could almost see it. Without the light, they were all done for. She knew that as well as anybody. Their worry was perfectly understandable. But she did not share in it. Grand Mother stood firm. She straightened out her creaking back, pulled back her ageing shoulders, forced her body as high as it could possibly go. If there was fear in her, she certainly wasn't going to let anybody see it. Sulla was out there. The light would return. Her people could doubt this as much as they wanted. Grand Mother refused. She would show them strength, as she always did. They might not believe in Sulla, but they could believe in her. She would show them the way.

The change, when it came, was barely perceptible at first. Many believed it to be a trick. Throughout the entirety of the Great Shadow, that half-cycle of suffering and strife, there had only been greys and blacks, shadow and shade. Sulla had slipped away and taken all of her colours with her. That hint of red the people saw now, the distant promise of an orange or a pink, they simply dismissed it as their own foolish optimism. Blind hope is deceiving me. It is but a mirage. Do not bow to it. There is nothing out there but the dark.

But then came the heat. A gentle warmth, drifting up off the black sand, that was impossible to ignore. All could feel it now. Excitement began to build. The people of Antar could not only see Sulla returning, they could feel her too. She was soothing the nervous with her gentle touch. She was reminding them of a time when they weren't terrified. She was flushing out their dread.

Grand Mother raised her arms to the sky. Her people held their breath. They dared not believe it was possible. But then, as Grand Mother leant back her head, the people saw it clearly for the first time. It was unmistakable - the light!

Her face shone out to them, lit up in the fire of Sulla's glorious return. For the first time in what seemed like an age, the people saw clearly cracks on Grand Mother's dark brown cheeks, each wrinkle on her tired old forehead, every chipped yellow tooth. Her grin stretched out far and wide, a beaming smile to welcome in the brand new dawn.

Grand Mother stumbled out into the surf, calling out in praise to Sulla, thanking her for the light. She cheered out wildly with uncontrollable joy, repeating the mantra that all Antar knew by heart - the Olds are wise, the Olds are true, with Sulla's light, they guide us through. Her people followed, erupting in celebration, charging down to the waves. The very youngest, who could barely remember a time before the Great Shadow, leapt up into the air, screaming out in delight. Caught up in the moment, they did not truly understand what was happening, the significance of it. This was something they would learn in time. The very oldest hugged and kissed, tears streaming down their cheeks. They knew how essential the light was. And they knew of the many who had not made it through the Great Shadow to see it. Sulla's return was a gift. It was a resurrection. The very land itself was ready to rise once more.

And so, as Antar celebrated, Sulla's glow moved on. It crept out over the waves and up onto the beach. It found new new homes across the land. The light spread itself far and wide and down to the saltgrass fields, which could once again start sprouting their crop. No more chewing on roots, sucking on stems, feeding off scraps. A new harvest would soon see to that. The light passed on, down to the harbours, which slowly awoke to the sound of tiny conical crafts clunking against one another, tapping gently away along the battered sides of the piers. Some lay crushed and broken, scattered in pieces over the water's surface. The darkness had been brutal. Only the most foolhardy would have attempted a fishing trip in the depths of the Great Shadow. With Sulla's return came the promise of a new catch. Her life-giving beams brought forth whole new opportunities. Soon the fisheries would be alive and bustling with the excitement of a people who finally knew where their next meal was coming from.

Beyond the harbours and the fields and the territory of the people, the light crept onto the huge dirtplains of Antar, and into the realm of its beasts. It caught the attention of the huge herds of hufa, woke them from their slumber. It raised them up, blinking, yawning and stretching to greet the brand new day. The animals had not eaten since Sulla departed. There was little else to do but sleep during the Great Shadow, hunker down and hope you were not the one the elements chose to take. The hufa would soon begin their long march, criss crossing this way and that across the land, searching for whatever morsels of plantlife that still remained. Not all of them would make it. Hundreds would fall. That was just the way of things.

Those hufa that did not succumb to starvation would be picked from the pack by the vicious chumpah, the brutal and bony beasts who scavaged on stragglers, ripping into malnourished flesh with hungry teeth and desperate claws. If the Great Shadow had been kind to them, presented them with a plentiful bounty of fallen bodies, then that would placate them for a while. If not, then they would be forced to hunt. As Sulla's light awoke the chumpah, a thousand pairs of yellow eyes peered up to greet her, as one by one the ruthless killers began the new cycle by licking their lips.

Beyond Antar's people and its harbours and its plains and its beasts, the life-quenching light edged further out across the land. As Sulla leaned forward, peering higher and higher above the horizon, her rays discovered the southern seas, the barren mountains, the desolate wastelands of inner Antar. It laid bare all that the Great Shadow had hidden away. It brought with it strange new discoveries, bizarre mysteries, and a whole new cycle of opportunity. And eventually, after the celebrations on the beach had long since died down, Sulla's light found its way to the far stretches of the shore. Her glow found itself curiously drifting up the body of a long, strange, white creature that lay silently against the sand, just waiting to be found. If Sulla had thoughts - and who are we to say that she doesn't - she would have wondered to herself what on Antar this thing could possibly be, and who was going to be brave or foolhardy enough to go searching for it.

*

Lesco loved the Find. Everybody in Murdo City did. The Great Shadow might bring with it the terrible storm surges and the scorching winds, but it also acted as provider. Its crashing waves and battering cyclones were the delivery service of choice for the Olds. What bounty they sent forth, the Great Shadow deposited all across the beaches and plains of Antar. And so, when the light returned and the land began to recover, that was when the Find began. It was a time for the very bravest amongst the population to head out and see just what treasures the Olds had sent their way.

Excitement had been building for the Find ever since Sulla's return. There had been jobs to do first, of course. Antar could not just jump back to its feet. It needed a lot of hard work and not a little sacrifice to get it there. Lesco had been eager to volunteer. When the call came in to help clear up the damage done by the Great Shadow, Lesco raced down to the nearest crumpled building and immediately got to work. Upon the request to help repair the fishing fleet, Lesco was one of the first to start constructing rafts. He helped out where he could in harvesting the early crop of saltgrass. He went out of his way to clear Murdo's streets of the wreckage. When patrols were required at all hours to keep a watchful eye for signs of chumpah, Lesco was first in line. He often lost track of how long he had been awake, working non-stop to assist wherever he could.

His reasons for all this were twofold. One - quite simply - was that Lesco was a good citizen of Antar. He had not seen much of it in his 15 cycles, being born and raised in Murdo City itself, but he knew enough to understand how special it was. Antar was his home, its people, his family. Working hard for them was his duty. But on top of this - and perhaps the far more pressing reason for Lesco's efforts - was that he desperately needed the Find to start, to get out there and win it, because in doing so he might be able to impress Isda. Lesco's number one motivation for all this hard work was that he had fallen in love.

It had all happened instantaneously. Prior to seeing Isda for the first time, Lesco would have stated with utmost confidence that he did not even believe in love. It was a pathetic distraction that drove people mad and forced upon them foolish actions. But after his first encounter with Isda, Lesco would proudly proclaim to anyone willing to listen that he no longer believed in anything else. Love was all there was.

His brain held little regard for anything non-Isda related. All thoughts, on any subject, eventually returned to her. All conversations finished with her name. Lesco saw her face everywhere he went. Each tent he passed, each hut, even the strung up hufa skins that scattered the markets - they all formed into a spectacular representation of her dazzling smile. When Lesco gazed down to the saltgrass fields, he didn't see sludgy green slime slipping around in the swamp, he saw Isda's shimmering black hair, bathed by Sulla's light, a halo of absolute perfection. To see her sparkling blue eyes, all Lesco had to do was look up to the skies and there they were, glinting back down to him. Isda had become his only focus, his entire world, his one true reason for living. There was nothing that existed but Isda.

Unfortunately for Lesco, Isda didn't really know who he was. This was of no fault on her part. After all, she had never actually met him. A lot of people liked Isda. She had a way of grabbing attention by simply being present. Eyes tended to be drawn to her. It was difficult to keep track of every single person who had chosen her as the object of their affections. Especially if, like Lesco, they hadn't actually bothered to talk to her. Lesco had spotted Isda from afar and his brain had clicked. He had found purpose. She had shone brighter than all around her, as if Sulla herself had selected this girl, picked her out from the crowd. "Here," the beaming light had told him, "witness your destiny, follow your heart. Your life will never be the same again."

For Isda, it had just been another day. She had not even known Lesco was there. She had two cycles on Lesco, meaning that he was not really the sort of prospect she was currently looking for anyway. And so she had not a clue about that fateful day at the market, when her incomparable beauty had stolen a young boy's heart. She had simply been looking to trade one of her clam shell carvings for a new hufa bone knife. If someone had told her that several feet away a strange young boy had been gawping at her and falling in love, she would have simply laughed it off and moved on. These sort of things happened to her all the time.

Still, to Lesco, the whole sensation was brand new. Obsession, lust and desire, all packaged up neatly in one clearly identifiable target. He had a clear goal now. He knew exactly what to do with his life. Love had shown him the way. But if Isda was to be his, he would need to work for it. He would need to fight. And, most probably, he would have to do something so spectacular that he could no longer be ignored. Lesco was going to have to go out there and win the Find.

So first things first, Lesco needed to get himself on the list. Not just anybody could be selected to join the Find. Antar had limited resources, its people being one of them, and it could not afford to send them all out to scour the land when so much needed to be done back home. The cycle must continue. The Great Shadow would come around again. Barriers needed building, stores needed stocking, and spears needed sharpening, should the chumpah ever become so bold. No, only the very best and brightest could be chosen for the Find, those who had proven themselves worthy. Lesco's best chance was to work himself to the bone until Grand Mother noticed him. Whenever a job needed doing, Lesco would be seen to be doing it. His sweaty face would be there, lifting, carrying, chopping and digging. He would make himself unignorable. Everyone would know his name. And so when he raised his hand to join the Find, Grand Mother would have no choice but to pick him.

The fateful day finally arrived. The grand market square of Murdo City had been cleared for the ceremony. Those from the surrounding towns and villages had travelled to the capital, often taking several days to do so. The Find was worth the effort. To Lesco, it looked as if the entire world had shown up. For all he knew, it probably had. A thousand faces he didn't recognise, all jostling for position to see who Grand Mother would choose. Those brave volunteers, lined up one by one on the platform, waiting for Grand Mother's decision. Lesco looked along them, the women and men standing beside him, arms at their side, waiting for their turn. He hoped dearly he had done enough to stand out. His heart pounded and his knees shook. His mouth ran almost entirely dry. There was so much at stake.

To calm his nerves, Lesco looked out into the crowd, scanning the faces for one he recognised. For the best among them. For his one true love. There she was, radiant as ever. Lesco didn't know how she did it, but again Isda appeared veiled in sunlight. Sulla obviously favoured her. That was the only explanation. Isda's elegance was worthy of all the glory that Sulla could bestow. Lesco could not argue with her selection.

And then, just after Lesco had spotted his love out there in the crowd, Isda smiled back towards the stage. She beamed right back at him. Lesco's heart erupted. Isda's eyes lit up, they sparkled, so brilliant and blue. Lesco had never seen anything like it. His stomach launched itself into a somersault. So much grace. And focused on him! It was almost too much to take.

To his side, Lesco heard a man chuckle. What could possibly be so funny, Lesco wondered. This was no time for jokes. Why was this simpleton ruining such a perfect moment? Lesco glanced across. And then he looked up. And up even further up. Lesco gulped. This was not a man standing beside him, it was a mountain. It was a hulking great mound of muscle, with arms thicker than Lesco's legs, and legs thicker than Lesco's entire body. Atop this beast sat a perfectly square and chiselled jaw, two stunningly prominent cheekbones and a pair of mesmerising brown eyes that Lesco found himself immediately drawn to. And then annoyed with himself for being so taken with them. This beefy idiot was being horribly disrespectful, chuckling and grinning away while Grand Mother prepared herself. Laughing at the Find. And waving now as well! Throwing a hand into the air, flexing those impressively sculpted biceps. Who did this hufa-brain think he was?

And then Lesco saw it. Who the hulk was waving at. Who was waving back at him. The person in the crowd who had not been flashing her brilliant blue eyes at Lesco, but in fact aiming them in the direction of the enormous slab of man-meat standing next to him. It was all too apparent now. Devastatingly obvious. Isda's sparkling smile had not been meant for Lesco at all. She wasn't even looking at him.

The world drained of colour. The low murmuring of the crowd faded away to a low hiss. Lesco felt heat flood his cheeks. His stomach stopped somersaulting and began to gurgle. His throat filled with bile. He sensed Grand Mother moving along the row, passing her judgement, but could not really focus on it all happening. He heard dulled cheers from the crowd, distant gasps, as each brave volunteer received their blessing or respectful rejection. But he didn't really register who was chosen and who was not. His life had lost all meaning. It was if he had lurched backwards, away from himself, removed from his body. He had become a blank space. Lesco wasn't really there any more.

Isda was his destiny. They were meant to be together. And yet here she was flashing looks at the Hufa-Brain, sharing a giggle with him, even exchanging a wave. A man who had nothing to offer her but his stunning good looks and charming smile, with no doubt some more-than-adequate hunting skills and a supreme talent for home-building, judging by the look of him. That was nothing compared to what Lesco could offer her - his undivided attention, his life-long dedication. The gift of love. What was the Hufa-Brain in comparison to that?

Grand Mother reached Lesco. She whispered her judgement to him. A cheer went up from the crowd. Lesco raised his pumping fist out of instinct. He wasn't really paying attention. His mind was totally elsewhere. The plan was faltering. There was now a huge, muscle-clad spanner in the works. Life had become infinitely more complicated. There was not just Isda to impress now, he actively had to out-perform Hufa-Brain too. A man twice his size and, even Lesco had to admit, significantly more blessed in the looks department. His Find was going to have to be so unbelievably spectacular that the walking bicep next to him was instantly forgotten about. In order to win Isda back, he was going to have to blow not only her mind, but everyone else's as well. This needed to be the best discovery ever. The ultimate Find. There was no other option.

*

On the far side of Antar, there was an ocean. And against that ocean, there sat a beach. And on that beach, there lay a monster. A huge, white and mysterious creature, sprawled out across the sand. It was so big, it stretched right from out of the dunes and down into the sea. Its tail - if it could really be described as a tail - disappeared out under the surf. Water crashed up around it. Every now and again a low whoomph would echo out along the shallows, a wave thudding up against its side. The monster did not seem to mind. It took its battering from the ocean without protest or complaint. It made no attempt to move. No sound was uttered. The monster simply lay there, still and silent, blocking the path of anyone wishing to walk along the beach. And drawing shocked gasps from any young adventurers out on the Find who just happened to have stumbled across it.

Lesco knew he had to go big. That much was obvious. Isda had been drawn from the path of true love by that stupid old Hufa-Brain. If he was to draw her back again, he couldn't just deliver any old nonsense. All the other hunters out on the Find, they'd be searching the nearby cliffs and rockpools, barely setting foot beyond Murdo City. They'd scour the nearby black sand bays for whatever might have washed up there during the Great Shadow. They might make the effort to head out onto the great dirtplains, where the herds of hufa roamed. It would be a risk, given that where there were great numbers of hufa, there would usually be chumpah sneaking around after them. But the scorching winds of the Great Shadow did often deposit treasures far and wide. It was not uncommon for the Olds to spread their gifts that far inland. But Lesco wanted more. And he was willing to take even greater risks to get it.

Lesco knew the tales of the Olds. Everyone on Antar did. Their lands beyond the poisoned sea were the stuff of legend. The Olds ruled the entire world up there. They had conquered it from top to bottom. All except Antar, anyway. Millions of them, all living their comfortable lives in their colossal cities, perfectly designed and constructed to attend to their every whim. They could cool their homes when they became too hot, they could heat them up when things got too cold. Clothes could be purchased from vendors, rather than having to scavenge and trade for materials. And they had all the food they could ever eat. They didn't even have to hunt for it. If they requested it, their succulent meals would simply arrive fully cooked and prepared at their door. And when they were finished, in need of relieving themselves, they had underground rivers that would take their waste away from them, deposit it at such a distance so that no one would ever have to smell it.

Lesco wasn't sure he believed all of the stories. Some were pretty far-fetched and beyond his understanding. Fire-chariots that sped the Olds across the land, faster even than the speediest hufa could gallop. Bridges that spanned oceans, whole citadels that stood *on the water*. Some even claimed the Olds had conquered the very skies themselves, zooming through the clouds at such speeds that made the air itself crack wide open. But Lesco had never seen them himself, soaring away overhead. None of it seemed very likely.

He had seen the ruins on the outskirts of Murdo City, though. Ancient and mysterious they were, a cobbled collection of crumbled square buildings. No one knew their true purpose, or why the Olds had left Antar, never to return. Grand Mother would often walk among the broken walls and cracked ceilings, communing with the fantastical peoples to the north. The ramshackle ruins were a conduit, she said, a way in which she and every Grand Mother before her could communicate with the Olds. It was how they got their messages to Antar. They had chosen Grand Mother to spread their word.

So with the ruins, and the strange bounty the sea gave up after each and every Great Shadow, Lesco knew that the Olds existed. He knew they were real. Those bizarre little objects that fell on the dirtplains, or appeared on the beaches to greet Sulla's return, they all had to have come from somewhere. The Olds was the only explanation. And surely the fact that the gifts they gave up, those colourful little trinkets and faded receptacles, all covered with the strange letterings and markings, the fact that they were made not from any material known on Antar - not wood, not rock, not skin nor bone - that in itself showed what the Olds were capable of. It was a clear demonstration of their power and stature.

But if Lesco was going to win the Find, he couldn't just deliver another bucket or basket. No, he needed something far grander than that. And if the Olds had built cities that spanned continents and bridges that crossed seas, surely they were capable of building something a bit more impressive than some tatty old netting. And maybe, just maybe, they were willing to send that mysterious and marvellous treasure his way, if he was just brave enough to put in the effort to look for it.

And so Lesco packed his bags for the long haul. He tucked away as much dried saltgrass as his pack would carry, as many hufa skins as he was allowed to wear. The journey would be long, the weather unreliable. He would need protection too, and so Lesco commandeered the grandest of spears from the armoury. That in itself had raised a few eyebrows. All who entered the Find were given the finest tools and provisions, prepared as best they could for what lay ahead. But no one had put as much effort into it as Lesco. No one before had attempted to travel as far. But Lesco knew the ultimate Find had to be out there. He knew he just had to look where no one else dared.

It was well beyond the thirty-fifth turn that he stumbled across the monster. Lesco had been smart, hugging the coastline. Chumpahs rarely drifted far from their food source, so to find one down on the beach was a rarity. He had been forced inland midway through his journey, searching for a crossing point for an unusually ferocious river (the Great Shadow must have done its damage up in the mountains too), but Lesco knew how to tread lightly, be cautious, remain downwind and out of sight. There had been no sign of chumpah tracks, no remnants of a kill. Lesco had not been overly concerned. But after returning to the sea, Lesco had been able to fully relax, enjoy himself, really cover some ground. He doubted very much any of the other hunters would have bothered trekking this far.

Much of his time on the Find was taken up with daydreaming. He would spend whole hours at a time imagining his life with Isda, what would happen when he returned to her victorious. There he would stand, proud and true before his people, the ultimate Find at his back. Next to him would be that dumb old Hufa-Brain, pathetically holding up some weather-beaten bag, or sea-stained container. Everyone would be pointing and laughing at the muscly moron for being so useless. Lesco would rise above it, though. He was better than all that. Then Isda would come to him, beam that dazzling smile of hers his way, take him in her arms. There would be hugging. Probably also some kissing. And then cheering from the crowd. They would call out Lesco's name and raise him high above their shoulders. He would be declared King of the Find. There would be much celebration. The crowd would chant for Antar, repeat its words - the Olds are wise, the Olds are true, with Sulla's light they guide us through. Everyone would be happy. Well, almost everyone. Hufa-Brain would probably skulk off somewhere, all lonely and miserable. Lesco didn't really care what happened to him after that.

It was all these thoughts of Isda and victory that had Lesco at a distraction when the monster finally appeared. If Lesco was being honest with himself, he probably should have spotted it a lot earlier, given how massive it was. He was on the Find, after all. This was exactly the sort of thing he should have been keeping an eye out for. But by that point his thoughts on Isda had turned substantially more graphic. Lesco was lost in a blur of skin and lips and various other body parts. His eyes had glazed over and was struggling to keep walking in a straight line. So it came as something of a shock when the monster popped itself smack bang in the middle of all of his rather inappropriate fantasies. The sight of it thrust him back to reality with a jolt.

Lesco screamed. A flash of white out the corner of his eye, a hulking great shape looming out of the sea mist. A monster coming for him. Something terrible. He dived to one side, burying himself behind a sand dune. There was no time to assess what the thing was, no time to study. Just get out of its way. He listened hard for the sound of thudding footsteps, for the scraping of its enormous belly across the sand. Nothing. Whatever it was, it hadn't spotted him. It was not on the prowl, trying to sniff him out. He was in the clear. For now.

With his spear at the ready, Lesco scrambled on his belly to the peak of the dune. He edged himself forwards, creeping carefully towards the top. Should there be any sudden movements, he was prepared to spring into action. He could be on his feet in a second, his spear raised and primed in less than two. Whatever it was out there, he could handle it. His confidence suppressed his fear. Still, this thing was big. It would be foolish to abandon caution altogether. And so Lesco ever so slowly peered down over the dune, to the titan that now stood in his way.

Upon getting a good look at it for the first time, Lesco let slip a little whimper. He just couldn't help himself. *This thing was huge.* As far as Lesco could work out, the monster was laying down. It was difficult to ascertain exactly which end was the front end and which end the tail, given they were both hidden from view by sea and sand, but it seemed safe to assume the thing was laid on its side. But even then, it remained wider than he was tall. He would have to clamber from someone's shoulders just to jump onto the back of it. And the length of it, stretching all the way from the surf and buried deep into the dunes, Lesco had to guess as being fifteen men laid out at least. Maybe even twenty. It was incredible.

Lesco could see that the monster's back, the section raised out of the water and up onto the beach, was absolutely covered in saltgrass. Tonnes of the stuff. Head to toe. It was coated in it, wearing it like a tunic. And where there was wild saltgrass, there were often crabs and clams and all sorts of tasty treats to be had too. Lesco had stumbled across a feast. That haul in itself would be a discovery worthy of celebration - a month's worth of eating just lying there, ripe for the picking. But of course, Lesco had no care for saltgrass and crab right now. Not when there was a monster to deal with.

It did not appear to be moving. That was Lesco's first thought, once the shock had subsided. Was it sleeping? Was it dead? Lesco allowed himself to slither forward a little, breaching the dune. The monster remained static. Cautiously, Lesco pulled himself up to a crouching position. The monster seemed uninterested. Lesco shuffled forward, spear raised and at the ready. Still no signs of life. Ever so slowly, Lesco crept down towards the waves. At all times he was careful to monitor his surroundings, asses the escape routes. This was no time for carelessness. But he knew he needed to get closer, get a better look at this thing. His curiosity simply wasn't going to allow him to do otherwise.

With each encroaching step, the monster came more into focus. It was truly a bizarre creature, unlike anything Lesco had ever seen before. Certainly nothing existed like it on Antar. Lesco guessed it must have come from out of the ocean.

Perhaps even crossed it, from lands far away to the north. What distance it must have travelled, he pondered, and what the world up there must look like, to be able to give birth to something so strange as this.

It had an odd colour. Probably white once, Lesco deduced, but a very long time ago. The poisoned sea had stained it a dull yellow. And it appeared to have no arms, no legs, and stranger still, not even a face. Lesco had been hoping for at least an eyeball, something to study and gauge for a reaction. No such luck. There was nothing there that Lesco could see that even came close to approaching a mouth. No sign of lips or teeth. No lolloping tongue. This immediately made Lesco feel a little more comfortable. It seemed unlikely the monster would be able to eat him if it didn't have a mouth. What on Antar was this thing?

Lesco's excitement grew. The closer he got, the more he began to suspect that the monster might not actually be a monster at all. To Lesco's eyes, it appeared to be one long, pointy, saltgrass-covered spear, not dissimilar in shape to his own. It looked sharp and straight and ready for stabbing. But this was no hufa bone carving. Not unless the hufa had been the size of a mountain. If this was a spear, then whoever had made it must have been enormous, a giant out of one of Grand Mother's ancient tales. Lesco shuddered at the thought.

The skin, those parts of the monster that Lesco could see poking out between the saltgrass, they didn't look like any kind of skin Lesco was familiar with. Even the chumpah husks he'd seen in the market looked nothing like this. They were all bumpy and tough, whereas this appeared all smooth and flat. There was no sign of a hair, a pimple, or even a wrinkle. It was possible to make out tiny patches, small blotches, which the sea had been unable to stain. They were brilliantly white, reflective, almost shiny. Certainly nothing alive Lesco had ever seen looked like it. The only material that even remotely resembled it was on some of the Find items. But they had all been tiny, no bigger than a human head, the length of an outstretched arm. Whereas this thing was as long as a grand market hut. No, bigger, the length of two!

Lesco gulped. His knees began to wobble with excitement. He felt a strange stirring in his belly. Everything about this discovery pointed to the Olds. They were the only ones capable of building something so huge, so impressive. What exactly was it? What did it do? That did not matter to Lesco. He only had one thought on his mind. This could be it. He might actually have done it. The most magnificent discovery, the ultimate Find. This could be Isda's prize!

First things first, Lesco had to do some investigating. It would do him no good to rush back to Murdo City, proclaim himself champion, and then lead a party down here to find what turned out to be nothing more than a rotting corpse of some long-dead sea creature stinking up the beach. No, he had to be sure it was a construction, an item. A gift from the Olds. And that meant getting in close. It meant touching it.

Lesco gritted his teeth. He edged forwards, raising his spear, prepared for an attack. Monster or no monster, he could not be certain that the thing was safe. If there was even a hint of movement, Lesco would be ready. With each tentative step, the bizarre discovery seemed to loom up over him. It was even bigger than he had initially thought. He would definitely need a ladder to scramble up on top of it. With eyes darting this way and that for any hint of danger, Lesco ever so cautiously pushed his spear forward. The tip nestled between the saltgrass, slipping and sliding its way through. With a gentle prod, the spear sludged onwards, squelching between the squidgy weeds. And then it stopped. A dull clunk as the tip found its target.

Lesco learned forward, applying a little more pressure. The monster did not budge. Lesco glanced along it, from the tail end overwhelmed by the surf below, to the head, stuck right up into the sand. No sign of any life at all. Not even a groan. He had touched the monster, his spear actually making contact with the creature's side, and nothing had happened. This thing wasn't alive. It most likely never had been. This was a Find item. And it was all his.

Lesco allowed himself a smile. The smile quickly spread. Isda had returned to him. He had banished her from his thoughts for good reason, but now the task was done, now victory was his, she could come sweeping back. His mind spun with a whirlwind of images - Isda smiling, Isda waving, Isda cheering, Isda moving in close to him, Isda taking him in her arms. His dreams all coming true at once. True love blossoming. It was just the right amount of distraction to prove costly.

Lesco was far away, forgetting where he was, what he was doing. That wasn't a spear he was gripping, it was Isda's hand. It wasn't saltgrass before him, but her flowing black hair. The sea mist he could smell was coming from her, off her smooth, brown skin, glistening in the daylight sun. He had lowered his guard. He loosened his grip on his spear for a mere second, imagining her soft fingers between his. He took his eye off his target. The movement above him was completely missed.

As Isda's body danced through his imagination and Lesco stood there grinning like an idiot, a large clump of saltgrass, loosened up by his prodding, slipped from the monster's side and landed squarely on his head.

The scream Lesco let fly at that moment would have awoken the dead. He staggered backwards, stumbling away from the monster, clawing at the slippy green tentacles that now covered his entire body. The stinking weeds had flopped down over his eyes, completely blinding him. They had found their way into his ears, slurping themselves inside. Lesco couldn't hear a thing. They had coated his shoulders, his arms, flopped down into his hands. He had dropped his spear in panic.

How could he have been so stupid? This was the monster's plan all along, to act all dead and dumb and Old-made, to act like an object, and then to launch a sneaky saltgrass attack at the last second. The slippery weeds had him beat. He was totally helpless. Now was the time for the monster to gobble him up.

Lesco crashed to the ground. He pulled himself backwards, clawing desperately at the black sand but failing to find any purchase. If anything, it just seemed to be dragging him in closer. In the end, he gave up and sat where he was, flinging the saltgrass from his face, uncovering his eyes, freeing his ears, crying and whimpering as he did. How pathetic he was, how dumb, walking right into this trap. And now Isda would never know what he had done for her.

He decided it best not to open his eyes. He wasn't entirely sure he wanted to see what was coming. Just hide in here, in the darkness, and hope that Isda arrived before the monster did. One last moment of bliss with her inside his own head before being munched and crunched to death. He prayed for his wish to be granted. The Olds are wise, the Olds are true, with Sulla's light they guide us through. He hoped they would hear him, forgive his foolishness, and send Isda his way for one last, brief, mesmerising moment. A second would be enough.

But as the time passed, Lesco began to realise he had been praying for quite a while. Close to a minute, perhaps. And nothing had happened. The monster hadn't come for him, nothing had eaten him. And Isda was nowhere to be seen. He'd just been sitting in the sand with his eyes closed, deliriously mumbling away to himself. Maybe it was time to find his courage, face up to his fate. He was a warrior of Antar, after all. A hunter chosen for the Find. He couldn't spend his final moments cowering away on the sand.

Lesco opened an eye. He had half expected that to be the moment the beast finally struck. But no. There was no marauding monster charging him, no gnashing teeth or ripping claws. In fact, nothing was really moving at all. Everything seemed relatively safe. His Find lay before him, just as it had before, silent and unmoving. As far as Lesco could tell, it had not shifted even a single inch. All that had happened is a wedge of saltgrass had fallen on top of him. There had been no attack.

Lesco opened the other eye, chuckling to himself. All that fuss over some silly old saltgrass. He was lucky no one had been around to see it. The weeds now surrounded him, scattered over the sand in a rough circle, creating a loose outline of his body. Some still hung over his shoulders, wrapped around his neck. It was slimy and unpleasant, but other than that, there was no obvious damage to either himself nor the monster. He had totally gotten away with it. There really was nothing to get so excited about. Except, that was, until Lesco looked up.

A significant chunk of the monster's side had been exposed by the falling saltgrass. More skin had been revealed. What had been green, dark and slimy was now smooth, shiny and white. And that was not all. A new colour had been revealed. There was something written there, across the monster, in large bold letters, bright and blue as the mid-cycle sky. Lesco gasped. His heart gave a flutter. He recognised the text immediately. All of Antar knew it. They had seen it a thousand times, scrawled across countless Find items before. Grand Mother had taught them what it was as soon as they were old enough to understand. It was the scripture, the sacred lettering of the Olds. And here it was, all bright and blue and printed across the side of the monster, now revealed by the dislodged saltgrass. Proof, if proof were needed, of exactly where this thing had come from.

Lesco leapt to his feet. He plunged forward, burying his hands into the saltgrass that still remained on the side of his monster. Almost gurning with excitement, he clawed it away, clump after clammy clump. Whole meals were flung over his shoulders, supplies enough to make it back to Murdo City twice over and then some. Lesco didn't care. There would be plenty more saltgrass out there. Supplies in Sulla's Cycle were plentiful. But there was only one Ultimate Find. And each handful he tore away revealed more of the lettering, stunning blue characters that were almost as big as he was. More and more and more of them, all running along its side. The monster had been branded, it had been named. And it had been gifted to Lesco himself. He truly had been chosen!

With his task finally done, Lesco collapsed back onto the sand. He sat there panting, admiring his handiwork. Before him sat the enormous, white, pointy treasure, covered head to toe in the writing of the Olds. He had no idea what any of it said, of course. The odd individual symbol looked familiar, but only the very privileged of Antar were blessed with the ability to read much more than their own name. But Lesco did know exactly what it meant, and that was all that mattered. It told him this treasure had belonged to the Olds. They had transported it to Antar, across the wild ocean, using the power of the Great Shadow. The storms had carried it here, all these many miles, a true gift from their great lands, far and away to the north. These symbols were proof of that.

It was a Find worthy of the ultimate hero. No one could deny it now. Not Grand Mother, not that meathead Hufa-Brain, and certainly not Isda. Lesco had won. It was confirmed. The glory was all his. He had travelled far and wide and proven his dedication to Antar. He had conquered the Find. He had demonstrated his love for Isda and the very Olds themselves had endorsed it. This incredible Find was their blessing. A beautiful future of love and light and unyielding happiness lay in wait. Lesco and Isda, Isda and Lesco, together forever until the end of all time. It was inevitable.

*

It had taken Lesco over thirty-five turns to cross the wilds of Antar and discover his Find. He made it back to Murdo City in less than twenty. It is amazing what true love could do for the energy levels. He had only eaten when absolutely necessary. He had barely stopped to sleep. He'd been cautious when he needed to, speedy when he didn't. If there were any chumpah around, like his journey out, he had not seen any sign. Whatever they were doing, they weren't doing it around him, which he was supremely thankful for. He had cut inside again at the river but, after several hours heading inland, decided to make even better time by taking the plunge. The current had slowed, the rapids mellowed. At least, that was what he told himself. Whereas on the trip out it had looked distinctly impassable, now it looked almost inviting. The elation pumping through his veins made Lesco feel like he could do just about anything. Swimming across the river would be a doddle.

As it turned out, it wasn't quite so simple. Several times Lesco was dragged under, tossed and turned around, before being deposited several metres further downstream. But with the promise of Isda's passion and devotion spurring him on, he fought back against the raging rapids, conquered the current, and clambered his way out the other side. He even laughed as he did so. Lesco was in love. Nothing could stop him now.

And so it was he arrived at the gates of Murdo City, exhausted and slightly soggy, with a tale of stupendous adventure to tell. He shouted it excitedly to the guards, recounting in great detail his awesome discovery. They nodded along, greeting each outlandish detail with a rather sceptical eyebrow raise. Clearly this poor boy must have lost his mind out there. A great Find the length of twenty men, the width of two standing on shoulders? With sacred scripture scrawled along the side? It was impossible. The Olds had never sent something so grand. The boy was clearly insane.

Nevertheless, word spread quickly through Murdo City. It rushed down streets and along alleyways, ducking its head into tents, around the doors of huts, throwing itself through windows. It passed through the great square, from stall to stall, handed over with every trade, taken home by every customer. Pretty soon, the whole town was awash with it. Have you heard? Lesco is home and his Find is as big as a mountain. He is shouting about it like a madman. Do you believe him? Not at all, but you should at least come and watch. He is a very passionate performer.

Eventually, the word arrived at Grand Mother's doorstep. She did not know what to make of it. She had a vague memory of an annoying young boy who had been pestering everybody for work. Something about a divine destiny. A great love for our times. He had been very irritating. It was possible she had selected him to go on the Find just to get rid of him. But she had her duties to perform, and so if he was saying he had discovered the finest treasure the Olds had ever sent to Antar, it would be remiss of her not to at least hear him out.

When Lesco was eventually presented to Grand Mother, he flung the words at her like a verbal typhoon. Unstoppable narrative spilled from his mouth. He did not appear to pause for a single breath. Several onlookers had begun taking bets on when exactly he was going to pass out, so much detail was there in such little time. It was a miracle that Grand Mother was able to understand any of it. A huge white spear, with giant blue lettering, she had asked. Lesco blurted out an enthusiastic response. Grand Mother nodded sagely. It was highly likely the young fool was delirious and imagining the whole thing. He looked like he hadn't slept for weeks and had possibly been living in a pond. But if there was even a chance his story was true, it was her Old-given duty to go and investigate. At the very least, it would give her something to do instead of pottering around waiting for all the hunters to return and present their prizes.

And so Grand Mother called forth her bravest soldiers. She instructed them to prepare her raft, commandeer the finest craft from the fishing fleet to accompany them. If the boy had made it back from the Find in twenty turns, by sea they should be able to make it in ten. Antar could cope without fish while they travelled. If the Find really was as magnificent as the boy had described it, then the sacrifice would be worth it.

The fleet set sail from the docks, Grand Mother's raft flanked by a phalanx of tiny fishing vessels. It looked to Lesco as if the whole of Antar had turned out to send them off. There was so much chattering, constant waving, and not a little cheering. Grand Mother took it in her stride, clearly used to this sort of thing. Lesco gawped around like an idiot, straining hopelessly to take it all in. He tried searching the crowd for Isda, to find calming comfort in her beauty. But he couldn't quite spot her. No doubt she was here. How could she not be? But there were so many people, she must have become lost in the crowd. If he had really been paying attention, he might have noticed Hufa-Brain was missing too. Lesco might even have wondered what it was they could be doing that they deemed more important than all of this.

As the fleet made its way along the coast, Lesco found himself as guest of honour on Grand Mother's raft. He believed he had been chosen because of his new-found grand status. The thought had not occurred to him that it was simply because the expedition needed a guide. Still, he could barely contain his excitement, pointing eagerly at every landmark along the shore he recognised, every identifiable outcrop he had previously passed. He squealed with delight when they approached the mouth of the river, knowing full well that they were fast approaching their target.

To pass the turns, Grand Mother would ask him questions about himself. Who he was, where he was from, what he wanted to be. Why he had travelled so far away from home, given he was so young and inexperienced. Lesco had told her the truth.

He was a simple son of Antar, a devoted follower of the Olds, on an epic quest of love. His passion had spurred him on. It had allowed him to achieve greatness.

When Grand Mother had pressed him for details, Lesco had not been shy in providing them. He had told her Isda's name, repeatedly described in great detail what she looked like, who she was, and what their life would be like together. Grand Mother noted more than a hint of obsession in his telling. She is the greatest person on Antar, Lesco had told her. The most beautiful, the most charming, the most delightful. All he cared about in the world was her. She was his whole life. Isda is all anyone could ever hope for.

Grand Mother had laughed heartily, seemingly finding great humour in the idea that Lesco could become so utterly infatuated with someone he had never really met, let alone actually held a conversation with. Perhaps you are getting carried away with yourself, she had suggested. Lesco had scoffed. Grand Mother might be an expert on the Olds and all things Find-related, but she clearly knew nothing about love. Grand Mother responded simply with a gentle smile, before gazing silently out to sea.

It was late into the eighth turn when they arrived at the beach. Lesco almost didn't recognise it at first - so much of Antar's coastline was frustratingly similar - but then a call went out from one of the lead boats. More of a shocked exclamation, a disbelieving shout. They had spotted something sticking up out of the surf, beached up onto the sand. Something huge, long, pointy and white. There was a great deal of fuss being made about it.

The fleet made landfall. Grand Mother was escorted from her raft as the boats were pulled up onto the sand. Lesco watched her closely for any sign or reaction. He was hoping to be able to gauge from her exactly what it was he had discovered. And, more importantly, how impressed she was by it. Alas, Grand Mother remained annoyingly stony-faced, silently shuffling up the beach in the direction of the great Find, not speaking a word. Her guards, however, were a mess of overblown reactions. They were jumping all over the place, marking out circles around her, forming ranks. They barked instructions at each other, flashed various hand symbols. Go here, stand there, watch that. Lesco observed humorously as they flapped and fretted, doing their utmost to protect Grand Mother from the enormous monster at the other end of the beach. Lesco knew she did not need protecting. None of them did.

He had conquered the beast already. There was nothing to be afraid of. It was funny to watch the finest soldiers in Antar become so agitated for no real reason.

When they finally reached Lesco's great Find, the small crowd stood before it in awe. Nobody could quite believe it. The boy had not been lying. This truly was a monster. Bigger than they had even imagined. They had never seen anything like it. Grand Mother bowed her head, spoke softly the sacred words - the Olds are wise, the Olds are true, with Sulla's light they guide us through. All standing beside her repeated them in unison. Once the prayers were done, Grand Mother turned to Lesco. Much to his relief, she raised her eyebrows, clearly impressed, before giving him a little pat on the back. He had been hoping for something a little more theatrical, maybe everyone down on their knees, bowing to him, chanting his name, but it was better than nothing.

What was it? The soldiers were eager for answers. Where did it come from? What does it do? And is it safe? They pleaded with Grand Mother to share her great knowledge. She hushed them, frustrated with their impatience. Silence was required. She needed time to think. Grand Mother looked the Find up and down, from one end to the other, taking in all its magnificent detail. She stood before Lesco's monster and studied the scripture upon it, spending several minutes deciphering the huge, blue text. Her travelling party waited patiently behind her. Grand Mother was supremely wise. They all knew this. If anyone was going to uncover the secrets of Lesco's magnificent discovery, it was going to be her.

And then she turned. She gestured for Lesco to step forward, to join her at the monster's side. She asked him if he could read. Lesco shook his head. Grand Mother pointed up to the text and drifted her finger through the air, reading the great letters aloud as she went. Three words that Lesco neither recognised nor understood. *SilverWind Industries Inc.* That's what it says, she told him. That is what you have found.

Lesco shrugged. It meant nothing to him. What was a SilverWind? What was an Industries? And Inc sounded like a noise someone would make when they were going to be sick. Grand Mother smiled, resting a hand on his shoulder. It is a sail, she said, part of a great machine, what would have once been called a turbine. The Olds use them to farm the wind. Lesco burst out laughing. He eyeballed Grand Mother sceptically, not entirely sure if she was toying with him or simply going mad in her old age. Saltgrass could be farmed, possibly hufas too, if you caught them on a good day. But no one could farm the wind. Not even the Olds. It was ridiculous. What on Antar was the crazy old woman babbling on about?

But Grand Mother had insisted. These great sails stood on huge towers, pinned to the ocean floor. As the wind turned them, the Olds would harness the power of the very air itself. There would be hundreds of them, thousands, all scattered throughout the oceans to the north. Like an immense forest, growing out of the sea. This one must have been taken out by a violent storm, or a huge wave. When the Olds could no longer make use of it, they had sent it Antar's way. And now Lesco had found it.

Lesco stood listening to her, mouth agape, shaking his head in disbelief. The insanity of it all was simply too much to get his young head around. Farming the wind. A forest on the ocean. Harnessing the power from the air all around them. Was there nothing the Olds couldn't do? The travelling party took a moment, standing together in respectful silence. There was a time for celebration. That would come soon enough. For now, they bowed their heads and gave praise to the Olds for this greatest of gifts. And then slowly, one by one, they began to wonder how on Antar they were going to get the thing home. Luckily, Grand Mother had a plan.

The operation to return the turbine to the sea was quite something to behold. No one questioned that the Find would have to return to Murdo City. After the Great Shadow they had just had, it would do the people good to see something so miraculous arrive in their capital. All of Antar must see this. With the manpower currently at Grand Mother's disposal, she knew they had not a chance of transporting the great structure by land. But she estimated with some confidence that the thing would float, if they could just get it back into deep enough water. Channels were dug, ropes and pulleys constructed, and a great deal of grunting and pushing was employed, but eventually the enormous sail slowly started to slide down the beach towards the waves.

Lesco had been tasked with sitting atop the great beast, coordinating the efforts, instructing the men which way to push. Of course, they all knew which way to push. It was blindingly obvious. Lesco's assignment was a fraud. Grand Mother just didn't want him getting in the way of their carefully crafted operation. The boy would no doubt get himself buried or squashed. Much better to have him safely stashed away where he could not cause any trouble. This was all completely lost on Lesco. He was convinced he had been selected for his fine people skills and project

153

management acumen. He sat proudly atop the sail as it shunted along the sand, believing himself to be of great use, shouting out words of encouragement to the increasingly irritated soldiers. If Lesco had not been the one to make the discovery, they would have been tempted to tip him off and slide the sail right over the top of him. But the Olds had chosen Lesco. The Find was his. They begrudgingly would have to show him some respect. At least for the time being.

Eventually, with a raucous cheer, the great turbine was freed into the ocean. Lesco remained on top of it, riding its back as if it really were some huge sea monster. He could barely contain himself, shouting and screaming and hollering away, celebrating his own success. The soldiers rolled their eyes at him as they positioned the various fishing boats around it, together with Grand Mother's raft, and bound them all together in one enormous flotilla. What a sight it could make, Lesco considered, riding the waves, cresting the horizon as it slowly emerged into view for the eagerly waiting residents of Murdo City. How they would cheer as they saw the victory party return. How they would gasp when they saw what had been brought back to them. The great sail, the immense turbine, an actual wind-farmer of the Olds. And how they would gaze up in awe at the young son of Antar who sat atop it, waving back to them, the brave soul who had risked his life to discover it and bring it home.

Lesco grinned to himself, the sun on his back, sea spray in his hair, and wished away the return journey. The sooner to be back home, the sooner Isda would be there to greet him. A speedy return and he would be running up the dock to her, embracing her, beginning the rest of his life with her. His heart swelled at the very thought of it. A romance for the ages, the greatest love of our time. It was meant to be. Lesco could not wait.

*

The turbine stood proudly in the centre of the festival circle, towering above the great square. It sat in a large pit, ropes holding it in place. Rocks at its base prevented it from toppling. Its tip, way up high above all the huts and the tents, could be seen for miles around. It was Murdo City's magnificent new monument. Laid out before it, surrounding it, sat the rest of the Find items, stacked in neat little piles, looking up to it, as if all were praising it. So many tiny trinkets and treasures, paling in comparison next to the gigantic wind-farmer. Around the sail and all the other fine

154

gifts, the people of Antar - the dancers, the revellers, the joyous celebrators - swaying and swinging, laughing and cheering, looping around the great bounty in time to the frantic drum beats. Their words were shouted and sung, with more joy than perhaps ever before. The Olds are wise, the Olds are true, with Sulla's light they guide us through. Goblets were clinked, toasts and tributes made. The greatest Find that Antar had ever seen. What a time to be alive. All joined in this unprecedented merriment.

All, that is, except one. A young boy, no more than 15 cycles to his name, sat alone on the very edge of the party. His knees were tucked up against his chin as he hugged them to his chest, trying to hide the tears now streaming down his face. This was supposed to be the greatest moment of his young life. It had turned out to be the absolute worst.

Lesco stared out into the mass of people, and at one person in particular, wanting desperately to look away from her, but finding himself unable. Everyone else was having too good a time to notice, but here he sat, heartbroken and abandoned, his entire world in tatters. How could she do it? Here, now, in front of everybody. After all he had done for her. How could she hurt him so? How could the Olds have let this happen? He was the Find King! What sort of reward was this? It just didn't make any sense. His intended, his destiny, his one true love. How could she have done something so insane as reject him in favour of that muscle-bound meathead Hufa-Brain?!

As Isda embraced her new lover, Lesco considered whether he should just go and throw up. It certainly seemed preferable to watching this horror continue to unfold before him. The love of his life was kissing another. In fact, kissing was an understatement. It looked very much more like she was trying to eat him, somehow absorb Hufa-Brain through a combination of flapping tongue and gnawing lips. It certainly didn't look like a suitable display for a family-friendly triumphant celebration. But for some inexplicable reason, not one other person present seemed to care one jot about what Isda and Hufa-Brain were doing to each other. If anything, the people nearby seemed to be enjoying it, laughing and shouting words of encouragement, cheering on the young lovers and celebrating their new found happiness. It was absolutely disgusting.

Isda had not met Lesco at the docks. She had not come running to him when she had found out he had returned. She had not sought him out at all. This was partly because she still had no real clue as to who Lesco was, but mostly because she had spent the last few turns in a passionate whirlwind of blossoming romance. She had heard about the great wind-farmer, the mission to reclaim it. People had excitedly recounted the story to her, and insisted she come and see the triumphant search party return. Isda had smiled politely, said she would come along if she had time. But in truth, she had found herself unable to care too much about the big, white, clunky object that was now being erected in the great square. It was just a thing, an item, that did not appear to have any practical purpose. Like most of the Find hoard that turned up each cycle, she found it difficult to get all that excited about any of it. None of these items the hunters dug up actually did anything, they just sat around Murdo City taking up space. If it was up to her, she would spend Antar's limited resources fixing Antar's not insignificant problems, rather than waste time scouring the land for useless junk that some people no one had ever met before had sent their way for frustratingly unclear reasons. To her, the whole idea of the Find seemed rather ridiculous.

Apart from the party, of course. Now, that was something she *was* looking forward to. Even if it was being thrown for reasons that didn't entirely make sense to her, that certainly didn't mean she wasn't going to enjoy herself. The dancing, the saltwine, her and her new man, enjoying the festivities, enjoying each other. Just being together. What fun that was going to be.

And so along she went, arm in arm with her beloved, eager to show him off. Eager to show them both off. The others could get excited about the giant sail that did nothing, she was excited about a very real promise of a brighter future. That's what Antar truly needed. Not a pile of silly trinkets, but a promise of improving prospects, of a life actually worth living once the Great Shadow breaks. It can't just be an endless struggle peppered by worship for the forever absent Olds. Antar's prospects needed to be greater than that. The happiness she had found could be a symbol far more inspiring than anything the Find could cough up. It was real. It meant something. It had a future. And in it there was a joy she was desperate to share. On such a spectacular turn such as this, surely no one could begrudge her that.

Lesco, of course, felt rather differently about this public display of affection. He was really rather keen on begrudging, on staring and sulking and angrily resenting. This really did seem like the ideal opportunity for it. However, even Lesco was ready to draw the line when he saw Hufa-Brain's hands going to places they really should not be going to in a public setting. Enough was enough. He could not watch for one second longer. Isda had clearly gone insane. To lose herself in Hufa-Brain and his excessive fumbling while all the celebrations continued to swirl around her, to simply ignore the centrepiece - Lesco's triumph - and keep sucking away on Hufa-Brain's face without even a thank you thrown in Lesco's direction, well, that was just insulting. He refused to take it any longer. Antar could keep its party. Let them blindly rejoice while this great injustice played out right in front of them. Lesco would have no part in it.

He stood to leave, wiping the tears from his cheeks. The last thing he saw before he turned away was Isda's welcoming smile and playful eyes glancing up to her lover. Despite his hasty retreat, that heart-crushing image burned itself into Lesco's brain and refused to budge. As he slumped away from the jovial masses, it just kept on coming back to haunt him. And his rage increased each time that it did. Every face he saw in the crowd, it beamed Isda's smile back to him. Each swinging body became Hufa-Brains hulking great arms. Even the tents he passed, hufa skins flapping gently in the mid-cycle breeze, they looked to him like exact replicas of one enormous slab-hand grabbing hold of far too much perfectly rounded buttock. Everywhere he looked, there they both were - his one true love and the beast who had stolen her. It was impossible now for Lesco to see anything else. Isda was lost to another and the entirety of Murdo City was mocking him for it. It was so unfair.

Lesco kicked out. It was almost instinctual. Rage had overwhelmed him. His body was beyond his control. He had stomped off to the edge of the celebration circle and, when no one was really around him, just swung his leg violently forward. It didn't really matter what it hit, he just needed to kick. He needed something to suffer. Lesco had assumed it had been a rock or a pile of dirt he had spotted out the corner of his eye. Certainly nothing worth getting excited about. It just needed to be booted. But there had been a sharp clack, rather than the expected dull thud. And the victim of his attack had spun off wildly between a couple of nearby tents, not just exploded and scattered up into the air like he had been expecting. For the briefest of moments, Lesco was distracted from his heartbreak and intrigued as to what exactly his foot had collided with. This needed investigating.

Find King or not, it would do him no good to be caught sneaking around someone else's property. Best conduct his search on the sly. So after glancing over his shoulder to make sure no one was looking, Lesco darted between the tents and hunkered down behind them. No one out there seemed to notice. They were all still having too much fun. Two of them in particular. But Lesco had a mission now, a welcome distraction from his torment. What was it his foot had struck?

It did not take long to discover his victim. There it lay, pressed up against the side of a tent. It appeared to be a bottle, small and yellow, and absolutely covered in tiny black letters. Lesco had seen enough of this text now to recognise it immediately. What his foot had collided with appeared to be a gift from the Olds, made from that strange material that bent rather than broke and gave off strange smells and colours when you burnt it. This was no rock or pile of dirt. This was a Find item.

Lesco crouched down between the tents, contemplating his next step. The bottle must have been dropped, or disturbed somehow from the Find pile. In the commotion of the party, it had spun out to the edge unnoticed. Or perhaps some other hunter had picked it up and tossed it aside, knowing full well that it was nothing in comparison to Lesco's wind-farmer. It had not been worthy of joining the collection of buckets and bottles, ropes and bags, cartons and containers that made up the Find pile. All those items, scarred or stained by the poisoned sea, deposited by wave or wind over the lands of Antar - all of them had found their way somehow from the land of Olds to here, to the celebration circle, to be saluted and worshipped and danced around and treasured. All of them except one.

Lesco gazed down at the bottle. In comparison to his giant wind-farmer, it really was rather pathetic. And someone had gone hunting for it. Whereas Lesco had brought back the greatest Find of all time, an unknown hunter had discovered this tiny, insignificant, pointless item and somehow thought it worthy of recovery. This inadequate piece of nothing. And whereas Lesco was being punished for his efforts, rejected by his love, abandoned by the Olds, this other hunter was probably out there in the throng somewhere, having the time of their life, being rewarded. For all Lesco knew, the conqueror of this useless bottle might even have been Hufa-Brain...

Before he really knew it, Lesco was gritting his teeth. Almost unbeknown to him, his hands had clenched into fists. His face had begun to glow red. That final thought had crashed through the walls of his consciousness and was now setting up camp, refusing to leave. His body was reacting accordingly. This bottle - it *did* belong to Hufa-Brain. Isda's conqueror. It must do. That was why Lesco had stumbled across it. He had been presented with an opportunity. Lesco had performed miracles out there on the hunt, yet had been ignored and betrayed, tossed aside. In contrast, the beast who had found this stupid bottle, the pathetic idiot who had brought it home with no effort whatsoever, was currently experiencing unimaginable pleasure with the one person in Antar that Lesco actually cared about. This bottle belonged to Lesco's love rival. It *was* his rival. It was his nemesis. It was everything he hated in the world. And so it had to be punished. Lesco had been brought here to enact justice. The bottle had to die.

Lesco kicked out again, picturing the hunter's face as he did so. He launched his foot straight through the bottle. There was Hufa-Brain, lying face down in the dirt. He was weeping. His arms were outstretched in a miserable display of cowardice. He was pleading with Lesco for mercy. He would receive none. Lesco chuckled as the bottle flew off into the air. In its place he saw blood and teeth splattering off across the dirt. He saw a tongue being rocked back inside an enormous meaty skull.

A pang of pain rocked through Lesco's foot. It didn't matter. Seeing the bottle - Hufa-Brain - flying off through the air more than made up for it. He grunted loudly. He cried out in triumph. He stomped his aching toes down into the dirt, beating the pain out of them. Stop complaining. This will all be worth it.

No one in the celebration circle seemed to pay much attention. The people of Antar danced and skipped and called out in praise for the Olds, while beside them Lesco stamped and kicked and grunted away all his frustrations at the sheer injustice of the world. He had never felt so detached from his people. And that, of course, was all the bottle's fault.

Off Lesco went, charging further and further away from the square, leaving the party far behind. Tent after tent whizzed by, all of them empty. No one else was back here. No one else had cause to be. Even the guards had abandoned their posts. All of Antar was enjoying the festivities. All except Lesco, on his hunt for the bottle. He found it again, nestled up against a stack of spears. He picked one, raised it high above his head. Lesco cried out in rage. And the spear swung right into the bottle - directly into Hufa-Brain's face. A nose shattered. A jaw cracked. The bottle cried out in pain. Lesco ignored its protestations. There was no room for leniency now. He swung the spear again, launching the bottle further into the air. And with a cheer, Lesco launched himself after it.

The game - Lesco's fantasy - continued for some time. All of Murdo City was at the party, celebrating the great Find. The streets were completely empty. No one was manning the guard towers or patrolling the walls. All the tents and huts had been left unattended. Everyone was in such carefree spirits, Lesco was free to batter the bottle wherever he pleased. And then go charging on after it. Each time he swung out or kicked, he would imagine the pathetic scream that accompanied it. Maybe he could not have Isda. Perhaps that was what the Olds had decreed. But if that was to be the case, in his imagination he was going to make damn sure Hufa-Brain could not have her either. There would be nothing left of that fool once Lesco was done with him.

Lesco had no real clue where he was going. It didn't really matter. Although he would be at pains to admit it, given he was supposed to be heartbroken, for the first time since the celebrations began, he was actually having fun. His game had proven itself to be a wonderful distraction. Kick, cheer, charge. That was all there was to it. He needn't worry about anything else.

Until, that was, he heard a clang. Out there in the distance, in the direction the bottle had just flung off too. A clear metallic ringing that sounded unlike anything Lesco had been expecting, a noise rarely heard in Murdo City. The bottle must have struck something unusual. Lesco looked up, took in his surroundings, tried to identify where he had ended up. Up until that point, the entire journey had been a blur. A pack of chumpah could have snuck past him and he would not have noticed a thing.

He was beyond the residential area now, beyond the market, beyond all the huts and the tents and roadside stalls. It was not a part of the city he recognised. Far off, in the distance, Lesco could still make out the sounds of the party. And there was the wind-farmer, standing tall and proud above all that surrounded it. It would be a clear sign for anyone or anything to follow, should they need to know exactly where all the people were. Lesco scoffed. Those idiots and their stupid celebrations. That fool Isda. All that she was missing out on. He was glad to be out here, all alone, playing his whacking game. It was exactly where he wanted to be. But… where exactly was he?

The road he was on was unfamiliar. It did not look built by Antar. It was far too uniform, too neat and straight. On either side of it lay half-built barricades of rock and iron. Beyond them, a collection of crumbled buildings, walls built out of metal that had been warped long ago into tiny waves. They had all been bent out of shape by countless cycles of damage and decay. The Great Shadow takes its toll on everything.

Lesco gasped, his brain suddenly clicking into gear. These were the ruins of Old Murdo! He had stumbled right into the ancient city. It was not really somewhere he was supposed to be, being sacred ground and all. But who was going to stop him now? No one was around to see. Before him stood a scattered collection of fallen down outhouses, strange circular storage spaces, clunky rooms built on huge chunky stilts. Lesco had not a clue why the Olds would have wanted to raise their houses above the ground. Or why they had not bothered to build any of it to last. No wonder they had all up and left, headed back north, if this is the sort of accommodation they were dealing with. If he had possessed all their strength and wisdom, he would have constructed huge palaces, giant monuments to all that was great and good in the world. Not this collection of tatty old rubble.

Lesco's Hufa-Brain substitute had clipped the edge of the marker that identified the border of Old Murdo. He saw it now, nestled against one of the posts that held the sign in place. That must have been the source of the clang. Lesco marched over to collect his battered plaything, now barely even recognisable from the bottle it once was. He paused for a second, taking a look at the sign itself. He had seen it before, long ago, and never really paid it much attention. But now he was here, all alone, he suddenly found it immensely fascinating. What on Antar had the Olds been thinking, putting this here, placing their entire town here? It did not make a lick of sense. The sign itself was snapped in half. Where the other half was, no one really knew. Perhaps it had been ripped away by the Great Shadow, the harsh winds flinging it out to sea. Or maybe an overly ambitious chumpah had swung by, took a disliking to it. Were those teeth marks along the serrated edge? Was the damage done by claws? It was impossible to tell.

What Lesco could see clearly, though, was the word Antar printed across the sign, together with a rough map of the land he knew so well. Lesco peered in closer. Looking at the sign now, it did look very much to him as if there might have been other letters beyond what he could see here. As if Antar was not the entirety of what had been originally written. The words printed underneath - *Research Centre* - were just gobbledygook to Lesco. Maybe Grand Mother knew what it meant. The Olds really were a strange bunch, with their ridiculous attempts at houses and their insane scripture. Lesco could not make head nor tail of what they must have been doing out here. And right now, he didn't much care. It did not really matter to him all that much. He just wanted his bottle back.

Lesco crouched, stretching out his hand to take up the bottle. And that is when he froze. That is when he felt a terrible chill run down his spine, when his stomach suddenly lurched for freedom. For it was in that moment that he spotted the pawprint. Or rather, paw*prints*. Now he was bent double, nose inches from the ground, he could see them all quite clearly. Just on the other side of the sign, out there in the dirt. So many of them, all heading in the same direction. Those terrible tracks that were familiar to every citizen of Antar. All had been trained to spot them. And all had been warned to fear them. That large round bowl, the size of a fist, with five smaller indentations ahead of it. With five scratches in the dirt beyond. Five deep cuts into the earth, from five razor sharp claws. Lesco gulped.

Ever so slowly, Lesco raised himself back up to full height. The bottle remained where it was. Lesco had completely forgotten about it. There was something far more pressing on his mind. He felt a shiver down the back of his neck, the hairs there suddenly alert. He could feel his heart pounding, hear the blood pumping in his ears. He could taste metal. Beyond the sign there was nothing. All was completely still and silent. It was almost as if the coast was completely clear. But tracks don't lie. Those pawprints pointed to only one thing - chumpahs.

Lesco tried to calm himself. Perhaps the pack had come through Old Murdo, found nothing of interest and moved on. With all the celebrations going on, the ruins had been unguarded. They had seized their opportunity to scout it out, dig for scraps, take what they could and leave. There was nothing to worry about.

Except Lesco knew that wasn't true. Chumpahs don't scavenge, they hunt. They sweep through, silent and deadly, taking their prey while it still lives. While the blood runs warm. There's no joy for a chumpah in feasting on long dead flesh. They like it twitching and still screaming. And those pawprints, they all led in only one direction. All of them together, heading further into the city. There was no mistaking that. It was all the noise and commotion that had drawn them in. It was the lack of guards that had made it possible. It must have just been blind luck that Lesco had not stumbled across them already, his whack and chase game taking him in all sorts of bizarre and unpredictable directions. But the chumpah were out there. There was no avoiding that fact now. And as much as it terrified Lesco to admit it, it was obvious what was happening. The pack were heading for the party. They knew exactly where the banquet was. And very soon they would be feasting.

Lesco looked up. Beyond the sign, beyond the crumbled ruins of Old Murdo, there - the guard tower. It was empty. Had the chumpah already attacked? Or had the idiot left his post to join up with the celebrations? It was impossible to tell from Lesco's position. There were no obvious signs of damage to the tower, no evidence of an onslaught. Although, as Lesco thought grimly, if the chumpah had taken the guard, it was unlikely they would have left anything behind to find. At most, a torn piece of tunic in the mud. A splash of red in the dirt.

What Lesco could see, however, was the alarm. The horn was strung up clearly atop the tower - stretched hufa skin wrapped around chiselled bone - and no one was around to sound it. Lesco knew immediately what it was he must do. The chumpah stalked slowly but pounced quickly. The screaming had not yet started. There was still time. If he could make it to the tower, blow the horn, raise the signal, he could warn them. The guards could arm themselves. They could organise. They could form barricades, prepare traps, hide the vulnerable. They could prepare. They would stand a chance. If Lesco could just get to the guard tower in time, lives would almost certainly be saved. That was what Lesco must do. He was the Find King, after all. An absolute hero. And Antar needed him now more than ever.

And yet Lesco paused. He did not launch himself into a sprint, full pelt towards the tower. He did not dash through the ruins in a glorious last-ditch attempt to save Antar from the chumpahs. He did not run for his life and the lives of his people. Lesco did not move at all. Instead he listened, a grisly smile upon his lips. The sounds of the distant party still drifted through the streets of Murdo City on the breeze. They were still out there, the people of Antar, enjoying themselves at his expense. All those happy souls, celebrating the greatest of Finds, though not with the actual person who found it. All those dancers and drinkers and cheerers and huggers. Those kissers. The entire crowd, oblivious to their fate, hopping and skipping around Isda and Hufa-Brain, just watching on, letting them get on with it. Allowing them to parade their cruellest of romances in plain sight. Where just about anyone could see it. Where it could break a heart in two.

Lesco was already a hero. He had discovered the wind-farmer. He had tamed it, presented it to Grand Mother. He had won the Find. And yet that still had not stopped him from being rejected. His remarkable achievements had not prevented him from being left out, shunted away and forgotten. The citizens of Antar had not saved him from his heartbreak. So why should he bother to save them from the chumpahs? What benefit was there to him in being the hero, if this was how Antar treated its heroes?

No, they didn't deserve their Find King. Isda, Grand Mother, Hufa-Brain - all of them, they had made their choice, brought this on themselves. They deserved the chumpahs. And Lesco wasn't going to lift a finger to stop them. Antar had it coming.

*

The true scale of the attack did not really hit Lesco until he saw the leg. Up until that point, he had actually been having quite a lot of fun. He had not been overly concerned by all the screaming. People scream when they see chumpahs. They raise all sorts of ruckus. It was a perfectly reasonable reaction. So the distant cries and shouts, coupled with the barks and the snarls, had not really bothered him. It was to be expected. Enjoyed, even. Antar was receiving its punishment. Tough as it may be, it was learning its lesson. This is what happens when you cross Lesco, the Find King. Don't you ever forget it.

He had not been particularly distressed by the people running past him either. Once the screaming had stopped, the noise died down, Lesco had emerged from his hiding spot. The chumpahs, wherever they were, had made their point and moved on. Lesco was fairly confident it was safe to do similar. Time to head back into town and take in all that well-deserved destruction. So off he went, trotting merrily back towards the great wind-farmer. And as he did so, he started to pass a few fearful looking faces heading in the opposite direction. It was hard not to smirk. Those idiots, those traitors, wailing and whining, stumbling around in shock. Where was all this concern when Lesco had been suffering? When he had been in pain? Maybe if they had been a bit more considerate when they had the chance, they wouldn't be in this mess. Lesco simply strolled past them, ignoring their cries for help. They were not worthy of his assistance. None of them deserved it. And he was having too much fun revelling in their misery to even think about offering it.

But then the leg came along. Lesco had turned a corner, trying desperately to suppress a smile, when he almost walked right into it. There, directly in front of him.

164

A leg. Just sitting there. And only a leg, lying right in his path. No body. No person. Just a single, solitary leg, very much in a place where a leg on its own should not be. Toes, a foot, a calf, a knee and then... nothing. A stump. A snapped bone, some nibbled flesh. And all just lying there, in the middle of the path. Right in his way. Impossible to avoid. Someone had lost a leg. Or, perhaps more accurately, a leg had lost the rest of its body. The leg wasn't lost at all. Lesco knew exactly where it was. But he was beginning to get rather concerned about the whereabouts of the rest of the person it belonged to.

Lesco sidestepped the leg slowly. He was finding it difficult to process - what it was doing there, what exactly had happened. There was a slight hesitation in his step. A few doubts were begging to circle. He had not been entirely sure what he had been expecting to happen when he let the chumpahs through. A few shocks, maybe, a couple of scares. The party ruined. Perhaps a couple of people would get bitten. A scratch here or there. But no worse than that. Certainly no one's leg was supposed to come off. The guards would have battled the chumpahs away long before that happened. They would run the beasts right out of town and everything would basically be OK. The people would realise the error of their ways and all would be forgiven. Because nothing drastically bad had happened.

Maybe it was just a coincidence. No need to panic just yet. Lesco nodded to himself, thinking it through. There was no reason to believe this severed leg was in any way related to the chumpah attack. It was more than possible there had been some sort of accident. An unfortunate misstep. Something sharp had fallen on the victim, severing the limb. These things happen. The unfortunate soul was being treated and comforted but in all the commotion, no one had thought to remove the leg from the road yet. It happens. Someone would get around to that soon.

Lesco had just about managed to convince himself the leg was unrelated to the chumpah attack when he spotted someone stumbling towards him. A young man - barely older than Lesco was himself - limping up the road, away from the party. He looked like he was struggling to stay upright. As Lesco approached, thinking he could help, he saw a deep red scar covering one entire side of the young man's face. Lesco winced at the sight of it, thinking how painful it looked, wondering why the young man seemed to be ignoring it. But then Lesco noticed something worse. A tear along the young man's chest. The poor fool was clutching it with both hands, trying his best to hold himself together. It didn't seem to be working very well. As the young man approached, he looked up at Lesco. Their eyes met. Lesco froze. There was a brief second - perhaps imagined, perhaps not - where Lesco was convinced there was a hint of recognition. Or realisation. *You did this*, the young man's bulging eyes seemed to say. *This is all your fault.* Lesco shook his head. It wasn't true. It couldn't be. The young man then attempted a further step forward before keeling over, landing face down in the dirt with a splat. The parts of him he had been trying to hold in now started to seep out across the path. The young man did not move at all after that.

How many pairs of pawprints had there been? Lesco tried to remember. He had seen them clearly enough, but had not bothered stopping to count. He did not think there had been that many. Surely not enough to do all this. Had the chumpahs been smart, moving in single file? Or had he simply been so eager to enact his plan of revenge he had not really paid all that much attention? Lesco could not say for certain. But what he did know, what he slowly began to realise as he made his way back towards the great wind-farmer, was that he could no longer avoid the truth of what was happening. Reality had dawned. Lesco had made the most terrible of mistakes.

He began to see tents strewn across the streets. There were huge rips in them, gouges, long, sharp tears. Hufa skins lay scattered around in the mud. Some even had little specks of dark red on them. Doors had been ripped clear from their hinges, walls had been battered down, whole houses crushed. And everywhere he looked, all over the ground, those huge, round pawprints that he had spotted and warned no one about.

Where he found people, he found shock and incomprehension, stunned expressions struggling to understand. They would be huddled together in little clumps, clutching onto each other. Or crowded around someone Lesco could not quite see, a bloody and battered body on the ground. The unfortunates that the chumpahs had not quite had enough time to finish off completely, or those who had put up too much of a fight to drag away. Chumpahs are smart. When they can no longer eat, they will gather up any food they can in their jaws and take it with them, no matter how much it kicks and complains. They will keep it with them until the time is right. Until their need is great.

The victims of Antar did not pay much attention to Lesco as he trudged back to the celebration circle. They had far more pressing things on their mind. The guards and the soldiers, those that had survived, ran to and fro, scattering their calls and their barked instructions. They tried to make it look like they knew what they were doing, that there was still some semblance of control. Deep down, they were just as confused as everyone else. Occasionally someone would shout out. "Help me! Come here! Help them! Go there!" Lesco wasn't sure if they were calling to him or not. They did not appear to be addressing anyone. Lesco wanted to do something, but just did not have a clue where to even start. Murdo City was in pieces. It had been attacked, invaded, chewed up and spat back out. And Lesco could not shake the horrible realisation that he had been responsible. This *was* all his fault.

When Lesco finally made it back to the celebration circle, that is where he saw the worst of it. It had been where the people of Antar had gathered, after all. Where the party had been in full swing. All that noise and commotion. That is what the chumpahs had been attracted to. It was where they had struck first. The wind-farmer remained standing. The rest of the Find pile had not been so lucky. The square was awash with all the tiny trinkets, cartons and bags and nets and bottles, all strewn across the dirt. The bodies lay between them, not all of them in one piece. There were bite marks and tears, deep scars and scratches. The ground was covered in running footprints and scrambling pawprints, scraping through the dirt. Attacks flying in all directions, prey fleeing wherever it could. The pandemonium of the attack laid bare in the tracks.

It was then that Lesco spotted a familiar face. A wave of relief washed over him, almost knocking him off his feet. He had not even been aware he was looking for her until he found her. Isda. She was still here. She was alive. There she sat, cross legged in the dirt. Around her were all the signs of destruction, broken stalls and broken bodies, but thankfully to Lesco, she looked relatively unharmed. He did not know what he would have done if she had been otherwise, if his terrible error had cost Isda her life too. But here she was, the one person he cared about more than any other. And she was still breathing. The chumpahs had not gotten to her. Despite the havoc and ruin all around him, Lesco found some hope in that.

In her lap, Isda held Hufa-Brain. Lesco stopped dead in his tracks when he saw that. The huge man lay sprawled out across the dirt, with Isda cradling his head against her belly. She wiped his brow and whispered to him. Tears slipped from Isda's eyes and landed on her lover's cheeks. Hufa-Brain was making no effort to stop them. Lesco wanted to be jealous. He wanted to hate the muscly moron that had stolen his love away. He wanted to rejoice in seeing his nemesis in such a state. But he was finding hate hard to come by. Especially when he saw what had happened to the man that Isda was now cradling.

Hufa-Brain stared blankly up, the life long since drained from his eyes. What remained of his body lay mangled in the dirt. There were bites everywhere. Scratches too. His legs and torso wore a deep red map of gashes and gouges. His arms were bruised and broken. Lesco dreaded to think how many chumpahs must have taken him on. And yet they had not made it past him. They had not laid a claw or tooth on Isda. Hufa-Brain had made sure of that. He had punched and kicked and grabbed and grappled. He had thrown himself between Isda and the chumpahs and fought until his very last breath. Lesco could see the fight carved out of Hufa-Brain's entire body. Every grim moment of it, ripped out of Hufa-Brain's flesh. He had lain down his life for Isda. Lesco's one true love was only still alive because Hufa-Brain had sacrificed himself to save her. While Lesco had been away sulking and booting bottles, allowing his bitterness to unleash terror on everybody he knew, Hufa-Brain had not left his lover's side for a second. He had stayed with her until the end, even when he knew it would kill him.

Isda looked up. She had sensed someone close to her, felt Lesco staring in her direction. Their eyes met. It had been the moment Lesco had been waiting for, hoping for, ever since he had first witnessed her incomparable beauty, bathed in Sulla's glow, all those turns ago. His heart had bound itself to Isda in that moment and had refused to let her go. He had trained so hard, worked so hard, and gone further on the Find than anyone had ever dared to dream before. And all for her. To win her love. For this very moment. For Isda to see him, acknowledge him, to need him as much as he needed her. And now finally it was happening. Isda was immediately in front of him, looking directly at him. Isda was right there. So was Lesco. For this briefest of moments, they were together.

But it did not feel as Lesco had expected. Far from it. He found not love and affection gazing back up at him, nor tenderness or devotion. There wasn't even recognition. When Lesco looked to Isda, cross legged on the floor and cradling her dead lover, he saw in her only confusion and dismay. The chumpahs had raged through her city and taken everything from her and no one had been there to stop it. There had been no warning signs, no protection. Because everyone had been looking the other way. In Isda's eyes, Lesco saw not love, but a furious fire that raged out of loss and injustice, a deep hatred directed towards a stupid ceremony, a pointless quest, an absurd tradition that had stolen the minds of all around her, distracted them from the truth. The Find had fooled everyone. It had dragged them from their responsibilities. And now her lover was dead. For Isda, there would be no forgiving it for that. It was the outrage Lesco glimpsed in that moment - Isda's realisation of what the Find had done to her and her own - that finally forced him to turn away.

*

The operation to clear the celebration circle began in solemn silence. Grand Mother directed her people as best she could, giving her blessings where it was needed. The wounded, those who could still be saved, were escorted away to the safety of their tents. For the less fortunate, it was simply a case of making them as comfortable as possible. When the time came, they would be wrapped in dried saltgrass, preserved in minerals from the sea, prepared for their long journey to the north. Grand Mother passed by each and every one, offering her hand and a kind word. "Do not fear. Soon the Olds will take you in, once the journey across the poisoned sea was complete." It was in these mournful moments that those close to Grand Mother observed a deep sadness within her, something beyond the tragedy of the attack. She walked solemnly, her head bowed, often seeking her own counsel when duty would permit. It was clear to all that she was deeply troubled, causing further worry for the people of Antar. If Grand Mother could not save them, then who could?

Lesco had found himself on water detail. Pails and pails of it were ferried back and forth from the seas and great rivers, chains of helpers moving it along into the heart of the city. What was not drunk was used to cleanse wounds, to wash potential disease from the battle scars. Once this task was done, they had been instructed to clean the streets of any grim reminders of the attack. It was no small operation. So much blood had been spilled.

Lesco took to his assignment gladly. Having a job to do was a pleasant distraction from all the chaos around him. He was glad for someone to tell him what to do. Through his work, he could slink away into the role of dedicated helper, another brave son of Antar doing his part for the relief effort. It was his hiding place, a safe space where no one looked at him the way Isda had. He could not be doing with any more of that.

Occasionally someone would recognise him - "You're him, aren't you? The one who brought us back the great wind-farmer!" - and Lesco would reluctantly nod. Those asking would smile, pat him on the back, congratulate him on all that he had done for Antar. All that he was doing. The Find King himself, here with us, selflessly helping Murdo City in its time of need. Truly he was a hero. Lesco would respond with a polite thank you, bow his head, before returning to his duties. People assumed he was just being modest. Look at brave Lesco, so stoic and respectful. If only we could all be more like him.

It was deep into the middle hours following the attack when Lesco finally stopped to rest. He had found himself a seat down on the docks, perching himself high up on a couple of upturned crab baskets. The water carriers had done what they could for now. Well-earned rest was encouraged. And so rest he did, relaxing after a hard turn's work, chewing on some old dried fish while staring out towards the calm ocean. As per usual, his first thoughts turned to Isda. He wondered where she was right now, what had become of her. Perhaps she was still in the celebration circle, hunched over the great big body of Hufa-Brain, venting her anger at the Find. Maybe she was out there helping, putting her rage to good use, fixing what needed to be fixed. Stomping around and setting Antar to rights. Lesco hoped so. It made him sad to think she might be as lost as he was.

Lesco had hoped to find calmness down by the ocean. If he sat and waited long enough, perhaps clarity would come to him. Somewhere in the gentle sound of sloshing water, the clack and clang of fishing boats bumping and scraping against each other in time to the tide, he would be granted the answers he so desperately needed. There had to be a conclusion that did not overwhelmingly point to all this being his fault. If he stared at the horizon and wished long enough, prayed to the Olds with sufficient devotion, surely it would come to him.

It was as Lesco sat struggling with this task that all of a sudden a conversation began to drift his way across the water. Two voices, out there somewhere across the bay, in hushed tones, presumably thinking themselves alone. Perhaps when they glanced across the harbour, the tiny outline of the small boy's body simply blended in with the crates and buckets around him. Maybe they just had not found the time to look. Either way, they spoke as if no one was listening, which made Lesco even more intrigued as to what they might have to say. He cupped his ears to the sound, guiding their words to him from across the water. The harbour amplified their exchange. Lesco was able to listen in quite clearly.

The two voices - one male, one female - spoke of the great loss that Murdo City had suffered. The tragedy of the attack. This was nothing new to Lesco. He had been there. He knew all this. But when the couple began to speak of the dire consequences for Antar's future, that was when Lesco sat up and began to really take notice. Their nation's survival held by a thread as it was. So much hard work was required through each Cycle of Sulla - supplies needed to be gathered, repairs needed to be made - just for Antar to stand a chance making it through the Great Shadow. And when the female voice began to accuse the Find of stealing resources from Antar that it really could not do without, it was swiftly hushed in paranoid tones by the male. And yet she continued. With the loss of people, would Antar even be able to bring in the saltgrass harvest in time? Would the repairs ever get completed? Antar's defences had taken such a hit, the number of guards now so low. What chance did it even have of protecting itself should the chumpahs attack again?

The thought had not even occurred to Lesco that the worst may not yet be over. That more hardship was to come. He had assumed that, terrible as the attack had been, that all he had to really do now was keep his head down, not expose himself, and things would basically go back to the way they were. Hopefully even better than the way they were, given Isda was now single. But this bleak portent that drifted his way across the water, it spoke of a very dark future indeed. Starvation, struggle and death awaited, the complete destruction of Antar itself.

The sound of weeping began to follow. Lesco could not tell which of the voices had succumbed to it. With a squint, he could just about make out a hunched figure on the far side of the bay, another next to them, offering a shoulder for support. It was difficult to tell exactly who was who, which half of this miserable couple was crying and which was not. Lesco's vision had become frustratingly blurry. Everything before him was a strange and hazy splodge. It was only as he blinked to clear his vision and salt water dripped onto this tunic that he realised that he had been crying.

Lesco rubbed his eyes. He did not need tears right now, he needed a solution. Antar had taken a great hit and was now in grave danger. He needed someone to tell him he was not responsible. Lesco thumped the crab box underneath him, venting his frustrations at the jetty below. If only he hadn't fallen in love with the wrong person. That was where this had all started, after all. If Isda hadn't come along, Lesco would never have become obsessed with her, he would not have worked so hard to get chosen for the Find and he would not have braved six days on the trail to bring back the great wind-farmer. The chumpahs probably wouldn't have made it so far into the city if not for the distraction that thing had caused. And he certainly wouldn't have felt so scorned by Isda's rejection as to let the chumpahs through for his act of revenge. That was the truth of it. He had acted out of great pain, a cruel and malicious hurt thrust upon him by his one true love. If anything, everyone should be blaming Isda, not him.

But Lesco doubted many citizens of Antar would believe all that if he explained it to them. He wasn't entirely sure he believed it himself. If Isda was responsible, if all this was truly her transgression, then why was he hiding out here away from everybody, tearful and alone on the edge of the ocean? Why did he avoid people's gaze? Why did he shy away from them when they aimed conversation his way? No, deep down, Lesco knew what was really going on. The truth was unavoidable. Antar was on its knees because he had been unable to contain his fury. That voice that had spoken to him earlier, when he had stumbled across the bloodied boy with the torn chest, had been warning him of what was to come. He was no longer able to ignore it. Finally, his guilt had caught up with him. It had wrapped itself around him and was refusing to let him go. *You did this. This is all your fault.*

Lesco wanted to scream but he knew that would just attract attention. He wanted to shout and curse, but if he did, the couple might realise he was there, come rushing over. They would enquire as to why he was so upset, ask him what was causing him so much trouble. And worst thing of all, he might actually tell them. It seemed very unlikely they would be willing to keep his secret. Soon everyone would know. Antar's pain would have a name. He would be Find King no more.

No, no good could come of wailing. Lesco shook his head, wiped the shame from his eyes, flicked the tears from his fingertips down onto the docks. There was no benefit in screeching and howling. Misery would get him nowhere. What he needed was a plan, a way of fixing the damage he had caused. But how? What possible chance did Lesco have now? He buried his head into his hands, growling deeply into his palms. There was no way he could bring the harvest in all on his own, repair the broken huts, fend off the chumpah hordes when they next came calling.

He was next to useless in the face of all that. And if there was a way to plead with Sulla, to ask her sweetly to reverse the turns, take her great cycle back to before the attack, then surely he would do it. He would not hesitate for a heartbeat.

Lesco would go anywhere, do anything, walk further, fight harder, go to the very ends of the earth if had to, if only it would make all these terrible dark thoughts just go away. And so he sat there, head in his hands, rocking back and forth on the edge of the crab box, whispering his prayers to the Olds to just show him a sign. Take all this torment away. Let him be rid of it forever. "Oh, great Olds, with all your power and wisdom, please just tell me what it is I should do…"

*

The Olds are wise, the Olds are true, with Sulla's light they guide us through.

*

A very light tapping caught Lesco's attention. At first he ignored it, believing it to be nothing more than one of those evil thoughts he had rattling around inside his skull. They had become quite vocal of late, eager to explode out of him in a rotten torrent of rage. But as the tapping continued, Lesco began to realise that his brain was not making the sound up to taunt him. The tapping was out there, in the real world, apparently coming from directly below him. And it would not stop. What on Antar was it?

Lesco slowly opened his eyes, peeking between his fingers. Down there, below the crab pots, below the wooden slats in the jetty, far below him the dark shadow underneath the dock - that was where the noise was coming from. Something unusual, that most probably should not be there, now tap-tap-tapping away gently against the wooden struts below just to get his attention. And at the very moment Lesco had been asking for help as well. It was all far too much of a coincidence for Lesco not to investigate further.

He slid down from the crab pots, spreading himself out on the jetty. His eyes went to the nearest slat, directly above where it seemed the sound was coming from. It was difficult to see much down there, the dock itself doing an annoyingly effective job of hiding the water from Sulla's gaze. But even so, Lesco could make out something bobbing around in the water, all shiny and white, sloshing around in stark contrast to all the darkness around it. It seemed to have tangled itself around the stanchion somehow and was now clanging against it. Long and white with a round clump at one end. Lesco squinted, trying to get a better look. It did not appear to be anything fish-related, or an item you would usually find drifting around in the harbour. It looked foreign made. It looked Old.

Leaving all his troubles behind for a second, Lesco crawled on his hands and knees to the edge of the jetty, before peering down underneath. It was terribly gloomy down there and home to several unpleasant smells. Some mixture of saltgrass and dead fish. It made Lesco's eyes burn. He had to concentrate in order to suppress a cough. But none of that was going to stop him. He wanted to find out what was down there, the nature of what called to him. He needed to know what the Olds had sent.

And so without wasting a second to think about the consequences, Lesco slid over the edge and dropped. The cold, stinky water rushed all the way up his body, so fast that he forgot to gasp as it passed his nethers and only really felt the chill when it reached his nipples. It was almost enough to cry out in shock. But Lesco resisted. This was his task and his alone. The last thing he needed was that silly old crying couple poking around after him. Or worse still, one of the guards. No, best keep all this to himself for now. Stay as quiet and as sneaky as possible.

He edged forward, turning his face from the worst of the stench. The strange item was just beyond his grasp, but hopefully he would be able to grab it without going too far under. Lesco flapped his arm out into the dark water, splashing it around until he found purchase. The mystery object felt cold and clammy, thin like parchment, but oddly tough. Like it would take some tugging to rip it. Luckily, it seemed not all that attached to the wooden stanchion, and came away quite easily with a bit of gentle persuasion. Lesco was able to pull the item and himself out from under the dock with the bare minimum of effort.

Lesco fell back, out into the light, taking in a deep hit of marginally cleaner air as he went. Excitement had dragged him through the worst of the stench down there but he had been wary of taking too much of it in. The last thing he needed was to pass out from the overwhelming funk of fish guts and land face down in the water. And so with some relief he turned, wading towards the shoreline, shivering as he went. There was an eagerness within him to examine what it was exactly he had pulled from the water immediately. But this was quickly repressed by caution, an awareness that he could not be certain there were no prying eyes ogling him from across the bay, suddenly taking a keen interest in what he was doing. Best get out of the open, back into the safety of the crab pots. And it would also be nice to be clear of the water, he considered. Certain parts of his body had begun complaining quite forcefully about the cold.

Up on the dock, Lesco scrambled behind the crab pots, into a nice little protected hidey hole. He took a quick glance between the slats to see if anyone had been watching, and when he was certain it was safe to continue, he finally looked down at the cold, clammy object still in his hand. It looked very much to him like one object wrapped inside another. The inner object was hard and long, roughly the length of his own hand, and was no doubt what had been causing the tapping. But the outer item - some sort of bag, Lesco supposed - was all scratchy and scrapy and wrapped up in itself, mostly a dull white but with a few faded patches of colour. And almost certainly made from that weird, everlasting material the Olds seemed to like so much, those crinkly sheets that could survive out there in the poisoned sea for cycle after cycle without taking any real damage. Feeling it between his fingers, seeing it right before his eyes, made Lesco's excitement increase. Another Find item had come to him, just at the point when he had called out for help. What was it the Olds were trying to tell him?

Lesco shook the bag, letting it stretch out in his hands, pulling the corners loose. As he did so, the item inside slipped out and slammed onto the floor of the dock with an uncomfortable amount of clattering. Lesco winced, gritting his teeth. He didn't think anyone had been around to hear it, but you could never be too careful. He grabbed the thing up, preventing it from rolling any further. Now in his hand, Lesco could see quite clearly that this was a Find item too. His grimace quickly morphed into a grin. It was a long tube, black and thin, scarred and rusted, with some sort of catch at the top - possibly a switch, maybe a button. The whole object was covered with unusual lettering, most of it faded and scraped away. What he could make out was simply gobbledygook, impossibly unknowable. Lesco frowned down to it, gazed at a couple of words in wonder - *anti-perspirant*. Such bizarre language, so strange and alien. It meant nothing to him. But there was an arrow at the tip of the object, some sort of dial. If Lesco was to hazard a guess, it would have been towards some instrument of navigation, pointing you in the direction you needed to go. But he could not possibly tell how it worked.

Lesco tried flicking the switch. There was a dull click but the tube did not respond. Whatever use this Find item had, it was far beyond him. Perhaps there was a trick to it. Maybe if he ran it by Grand Mother later, after she had finished with all her diligent solemnities, she could point him in the right direction. But for now, the message the Olds had sent him remained frustratingly vague. There had to be more to it.

Lesco placed the tube gently onto a nearby pot, turning his attention back to the bag. Maybe there was another clue there, a key to unlocking the secret. The switch had to do *something*. The Olds would not have sent a useless piece of tat his way, after all. And so Lesco pulled the bag out flat, stretching its four corners, and the coloured lettering upon it came into view for the first time.

Lesco's eyes widened. He let slip a high-pitched squeak. The bag was almost dropped immediately, so in awe was he of what he was witnessing. Five big, red letters, standing on a dotted line of blue, all still clear and largely unblemished by the harsh conditions out on the ocean. And letters in an order that Lesco very much did recognise. One of the few words he could read. A clear sign that this was his moment. He was the one, the Olds had selected him. And now they called to him personally, written right there in red and bold on the bag he held in his hands - L-E-S-C-O.

Lesco's knees began to shake. The tears flowed down his cheeks. To witness this, his own name printed across a Find item, was to him as if looking into the eyes of the Olds themselves. To see glory itself. It was almost too beautiful to observe, as if he should not look directly at it. But he could not help himself. He was overwhelmed. So overwhelmed, in fact, that he might have missed the unavoidable fact that the L did not really look all that much like an L at all. It could even, given proper examination, possibly have been another letter entirely. And there was also the issue that the words underneath his name - *every little helps* - meant absolutely nothing to him either. He could not read them. This message the Olds had sent him, whatever it was, was so outlandishly oblique as to be almost interpreted as not even a message at all.

But Lesco had faith. He believed in the Olds, as he believed in himself. They had sent him the great wind-farmer and, in his time of need, they had now provided him with this - a weird rusty tube with a broken switch and a clammy old bag with his name (possibly) written on it. He had prayed to them to take his guilt away, to help him restore Antar and save his people, and the Olds had responded. Now all he had to do was decipher what it was they were trying to say.

Lesco scrambled through his thoughts, flipping them over and pulling them apart, trying to recall what exactly it was he had been asking for. What his prayers had requested. What he had said. How he had been desperate for a solution, willing to do anything for it, promising even to go to the very ends of the earth to find it...

The idea formed in his brain with such absolute clarity that Lesco immediately doubted it had even been his. It felt almost like it had been placed there, sent there, by people who knew much more than him. By a mighty civilization across the oceans, one that could float fortresses on water, that could soar through the clouds, that could construct immense cities that touched the skies. And that could save all of Antar, if only one mighty hero was brave enough to make the journey to find them.

Lesco looked down to the bag - his name, printed in red, above a blue dotted line... that could only mean one thing. The blue dotted line was the ocean. His name was above it. The Olds were asking him to traverse the poisoned sea, to sail north to the land of plenty. And the tube, long and thin, with its strange switch and mysterious arrow - that was his tool for navigation. He could point it to the skies and the arrow would surely tell him which way to go. It was all so obvious now that he could see it, all the pieces of the puzzle neatly slotting into place. The Olds had sent for Lesco in person. This was the answer to his prayer. They were calling him to them!

The crossing would be fraught with dangers. Lesco knew this as much as anybody. The storms, the poisoned sea, not to mention the variety of sea monsters that were rumoured to be out there. To his knowledge - to anybody on Antar's knowledge - no one had ever made the crossing before and lived. But he was Lesco the Find King, selected specifically by the Olds themselves. And they had sent him the required tool for the task, the rusty black tube with its arrows and its switches, which he knew would point him in the right direction when the time came. He could not fail. *He must not fail.* Antar needed him.

And so it was that Lesco found himself pushing his tiny boat out to sea, a pack full of dried saltgrass at his side, and armed with nothing but a fishing rod and the mysterious navigation tool. As he pulled back on the oars he would gaze down to it confidently, so proud to have been given this chance, so determined to make the most of it. He bounced his tiny conical craft across the break, beyond the boundaries of the harbour, and waved back to the shoreline, to the slowly building crowds of curious onlookers who had gathered to watch this strange young boy rowing away to what they perceived to be certain death. Some even shouted obscenities his way, demanding he return the much-needed supplies to them, as they would do no good stranded at the bottom of the ocean. Lesco laughed back at them. If only they knew the truth. Where he was going and why, and who had called out to him. They would not be shouting and screaming at him then. They would most probably drop down to their knees in admiration, sending their prayers along with him on his long and arduous journey. He knew deep down that was probably what they meant, despite all the abuse.

Lesco wondered how many turns the journey would take. He hoped he would make it before the end of the Cycle of Sulla. The thought of travelling across the poisoned sea during the Great Shadow did not really appeal to him at all. There had always been talk among the people of Antar that the further north you went, the shorter the cycles became, until eventually each turn held both light and dark within them. Lesco doubted that could be true. Surely Sulla could become exhausted travelling all that way so often, rising and falling in each and every turn. It did not seem very likely. And he certainly could not plan for that outcome. No, best make the crossing as quickly as possible, with Sulla on his side. No need to take any chances.

Slowly and steadily the giant land of Antar began to drift away into the haze of the horizon. The last thing Lesco could really make out before it disappeared was the enormous wind-farmer, towering above Murdo City, sparkling in Sulla's gaze. It seemed fitting that was the final thing he saw - the great gift of the Olds sending him on his way to meet them. The wind was light, the ocean calm, and the warm glow of Sulla's love beat down onto the back of his neck. The conditions really were perfect, as if the Olds had decreed it themselves. After all, they could heat themselves up when they got too cold, cool themselves down when they got too hot, so it was not beyond imagination that they could control the weather too. They really could do anything, after all. His heart leapt at the thought of finally meeting them, witnessing their magnificence in person.

Lesco dreamed of the tales he would have to tell, the wonders he would get to show the people of Antar that the Olds had blessed upon him. And how grateful Antar would be when he finally returned, with all the gifts he could carry, sharing the great knowledge the Olds had bestowed on him to rebuild Murdo City ten times over. There could be no doubting his heroism then, even taking into account that slight hiccup involving the chumpahs. Perhaps even Isda would find it in her heart to forgive him. Lesco's smile widened at the thought. Isda standing there, on the beach, bathed in Sulla's glory. He could almost see her. Her smile sparkled as she waved out to him, wishing him well as he triumphantly soared across the waves. She called out to him, sending him the gift of her love as he began his long and perilous journey. "Come back to me," Isda called softly, beaming her words directly into his brain. "You are the one I truly love. I'll be waiting here patiently, turn after turn, for you and you only until you return. "

Lesco knew it to be true. It just had to be. Because he was Lesco, the Find King of Antar, discoverer of the great wind-farmer, and he was going to see the Olds. He was going to save everyone. If that wasn't good enough to prove his love for Isda once and for all, then Lesco did not know what was.

*

Antar stood in bright sunlight. Its people waited on black sand, hungry and afraid, gazing mournfully towards the horizon. They held each other - some for comfort, others for balance, their wounds making it difficult to stand alone. Above them all sat Sulla, proud and magnificent, at the height of her great cycle. This much warmth would usually be the cause of much celebration. The very young would be splashing around in the shallows, making the most of one of the rare opportunities to do so. The very old would be singing songs, cheering and chanting, praising Sulla and the Olds and championing the unyielding strength of Antar. Not so much now. A lot had changed. There was no splashing, cheering or singing. There was nothing to cheer and sing about. The people of Antar gathered there on that beach knew exactly what was coming for them.

Soon Sulla would begin to drop. Each subsequent turn would darken, the light dimming, until eventually Sulla would disappear altogether. She would hide herself beyond the horizon, taking all of her colour and warmth with her. After that, there would be no farming, no fishing, no building, no Finding. There would be only darkness and gloom. And the dread things that lurk within it. The Great Shadow was coming and Antar was unprepared. Each and every soul standing on the beach knew it. They were all gripped by the fear of their time running short.

The dead were lain out across the sand. Their numbers were greater than Antar had seen in a lifetime, a grim reminder of the terrible nature of the chumpah attack. One by one, they would all be released into Sulla's path, that glowing road of sparkle and glimmer she had laid out across the ocean. With luck, her beam would show them the way north. There they would find a new home with the Olds, resurrected and restored. Way up where, beyond the raging currents and the terrible storms and the poisoned sea, Antar knew its fallen were living out brand new, bountiful lives, in a place where they were never hungry, never scared, never too hot and never too cold. Disease and famine were no match for the power of the Olds. They could cure all. Even death. The Olds are wise, the Olds are true, with Sulla's light they guide us through.

Grand Mother stood beside the line of bodies, her bony toes tickling the surf. Her eyes were closed, her body still. She was waiting for the right moment. Deep down she had begun to doubt whether it would ever come. There was so much sadness in the gathered crowd behind her. If she turned, she feared she would see it, a dark cloud of uncertainty hovering above them, ready to unleash a deluge of torment and despair. Her people looked to her for guidance. Yet Grand Mother feared she no longer had any to give. She had told her people that all would be well, she had reassured them all that they still had a chance. If they stood as one, bound together, fought for each other, Antar would rise to greatness once more. There was still hope left. But each and every time she said it, the sentiment was like a chumpah tooth to her heart. For Grand Mother knew she was not telling her people the truth. For her, the words had lost all meaning. She did not know if recovery was even possible. If Antar *could* rise. Or whether the next Great Shadow would take them all. She had no knowledge of the future. The Olds had been silent. And so how could she encourage her people to fight, if she had no fight left in herself?

As Grand Mother allowed Sulla's warm glow to soothe her troubled brow, she thought back to her own coronation. It was so many cycles ago now. How proud she had felt to be selected, how bright the future had appeared. How, after the ceremony, her mentor had led her deep into the ruins of Old Murdo, far away from the celebrating crowds. There Grand Mother had been shown the great secrets of the Olds, the ancient scrolls and parchments they had left behind. There were so many strange drawings and texts, pictures and charts, sketches of unimaginable machines and impossible structures. A window into their world, far and away to the north. She had asked her mentor the same questions all the uninitiated ask - "Why were they here? Where did they go? And will the Olds ever return?" Her mentor had shook her head, hushed Grand Mother and held her gaze with a warm smile. These were questions that Antar had no right to know. The Olds will make their move in time, when they are ready. Until then, all Antar and its people can do is wait.

And so Grand Mother had spent all her life studying the ancient scripture, absorbing all she could about the ways of the Olds. She had studied the graphs, pored over the charts, learned to read their language and decipher their codes. She would have to admit, if truly pressed, that much of it went over her head and she did not fully understand all the finer details. To her, the texts had always seemed to hint that the Olds had never actually left the shores of Antar. That they had settled here, started life anew, after being forced away from the north by a terrible scouring of their homeland, the dour consequences of their own overreaching actions. But if that were true, that would make the people of Antar direct descendants *from* the Olds, and the world above simply an empty, uninhabitable wasteland. Which contradicted everything that she had been taught by her mentor, went against what all of Antar knew to be fact. To even think it was heresy. And so Grand Mother had dismissed these troubling readings, ignored them, put it all down to an error in her own interpretation. That was the only logical answer.

Grand Mother had lived her life from that moment in service to her people. She had used her supreme knowledge to great effect, solving dilemmas, quelling quarrels, answering any and all questions her people put to her as best she could. When doubt had struck her down, an unanswerable query, she had walked among the ancient ruins of Old Murdo and prayed for guidance. When it arrived, it always seemed to be in the form of her own thoughts, rather than any external voice or instruction. Her mentor had warned her about this. That is just how the Olds communicate, the old woman had said. Don't worry yourself about it. But after the chumpah attack, she had found not even a single positive thought implanted in her brain by the wondrous peoples of the north. No solution had come. For the first time in her life, Grand Mother had found herself without any of the answers.

And so it was then, with her toes dug into the warm, black sand, that Grand Mother made her decision. Her time had come. With a long, sad sigh, she considered whether she should have realised it sooner. Had she done so before the chumpah attack, before the great wind-farmer had returned to Murdo City, before she had even sent Antar's bravest and strongest out on the Find, could more have been saved? There was no way of knowing. All she could do now was make her final choice and see it through. If she could no longer lead her people, if the Olds had stopped talking to her, then it was time to hand that responsibility to another. Let the new generation take over. This old one has failed.

At that, Grand Mother gave the signal. She squinted up into the blazing mid-cycle sunlight and raised her arms, beckoning her people forward. One by one, slowly and respectfully, they gathered up the fallen. Each was wrapped in dried saltgrass, sealed at both ends, prepared dutifully for their journey. The people stepped forward, into the surf, and handed their loved ones back to the waves. Let the ocean take them. Their time on Antar is at an end. May they find peace in the great lands to the north.

As the dead slowly bobbed past her, Grand Mother turned her head to see a young woman - barely older than a girl - struggling in the shallows, fighting against the weight of a body nearly twice her size. The young woman was up to her waist in the water, often losing her footing and stumbling out under it. Others were approaching to help, but all offers were refused. Onlookers were dismissed politely but firmly. "Please, I must do this alone."

Grand Mother watched on as the young woman hauled the great hulk of a body forward, pushing it deeper and deeper into the sea. The girl battled hard through the breaking waves. Each one forced her back several steps, often smacking the body against her with some force. And yet she persevered. She pushed and she pushed, with barely a grunt or a groan to show her displeasure. It was her duty. She must see it through. And after much stumbling and splashing, her own body battered and bruised, the young woman finally overcame the breaking waves and released her lover out into Sulla's path. The light took him, calling him out to sea. And the young woman stood back, panting and exhausted, but clearly satisfied she had completed the task alone.

It was a strange sensation Grand Mother experienced at that moment. She could not work out exactly why, but there was a distinct sense of familiarity about this stoic young woman. If they had met, Grand Mother could not recall it. But she was certain she recognised this girl, standing there red faced and panting waist deep in the surf. As if someone she could not quite place had described this young woman in great detail - repeatedly - so that she was now impossible to forget. And the way the girl was standing, where she was standing, right in the path of Sulla's gaze, it seemed to illuminate her against the background of Antar's black sand behind. It was as if Sulla had selected her, chosen her, made her stand out from the crowd. A voice spoke in Grand Mother's head. *With Sulla's light they guide us through.* Perhaps these were her own thoughts, or maybe the Olds had chosen this grand moment to send her one last message. It did not truly matter either way. Grand Mother smiled. She had been given a sign. It would be foolish now to ignore it.

Grand Mother reached out a hand, gaining the young woman's attention. Their eyes met. The girl bowed respectfully. Grand Mother asked for her name. The young woman replied. And again came that pang of familiarity, a note of significance in the response. Someone, somewhere, had mentioned this girl before. Several times. Grand Mother was sure of it. She just could not quite recall who or when. Damn her old age. Curse her receding memory. But what Grand Mother could recall, with almost unnerving clarity, was what this unknown someone had said, their description of this brave young woman that stood before her, bathed now in Sulla's warm glow - *She was all you could ever hope for.*

After their brief exchange, the young woman turned, heading back towards the beach. As she fought her way through the water, Grand Mother gazed back up to her people, the throng waiting patiently up on the sand. And it was there she saw something strange. Perhaps a trick of the light, perhaps something more, but the cloud of uncertainty that had hung above them only moments previously appeared to have faded in its entirety. As this young woman approached, Grand Mother saw nothing but Sulla's beautiful bright light embracing her people, holding them tight and together as one. Grand Mother could not help but grin. She felt her eyes swell with tears. The Olds had spoken to her, one last time. A clear instruction as to what to do next. Antar had hope once again. She saw it before her, clambering out of the water and standing tall and proud, back up there on the black sand beach.

And so Grand Mother called out, asking the young woman to stop. Her protégé did as she was told. Grand Mother smiled to her. The young woman smiled back. And then Grand Mother spoke the fateful words that paved the way for Antar's great recovery -

"Isda, wait there, I have a task for you. I think you are going to enjoy it."

Returning

The light took her once again. It was at once searingly hot and fiercely cold, a confusing moment of unplaceable pain. Her body lurched forwards. Her ears popped. She could not control any of it. It felt to her like falling in all directions. It was unclear what was above and what was below. There was still sensation, though. Still feeling. Still life. The pain and the popping and the constant spinning was to her bizarrely reassuring. It was all she required to understand that she had made it back.

Through blinking eyes, the launchpad slowly came into view. Faces were there to greet her, at the far end of the room, staring back through a thick pane of glass. They seemed to be pleased to see her. She looked down to her body, the protective suit that housed it. There were her feet, still thankfully where she had left them. Her arms too, exactly where she hoped they would be. And beyond them, her hands, so tightly gripped to the arms of the chair that they had begun to shake violently, clinging on for dear life throughout the traverse. She was still in one piece, her body intact. The worst was over. She allowed her fingers to fall away from the handles. Her burning knuckles thanked her for it.

A voice boomed through the speaker in her headset. A word repeated. A name? She wasn't sure. It sounded so familiar and yet strangely distant, as if it had come to her from another time, belonging to a whole other existence she could not quite fathom. So much had happened since she had last heard it. It took a few disorienting seconds to realise the name belonged to her. She spoke, confirming acknowledgement, doing just as the voice had asked. Her memory of this place was hazy, almost as if she had dreamed it. Or had she imagined everything since? In that brief moment, it was impossible to tell.

A door beside her hissed. She turned her head, bringing on a bout of nausea. A stale burp escaped. She was thankful it was not followed by vomit. The dizziness was almost too much to contain. Beside her, people in helmets, intruders in her space, visors dark and clouded. They wore thick, black gloves. Protection for them or for her? She tried to pull away, unsure of their purpose. The seat held her in place. The voice spoke again, calm and reassuring, placating her panic. This is all normal, the confusion will pass. Take deep breaths. You're fine now, you're safe. It's all over. You are home.

The intruders released her. Clips were undone, bolts unfastened. She felt some relief at that. The straps had been too tight, leaving red marks on her wrists and ankles. Her chest ached, as if she had been tensing it. The lump that had been poking her in the back finally ceased its digging. She remembered wishing it away, hoping that it could one day be fixed. She would have to remind everyone, remind herself, when the time was right.

The voice spoke again, rapid and excited, eager for information. Tell us what you saw, where you were, who was there. She searched her memories - a garbled collection of faltering images - none of which appeared in any clearly identifiable form. She told this to the voice. The reply was apologetic. Recover your strength, regain your composure. I should not rush you. We have time.

She was led through the complex, assessed by medical experts, given a change of clothing, the world around her slowly morphing into familiarity. I know this place, these rooms and corridors. I know these people. I came here for a reason. She was handed water and pills. These will help. In one swift motion she took them and swallowed, eager for the fog to clear.

When assessed as healthy, she was released to the briefing room. She took to the chair, much more comfortable than the one used for the journey. The voice was before her now, sat opposite. It had form and a body, a face some deep part of her insisted was friendly. It spoke warmly, praising her work. It spoke to her of who she was and what she had done.

Slowly but surely, the memories began to rise up from the depths. The familiarity of the voice brought everything back. She smiled. The smile grew into a chuckle. The chuckle blossomed into a laugh. Her eyes filled with tears. Finally, she remembered what it was she had been doing, why she had gone away. And the home she had now returned to. She knew again what she was. She was a traveller, just like she had hoped. Her journey had been long and full of strange encounters. The voice asked her to elaborate. He gathered up a pen to write. She began to talk.

She spoke of the other worlds she had visited, both familiar and strange, terrifying and enticing. Places she wanted to go back to, places she never wanted to see again. A man she had met who hated what he might become. Another who believed he had all the answers. She had visited a dark dream in which laughter could kill, witnessed a society hanging on by a thread at the end of the world. There had been a party when all hope seemed lost and a town swallowed by the very earth itself. It had all seemed so real to her at the time. She was no longer sure if any of it was. The voice continued to write without judgement.

She just kept on talking, recounting her experiences. There was just so much she wanted to say. The voice sat there patiently, listening and nodding, not wanting to stop her now she was in her flow. It seemed unlikely he could even if he tried. She had started and so she would finish. There was an inevitability to it.

One by one, the tales of her travels came spilling out of her. All these bizarre thoughts and ideas she could not quite explain, that appeared to arrive from nowhere and were now impossible to forget. She found it almost annoying, how they stuck in her mind, dug their claws in deep, refusing to let go of her. The stories felt heavy as they rolled around inside her brain. They battled it out with more practical reasoning and too often came out on top. The only way to be free of them, to find a release, was to speak them out loud to anyone willing to listen. And so that's what she did, time and time again, threw them towards the voice with as much gusto as she could muster. He wrote it all down. She continued to speak. They both had their roles to play.

And then finally, eventually, thankfully, she reached the end of her telling. Her debrief was done. The voice had what he needed. Before him sat his notes. She looked down to them, curious, as if unsure if that was the end of it. He reassured her that it was. It's over now, it's done. You can move on. We have your statements recorded, your logs on file. Everything you told us, from the start to the finish, the tunnel and everything after. She smiled to him at that. It felt good to finally have an ending. The voice nodded but gave her a worrying look. Rest up, recuperate, celebrate if you must, but don't get too comfortable. It's only a matter of time before we send you back out there. She let loose a sigh, unsure if that promise of his made her happy or terrified. But then she thought of the alternative and shrugged. It was not as if she had much of a choice. When it came down to it, what else was she going to do but this?

Printed in Great Britain
by Amazon

21058138R00108